*"What exac...
Mr. Black?...
of a sudd...
sharing a room with me?"*

Please, *please* let her suspicions prove un-true! For several days things had been go-ing well—right up until Mr. Black made his entrance. No one at the inn suspected she was a girl. And if her ruse were discovered now, the game would be up. Juicy news traveled quickly through the countryside.

Christian shrugged carelessly. "I could stand to save a few pounds. I'm down on my luck, as well. Too many bets on the races."

Kate narrowed her eyes. She had been right about his character. All smiles, affecta-tions, and hidden agendas. A man who al-ways took what he pleased and thought nothing of others. One who would ignore the people in his life if it meant risking his own pleasure. Men like that were driven by self-interest and blind to others. They didn't look any further than what they wanted to see.

To be noticed as a female, she would prob-ably have to be stripped naked and dancing in front of him.

He drew a lazy pattern on the counterpane with his finger. "What's your real name?"

She blinked. "What?"

"Your *real* name, *Miss* Kaden?"

Anne Mallory

The Earl Of Her Dreams

AVON BOOKS

An Imprint of HarperCollins*Publishers*

AVON BOOKS
An Imprint of HarperCollins*Publishers*
10 East 53rd Street
New York, New York 10022-5299

Copyright © 2006 by Anne Hearn
ISBN-13: 978-0-06-087295-3
ISBN-10: 0-06-087295-0
www.avonromance.com

First Avon Books paperback printing: November 2006

Avon Trademark Reg. U.S. Pat. Off. and in Other Countries, Marca Registrada, Hecho en U.S.A.
HarperCollins® is a registered trademark of HarperCollins Publishers Inc.

Printed in the U.S.A.

10 9 8 7 6 5 4 3 2 1

Acknowledgments

*To Matt, for the wonderful maps
and the endless support.*

Special thanks to Mom, May, and Paige.

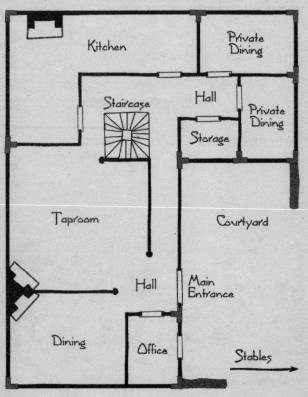

The Dragon's Tale Inn
Ground Floor

Kitchen

Private Dining

Staircase

Hall

Private Dining

Storage

Taproom

Courtyard

Hall

Main Entrance

Dining

Office

Stables →

The Dragon's Tale Inn

First Floor

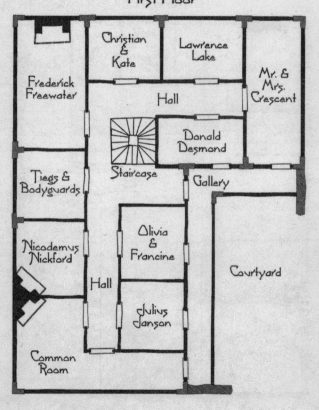

Frederick Freewater

Christian & Kate

Lawrence Lake

Mr. & Mrs. Crescent

Hall

Staircase

Donald Desmond

Tiegs & Bodyguards

Gallery

Nicodemus Nickford

Olivia & Francine

Courtyard

Hall

Julius Janson

Common Room

The Dragon's Tale Inn

Second Floor

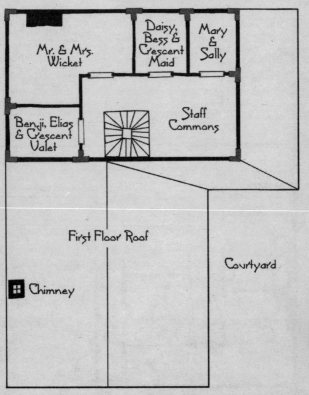

Mr. & Mrs. Wicket

Daisy, Bess & Crescent Maid

Mary & Sally

Staff Commons

Benji, Elias & Crescent Valet

First Floor Roof

Courtyard

▪ Chimney

Chapter 1

You're just like your uncle. All you think about is women and pleasure.

The Marquess of Penderdale
to his son Christian, age eighteen

Christian Black strode with long, purposeful steps into the bustling courtyard. The overhead sign proclaiming the Dragon's Tale Inn swayed gently in the cool breeze. Even with a winter storm approaching, the action at the coaching inn refused to still.

Christian ducked. A whiff of leather and a fluttering whisper were his only warnings as a stable boy accidentally tossed the ribbons too far. A quick "Sorry, sir!" and the boy fetched the

1

ribbons and was swallowed by the milling crowd.

Christian smiled. The activity at the coaching inns provided the best entertainment in country towns.

Ostlers jockeyed horses around weaving carriages, and bystanders yelled out encouragement as the drivers displayed their coaches and finery to best advantage.

"Come stay the night here, love. Best service in town."

Christian looked up to see a buxom blonde leaning provocatively over the rail, her assets nearly spilling over the wood as she showed *her* finery to best advantage as well. He did so love the cold weather when it displayed such bounty so beautifully. Her tight calico bodice strained against her perked breasts, practically begging him to release them from their confines. In his twenty-five years he'd never had a problem coaxing any woman from her confines.

He winked at the blonde, and she tossed him a saucy, provocative smile before sashaying inside. His blood flow concentrated in one specific area as he chronicled all he could do with those two luscious offerings. *After* his business was seen to, of course.

A long-legged, curvaceous diversion was already responsible for his current predicament. He'd have to revisit that curvaceous diversion at some point. He had left far too early. What had she said her name was? Samantha? Sarah? It was something that started with an S.

Not that it mattered. It was his name they always screamed, and not the other way around. He was good at *something* after all, no matter what his father said.

Christian glanced at the rest of the onlookers leaning against the wooden railing to catch a glimpse of the courtyard spectacles. Guests and workers hung over the inn galleries, even now, in the dead of winter, their breaths released in cold puffs, to watch the fanfare of the entering and exiting carriages.

The audience oohed over the livery colors of the rich, and sympathized with the gaping faces of those relegated to taking their first trip in the rumble-tumble baskets on the public coaches. They cheered the freshly scrubbed and harnessed horses that were proudly, or impatiently, waiting their turn, aahed over a coachman putting on a dramatic show in his many-caped driving coat, and laughed outright as every once in a while a reckless driver too preoccupied with strutting to his coach stepped in the present a restless horse had left in his path, uncovered or hidden by the fresh straw.

The postman blew his horn and galloped through town, the other horsemen giving him wide berth. The crowd cheered at the sight. Christian tugged at his left glove, paying little heed to the departing coach. Perhaps switching clothes with one of his servants hadn't been such a grand idea after all.

His valet, Bertrand, had nearly had apoplexy as it was, exclaiming the clothes far too coarse for his master to wear. But Bertrand had finally given in, accustomed to Christian's whims, and he was nothing if not steadfastly loyal. It was just a good thing Christian was stubborn; otherwise Bertrand would have resigned him to dandy hell years ago.

He looked up from his examination of the glove and abruptly stopped.

Two stately carriages were lined up for departure, and he recognized the coat of arms on the second as that of a lesser family of the ton. He discreetly donned his hat, tugging it lower until a few dark strands obscured his face. It had been arrogant to remove the hat in the first place. Not that arrogance had ever stopped him before.

Slipping into the crowd, Christian waited for

both carriages to process out before tipping his hat back up and sauntering into the inn. The din of the raucous crowd was replaced by muffled noise from the adjoining taproom, and the smell of straw and animal droppings swapped for that of baked chicken and ale.

"Good afternoon, sir. Be with you in a thrice," the cheery innkeeper said. He turned to give last-minute instructions to the buxom blonde maid from the gallery, who sent Christian a lascivious wink before exiting the room.

"Now then, how may we be of service? Post or travel?"

Christian slipped on a charming smile. "Actually, I would like a room for the night."

The innkeeper tugged his bushy auburn mustache, which was at odds with his balding pate. "My apologies, good sir, but we are full for the evening. Perhaps the Green Toad on the other side of town?" He grimaced, obviously chagrined at having to turn away business.

Full? That wouldn't do at all. Christian increased his smile from amiable to charming. "That's most unfortunate. My good friend Anthony told me how excellent the service is here, and that the Dragon's Tale is a much finer establishment than the Green Toad."

The innkeeper's chest puffed out. "Too true, too true." He looked down at a logbook. "But all our rooms are full. The traffic is especially good around the holy days, and we see a fair number of visitors on the post road. Coaching traffic continues to increase our load."

The innkeeper eagerly rubbed his hands together. "Thinking about adding a third section to the Dragon. Possibly making it into a triple gallery like the Four Swans in Bishopsgate. Could hold plays and the like. Would have to move the stables of course, seeing as we only have the two sides currently. And the—"

"That sounds lovely." Christian interrupted the rambling little man and tried his most cajoling voice. "But tonight? Surely there is something that a man of your stature could do?"

The innkeeper's bushy eyebrows drew together and he tapped his equally bushy mustache. "The Crescents, a distinguished couple from London are staying in the far corner, and Mr. Desmond, a fine cricket player is in the state gallery room. Nickford—eccentric fellow—and Julius Janson—the finest cricket player in four counties, didn't you know!—are in the south fire and gallery rooms. Mrs. Trent and her companion, and the mysterious Mr. Tiegs and his two friends occupy the middle rooms on each side of the inn. Mr. Freewater, strange lad, is in the large fire room. Then there's—"

"This Mr. Freewater—his room, it is a large room?" Christian asked, cutting short the innkeeper's overload of uninteresting and useless information.

"Oh yes, one of our largest. And with a fireplace, one directly above the kitchens, so it is nice and toasty."

"Nice and toasty sounds perfect."

"Oh, it is!"

"And it's large?"

"Quite roomy."

"So if there were an overflow, a pallet could always be arranged, especially in a warm, toasty room to ward off the chill."

"No chill there, you can be sure!"

"So in an overflow—"

"Oh! We can ask Mr. Lake if he still plans to stay," the innkeeper said, blithely ignoring Christian, something he was wholly unaccustomed to outside of his family. "Lives in Lehigh, the neighboring town, didn't you know. Don't really know why he is staying, but perhaps it has to do with Julius. Always at odds those two." He chuckled. "Good old Julius, a fine, strapping lad.

Great all-rounder on the field." He leaned forward. "He and my daughter Mary are quite compatible, don't you think?"

Christian stared at the daft man for a few long seconds. The innkeeper beamed back. Christian decided that ignoring his babble was as good a plan as any other. "But if the Freewater room is one of the largest, why not ask him about bringing in a pallet for the night?"

"Oh, definitely not."

"Just for one night."

"Oh, not Mr. Freewater."

"Surely we can work something out with Mr. Freewater?" Christian idly twirled a crown between his fingers.

The innkeeper's eyes followed the coin's lazy movement as it tantalizingly disappeared and reappeared. His shoulders drooped a bit and he resignedly shook his head.

"No, no. Mr. Freewater explicitly expressed that he was not to be disturbed. The Dragon has an impeccable reputation to maintain, and I doubt Mr. Freewater would forgive the disturbance. Terribly cheerless man, don't you think?"

Christian kept a rein on his temper and simply stared at the irritating little man.

"Oh, but then you don't know him." The

innkeeper paused for a moment, then exclaimed, "Oh! I have it. Young Mr. Kaden. Yes, yes, he is exactly who we should ask."

Christian pulled his reins tighter, his impatience straining to be free. He needed to lodge here, whatever it took. He couldn't afford to lose his quarry. And if this Mr. Kaden was his only chance . . .

"Excellent. Where can we find him?"

"Oh, right, too right. Elias, take over until I return."

Elias, a friendly, happy-go-lucky type whose eyes didn't quite reflect the happiness he was trying to project, stepped forward as Christian and the innkeeper exited. Perhaps if he completed his task and was feeling overly celebratory, Christian would buy the man a pint and teach Elias how to better fake a happy demeanor. He considered himself quite the expert.

"Dear, dear Mr. Kaden," the innkeeper continued in fragments as they walked. "Just happened in yesterday, didn't you know? He's helping around a bit, reduced rate on the room and all. Will probably agree right away to split the room. I'll still have to charge you the extra bit, though. Unless you want to help as well?"

Christian's immediate response was an emphatic *no*. He could only imagine his father's apoplexy were he to discover that his only remaining off-spring, hated though he was, would consider sharing a room with a complete stranger, not to mention *working*. Anyone with the surname Black just didn't *do* that. But then again, Christian reflected, he wasn't fit to be a Black, as his sire oft mentioned.

"Fine young fellow, Mr. Kaden. A bit on the small side, head injury too, but dedicated to work. You have to like that in a servant or helper. Interested? I could surely use someone in the stables. I've had to hire a number of day workers in the village. Good year for the coaching inn, good year I tell you. Can't rightly wait to get out the books and do the tallies in a few weeks for the entire twelve months. Can't remember a better—"

"You only need help in the stables?"

"Oh, well, yes." The innkeeper seemed slightly nonplussed at being interrupted yet again. "We are all taken care of inside the inn proper. Our girls do twice the load in half the time as any other inn around. And won't be quite as crowded soon as the teams clear out—we won against Lehigh today in an informal cricket match, didn't you know? We like to keep our skills up, even out of season. Mr. Lake is likely to be in his cups tonight if he stays—on the Lehigh team, didn't you know?—then things will settle down for the night. Were you a woman, there'd be plenty of need right now, but seeing as you are not—"

Christian sent him an unimpressed look.

"—the stables could really use the help. Could put you up there too."

The stables were not even in consideration unless he couldn't find an alternative. He needed to be inside the inn, preferably as close to Mr. Freewater's room and belongings as possible.

"Let me consider it, sir. If we could talk to Mr. Kaden, first?"

"Oh, right, too right!"

They walked through the public dining room, Christian's quarry nowhere in sight, and continued through the taproom and into the stairwell corridor.

Cheerful baking smells—apple pie, if he was any judge—and a faint breeze of lemon oil intensified as they neared the stairwell juncture, indicating the kitchens and larder as the doors on the left and what appeared to be private dining rooms and storage areas to the right.

Christian considered his situation as the innkeeper's head disappeared into one room after another looking for the elusive Mr. Kaden. It wasn't as if he actually needed to sleep. He just needed a place to stay and remain discreet as he inconspicuously rummaged through Frederick Freewater's belongings. He would consider the ramifications at some other time, per usual.

"Oh, there he is."

Christian looked up to see a short, gangly young man carrying what looked like two shirts.

"Tailor's apprentice, Mr. Kaden is. Father died. On his way to London to see if he can get work in one of the big shops. Said he would do our mending for the week. Right good lad, Mr. Kaden is, and decent with the needle too. Good deal for me to give him a discount. And now that you're here"—he smiled cheerfully at Christian, who managed a strained smile in return—"we can give Mr. Kaden a bigger break. Oh, Mr. Kaden! Mr. Kaden, a moment of your time, please."

The young man turned and walked somewhat apprehensively back to the proprietor.

"Good afternoon, Mr. Wicket. What can I do for you?" The apprentice's voice was very smooth. Like fine brandy. Christian twitched at the odd thought.

"I have excellent news, Mr. Kaden. This gentleman, Mr.—" he looked at Christian as if suddenly surprised he hadn't asked his name during a nonexistent pause in his nonstop babble.

"Black."

"Right. Mr. Black is willing to offset the cost of

your room for the night. More than half your current price for tonight, isn't that good news?"

Christian watched the tailor's apprentice stiffen. Interesting. If Christian were traveling as himself, he wouldn't give two thoughts to sharing a room. It would simply be out of the question. But this man, who obviously was in need, was waffling.

"Are there no more rooms at the Green Toad or White Stag?"

"Mr. Kaden! We don't discuss the White Stag, don't you know?" the innkeeper asked in a scandalized tone.

"My apologies, Mr. Wicket. But the Green Toad then? Surely they have available rooms?"

The innkeeper blinked rapidly, and Christian frowned. A hardworking lad not leaping at the opportunity to pay less? Most commoners wouldn't mind sharing a room. It was done all the time.

Christian took a deeper look at the boy. Clothing that was slightly too big, a brown head wrap that at first glance almost looked like hair circling his crown and ears, and a hat pulled down to secure it in place. A tailor dressed sloppily in ill-fitting clothes? No, something was definitely wrong here.

The boy must have realized how odd he was sounding because he quickly stated in his brandy voice, "I mean, the Green Toad isn't even close to

13

the same level of quality as the Dragon's Tale, but it will do in a pinch."

Christian's eyes narrowed on the bent head, disregarding for the moment that something about the boy's voice was peculiar. Stay somewhere else? There wasn't a chance in hell.

"How about I offer to pay you to stay there instead? I'll even give you a note for your trouble," Christian said.

The boy stiffened again, and the innkeeper looked askance at Christian. Damn. So much for being unobtrusive. Damn it all, and double damn Anthony for placing him in this situation. It had seemed a lark at first, finding an outlet for his love of puzzles and the chase, but it had turned into a royal mess.

Christian shrugged and laughed, hoping to lighten his tone. "I really don't want to be an inconvenience to either of you. Surely we can share a room for the night, Mr. Kaden. I promise I will be no trouble and will be gone in the morning."

The innkeeper looked mollified; the boy's posture remained stiff.

"You will be gone in the morning then? It will be just the one night?" The boy's smooth voice grew low and a bit pensive.

Christian frowned at the tone. Odd situations

were normal for him, but this one felt especially off. He almost felt the need to reassure the boy that he didn't plan on spending more than an hour or two in the room. Just time enough to scout Freewater's room. "Yes, I am only in town for the night."

The boy looked up at Christian for the first time; light blue eyes rimmed with gray met his. Christian smiled his most disarming smile. The one that made women swoon and men want to befriend him. In no less than four countries, it had worked every time. Well, outside of his family, that is.

The boy's mouth pulled taut. Obviously Christian was going to need to revise his statement. It was more important that his charm work on women anyway. And if he finished his mission early, he could spend plenty of time rehoning his technique while unwrapping the saucy blonde serving wench.

He had no intention of sleeping in the same room with a gangly boy when there were more buxom options available.

The boy looked at the innkeeper, a torn expression on his face, before resolutely turning back to face Christian. "I suppose we will have to make do for the night, Mr. Black."

The boy held out a hand, a slender hand, to agree. Perhaps it was Christian's previous train of thought about seduction or the increasingly loud alarms about the boy's voice; either way, the hand was a giveaway.

Christian looked back to the tailor's face. "Mr." Kaden almost unnoticeably chewed at his lower lip; his left hand, also slim and dainty, tugged at the brown wrap around his head, which covered his hair and ears, deliberately causing him to look more androgynous.

Christian's gaze traveled down to observe a smooth neck mostly hidden by the oversized clothing, and back up to flashing light blue eyes, resentful and enigmatic.

How delightful. Perhaps he would spend more than an hour or two in his room after all, his fondness for puzzles and mysteries overriding the easy availability of a maid like the buxom blonde.

Christian smiled his first real smile of the day as he grasped the warm, soft hand. And anyway, he'd have time to try out that smile again on his new female roommate.

Chapter 2

Be a good judge of character, my dear. Distrust a wolf in sheep's clothing. Many a smart lady has fallen prey to a rapscallion.

George Simon
to his daughter Kate, age eighteen

As Kate Simon shook her new roommate's smooth hand, the weathered clock on the mantel struck the hour. Her hand jerked with the chime, and the warm clasp of the man's hand tightened fractionally. Kate shivered as a lick of fear swept through her, momentarily replacing her indignation.

It had been one month and one hour since her life had literally fallen around her ears. All day she had avoided rooms and areas that were near the chiming clocks. If only she could avoid the nightmares they stirred as well.

The hand holding hers tightened again, and she studied the confident face of the entirely too attractive man across from her. It seemed her full quotient of bad luck and trouble had not yet been reached.

She scowled, but instead of responding in kind, his full lips curved into a long, sensual smile. Here was a man who obviously knew his appeal and how to manipulate others by using it.

Kate pulled her hand from his warm, firm grasp and tugged the left portion of her head wrap again to make sure it covered her still bruised and damaged ear. She could only imagine the cutting comment a man such as the one across from her might make if he were to see the bruises and patchy hair surrounding the area.

She could still hear the echoes of Connor Lanton's disgust ringing in her ears, both the perfect one and the not-so-perfect one. Which just went to show how fickle men could be—a man could be an ardent suitor one week, a cutting adversary the next.

There was no reason to think that this man across from her would be any different. He looked to be cut from the same cloth as Connor and her half-brother, Teddy. Mr. Black appeared to have the same natural indifference to anyone who couldn't provide some type of aid or amusement, the same charming yet cunning smiles for those who could, and probably the same sneering disdain when casting someone aside. What made the situation worse was that she could already sense that both men were neophytes compared to Mr. Black, who held himself with an innate aristocratic demeanor.

She disliked him on sight.

Whispers of her father's voice brushed through her mind, telling her it wasn't wise to judge someone based on his appearance or on one's biases, but the agony of her loss was still too fresh and she pushed the voice aside. Lashing out was much easier than looking inside and dealing with the pain.

Besides, there was something about Mr. Black—a discrepancy between what was and what should be. His clothing was of quality, but it didn't look like it belonged on him, as if the material was slightly too small to cover his shoulders and too large at his waist. His gloves were in his hands, showing that his well-manicured fingers hadn't seen a day's work, and the cap he wore was that of a workman, one she was sure didn't belong on his head. His dark blue eyes were wary and watchful beneath the heavy lidded, too-charming gaze.

"So we have an agreement, Mr. Kaden?"

Kate hesitated and looked to the innkeeper, who was sending her a questioning, hopeful glance. She had made an arrangement with Mr. Wicket to stay the entire week at a greatly reduced rate. It had taken a great deal of haggling, and she wasn't going to get a better rate elsewhere, regardless of the unnerving clocks. Not if she was going to continue to stay one step ahead of her brother and his minion.

No doubt Teddy was searching London and questioning their aunt, assured that he would find her a day or two before she had any chance of finding their solicitor. Teddy prided himself on being a skilled hunter, but often made the mistake of believing that deer and women possessed similar reasoning abilities and instincts.

"Mr. Kaden?"

"My apologies. Yes, of course, as I said, we will make do." She mentally winced, but perhaps she could strike a deal with Mr. Black outside the innkeeper's curious ears. There was a slightly desperate edge to Mr. Black's perfected smiles and easy acceptance of the situation that had her on alert. Desperation was an emotion she had come to know intimately over the past month. Perhaps she might even work out a way to pay for a seat in the stage to London. She didn't fancy the rumble-tumble—the outside seat she would be occupying otherwise.

"Excellent! Perhaps you could show Mr. Black to your room? Talk with Sally about getting some extra linens?"

"Of course, Mr. Wicket. Thank you for your concern and continued hospitality."

The jolly, rotund man puffed up at the compliment and bid them adieu.

"Shall we, Mr. Kaden?"

There was something unsettling about Black's statement. She narrowed her eyes at his tooth-grinding good looks and arrogance—the plain wool cap doing nothing to hinder either. The man was either a consummate actor pretending he had money, or else he was doing a poor job of hiding the fact that he really did have money. Either way, Mr. Black was hiding something, and that made him more dangerous than if he were just a common variety rake.

"This way, Mr. Black."

Kate grabbed the clothes that required mending and proceeded up the winding wooden stairs to the first floor, neatly avoiding the creak in the seventh step. Black either wasn't paying attention or didn't care as he stepped on the middle section of the riser, which immediately protested his tall, athletic weight.

As they reached the landing, two giggling girls descended from the upper floor.

"Good afternoon, Mr. Kaden."

Kate nodded at Mary, the apple-cheeked inn-keeper's daughter, and at the shy linen maid, Sally. "Mary, Sally. This is Mr. Black."

Black nodded, and the girls blushed and bobbed in unison.

"Since the inn is full, he will be sharing my room for the night. Could you bring a pallet, Sally?"

Sally bit her lip and shifted. "Sorry, Mr. Kaden, Mr. Black, but the pallets have already been re-quested and given. Both Mr. Nickford and Mr. Freewater requested them earlier. I'm sorry, sirs."

Kate was appalled . . . no pallets left? But that would mean . . . no! Her head snapped up to look at Black before turning back to Sally to argue their case.

"But . . . there are only two?"

"Yes, Mr. Kaden. I'm sorry, sir." The maid's eyes were firmly focused on the floor. In her short time in the inn, Kate had come to like the timid maid and knew the girl wished to please.

Kate worked up a reassuring smile. "It's not

your fault, Sally. We will talk to Misters Nickford and Freewater."

Sally gave a small, shy smile in thanks and followed her more gregarious friend down the stairs to the ground floor.

"Whatever shall we do, Mr. Kaden?" her unwanted roommate drawled.

Kate tasted defeat for a brief second, then walked briskly to her room across from the steps. Motioning Black inside, she shut the door behind him and set the clothes that required mending on the small oak side table. She couldn't afford the weekly rates at the Toad on her own without the type of deal Mr. Wicket had been offering, clocks or no clocks, but perhaps she could get Mr. Black to foot the bill.

Spinning around, she faced her foe. "Listen, Mr. Black, if you are so adamant about staying here, perhaps we can work something out. I'm traveling to London next week, and if your offer is still good to pay for me to stay the duration at the Toad—and if you throw in stage fare to Town—then you can be rid of me and have this room to yourself."

"Now why would I do that, Mr. Kaden?" There was that strange stress on her name again.

"Fine, forget the stage fare. I'll accept your offer for the week's stay."

23

She watched warily as he walked over and tested the four-poster bed by bouncing on it.

"Again, why would I do that, Mr. Kaden?" He patted the bed. "There is plenty of space for us to share, so neither of us need be displaced."

"The bed is but a double," she felt it necessary to point out. Why wasn't he jumping at her offer as he would have earlier? She fingered the cold, smooth planes of the water pitcher on the washstand, trying to settle her nerves and remain calm.

"How much space do you require?" There was a lascivious tone in his voice that had her feminine side taking unfortunate notice. She knocked the ceramic pitcher onto the floor. It clattered and rolled toward his feet.

"More than that, I assure you," she said as calmly as she could, all the while firmly repressing the sudden surge of heat pouring through her body.

He smirked and reached down to pick up the jug. His hair flopped across his eyes in a rakish manner as he straightened. Long fingers smoothed over the surface of the container as he quirked a brow.

She was obviously imagining things that were not there. Words that she secretly yearned to hear from an attractive man. She had grown accustomed to a fair amount of male attention during the last few years, perhaps not the bevy of admirers that some of the other village girls had, but enough for Kate to recognize and grow warm under a suggestive comment. Not that she would be getting any more of those—even if she had initially discounted her brother's taunts, Connor had proved Teddy's words true when he had turned his viper tongue against her.

Still, her body hadn't quite seemed to realize yet what her brain did, and Mr. Black fairly *oozed* sex and virility. She forgave her body the lapse.

Black put the pitcher down and leaned back on his elbows, staking out a spot on the bed like a giant house cat lying on a velvet counterpane.

"What are you doing?" Her voice rose a bit higher than her already unmanly tone. She didn't know what made her more nervous, his lack of attention to their dilemma or his obvious disregard for it.

"If it bothers you, we can ask Freewater or Nickford for their pallets." He crossed his legs at the ankle, raising them a bit off the floor in a parody of a stretch.

She tried to focus on the uninspired watercolor above the bed instead of on its lounging occupant. "You don't want to make the deal you proposed earlier in front of the innkeeper? The one where you can have this nice cozy room all to yourself?"

"No." He stretched his neck in one slow circle and stood. "Do you want to ask the gentlemen for their pallets?"

Her eyes followed his stretch against her will. What she wanted was to throw him off the nearest balcony. "Fine. Mr. Freewater's room is right next door."

If she had thought his previous smiles had been sensual, this one was purely predatory, almost bordering on feral. A shiver of dread passed through her. A hunter's smile.

"Then by all means, let's talk to Freewater," he drawled, the unnerving smile still in place.

Kate gladly led the way from their small, sparse room to the larger corner room next door and knocked. Then knocked again, louder this time, aware of the disquieting presence directly behind her.

A harried-looking man opened the door a crack and peered through the narrow slit. Kate got an impression of gray streaks running through dull brown hair, watery pale blue eyes, and unshaven jaw.

"I said, I don't need more linens!" Freewater narrowed his eyes as he took in Kate and her much larger shadow. "You aren't the maid. Who are you and what do you want?"

Kate pasted on a smile. "The maid said she brought you an extra pallet. Since the inn is fully booked, we are in dire need of it. Would you mind terribly giving up yours?"

"Yes, I would mind. Terribly, you insolent boy. Wouldn't have requested it otherwise now, would I have?"

Kate frowned at the scrawny man. "Yes, well, I understand that you are staying alone in this room, whereas some of the others have multiple occupants—"

"That fact doesn't concern me. The bed is lumpy; I need the extra pad for layering. Blame the inn for overbooking. Now, don't bother me again."

He slammed the door abruptly.

Kate blinked, the tip of her nose two inches from the wood, the smell of recently varnished oak infiltrating her nostrils.

A smooth voice interrupted her staring contest with a dark knot of wood. "I believe the innkeeper referred to Freewater as 'terribly cheerless.' I must admit that he's a better judge of character than I thought."

Kate turned to Black, who was leaning against the wall. "You could have helped."

"Not sure anything would sway Freewater. He's terribly cheerless, didn't you know?"

She frowned at his smirking expression. "But still, you want that pallet, don't you?"

"Not particularly."

"No?! Why ever not?"

He smiled lazily, and a dimple appeared in his left cheek. "I have no problem sharing a bed with you."

There it was again. That slight emphasis, just as when he had addressed her as mister. Mister . . . Kate froze. He *knew*. "We'll—we'll just try Mr. Nickford now."

She walked blindly down the hall to Nickford's room. He couldn't know. He just couldn't. If Connor or Teddy were in this situation they would blackmail first, ask questions later. She was in deep, deep trouble if he knew. She didn't have the funds to stay somewhere else for a week *and* get to London, and there was no way she could go to her aunt in London without her brother finding her. Timing was of the utmost importance.

A languid drawl interrupted her panic. "Are you going to knock on the door?"

Kate swallowed her incipient numbness and knocked. Six pairs of dangling brown eyes answered.

"Mr. Nickford?"

"Jolly good. You've brought me the mugs. Need them for my experiment, I do." Jiggling from his bright red head were three pairs of dangling eyeglasses attached in various ways to a contraption. "Bring them in, bring them in."

Nickford jostled her inside, and she saw Black enter with barely concealed curiosity.

"Mr. Nickford, we are here to—"

"Yes, put it over there." He motioned to a side table and set something up on top of the prized pallet.

"No, you misunderstand. We are here to talk about the pallet."

"The pellets? Don't need any pellets. Just the mugs. Hold still while I test this out."

"Pallets," she enunciated.

"Yes, the pallet works fine."

Black tried unsuccessfully to hide his mirth behind his hand and Kate glared at him.

"Watch out now."

Before Kate had an opportunity to follow the instruction, Nickford pulled a handle and a giant object sped straight toward her.

Kate momentarily forgot how to breathe.

The projectile barely missed striking her, instead hitting the side table with a resounding thwack.

"Where's the mug?"

"What?" Kate tried to catch her breath.

"The mug? Oh, failure again! The mug. Oh, why?"

Kate regained the ability to breathe and didn't know whether to give the man's cheek a hard slap to stop his fit or to join his wailing chorus.

Nickford stopped howling abruptly as if nothing had happened, straightened, and announced, "One test is nothing. There will be more, oh yes. Help me set things up again, my boy."

Kate swore she heard muffled laughter from the corner of the room, but she refused to look at Black. "We are here to commandeer your pallet." Directness seemed the only way to handle Nickford. "Now hand it over."

Nickford's face fell. "But my tests? You are taking my pallet away? I need it to prop up my items; you saw what happened. I need it!"

Kate breathed in deeply and held on to her patience. Nickford was like the baker from her village, temperamental one minute and jolly the next. "Mr. Nickford. Your shot was straight and true. I'm sure if the mug had been in position, you would have hit the mark. Now really, one night without the pallet will do no harm."

"But it was supposed to go *in* the mug."

30

At that speed? He was lucky it hadn't left a hole in the table.

"Be that as it may—"

"We are sorry to interfere, Mr. Nickford. We'll leave you to your work." Black tugged her arm through the door, and the last thing she saw was Nickford's jaunty wave before a warm hand pressed into the small of her back and prodded her down the empty hall and into her room.

"What are you doing?" She hissed.

"Surely you weren't going to steal the poor man's pallet. He was already starting to weep at its loss."

"Weep? It's a pallet! Not a Rembrandt!"

"And we don't need it."

Kate fought her temper and outrage as he strode past her, his fingers brushing her side. "I am not sleeping with you in this room without a pallet."

He resumed his previous position on the bed. "It will be mighty cold outside tonight. Heard someone say we were in for a bit of a storm."

She pointed a finger at him. "What exactly do you want, Mr. Black? Why are you all of a sudden so intent on sharing a room with me, when you were so opposed to it before?"

Please, please let her suspicion prove untrue . . . for several days things had been going well—right up until Mr. Black made his entrance. No one at

31

the inn had suspected she was a girl, at least no one with any wish to expose her. And if her ruse was discovered now, the game would be up. Juicy news traveled quickly through the countryside, and although her brother was dim when it came to the female mind, outside of gambling he rarely made the same mistake twice.

"Because you seem like such interesting company, Mr. Kaden. Besides, I could stand to save a few pounds. I'm down on my luck as well. Too many bets on the races."

"Then why did you offer to pay for me to stay a week at the Toad earlier?"

He shrugged carelessly. "It suited my purpose at the time, but on second thought, this is a better arrangement. I seem to forget I'm bereft of cash now and again."

Kate narrowed her eyes. Just like Teddy and Connor. All smiles, affectations, and hidden agendas. A man who always took what he pleased and thought nothing of others. One who would ignore the people in his life if it meant risking his own pleasure.

Sell his own sister to pay his debts? Sell his honor to enter just one more game? Borrow against the promise of an inheritance?

Men like that were driven by self-interest and

blind to others. They didn't look any further than what they wanted to see. She snorted. And she had been worried.

To be noticed as a female, she would probably have to strip naked and dance in front of him.

He drew a lazy pattern on the counterpane with his finger. "So what's your real name?"

She blinked as she met his eyes. "What?"

"Your real name, *Miss* Kaden?"

Chapter 3

It is never too late to extricate yourself from a bad situation. Be strong and cunning and never underestimate your foe.

George Simon
to Kate, age fifteen

"**P**ardon me, Mr. Black, but did you just question my manhood?"

Kate would not sweat. She would not sweat.

"Most definitely."

"Sir, I'm going to have to ask you to leave. I withdraw permission for you to share this room."

When he continued to lounge on the bed, she motioned toward the door. "Go now before I must prove my manliness with violence."

"Welshing on your agreement?" Instead of the angry or seductive tone of voice she expected, a good deal of humor had been injected. "I don't think you really want me to leave, Miss Kaden."

"I most definitely do. And stop calling me that."

"What should I call you then? Lady? Missus? Lassie? Maiden? Maiden Kaden has a nice ring, don't you think?"

"What? No! Leave!"

"I repeat, I don't think you really want me to go." He tapped a finger against the counterpane.

"I do. I really, really do," she insisted fervently.

He stretched and rose from his position on the bed. Kate's breathing increased as he stalked toward her, every bit the hunter she had thought him previously.

He leaned close to her good right ear, his breath tickling the skin just behind and sending shivers to her toes. "Oh, I don't think you do, unless you want everyone to know you are pretending to be a boy."

"You have taken leave of your senses, Mr.—"

He pulled away from her and snatched off her cap. Short brown curls tumbled over the side of the head wrap to brush her chin.

"Much better, maiden." He twirled a silky tendril in his fingers as she frantically put one hand to the left side of her head. Relief washed through her as she felt the band over her ear still in place. "Much, much better, in fact."

She swiped her scratchy wool cap from his fingers and with trembling fingers put it back in place. As soon as she had the curls tucked beneath the cap and was sure the head wrap hadn't come loose, she looked up. She couldn't see any disgust on his face, so he must not have seen her ear. Thank goodness. She didn't think her damaged femininity could take another bruising.

She caught the flicker of interest in his eyes as he smiled in his seductive way. That wouldn't do either. It would only delay the inevitable abhorrence and crush her in the end.

Besides, her racing heart was due to being unmasked, that was all.

"My hair is no longer than that of many men my age," she said, trying to recover whatever tendrils of the doomed masquerade she could. Somehow her voice emerged steady and calm, in complete opposition to the rest of her.

He bent his head and lifted her chin. "You look nothing like a boy. Your features are too fine and your skin too smooth." A thumb brushed her lower lip, and she could do nothing but stand there frozen, her body a statue in the hands of a master carver.

36

"You have beautiful long lashes, a generous mouth, and your stride is definitely feminine. Also your clothes are not those of a tailor's apprentice. To the casual observer, you may not be noticed in this garb, but on any closer inspection, you would never pass as a boy. Not by anyone of discerning intelligence. Two points deducted from the innkeeper and every other man in residence. You are far too fey."

Kate took a step back, her heart beating even faster, and his hand dropped from her chin, his thumb from her lips. "What do you want?" Her words came out on a breath. She studied the worn red and blue rug on the floor before remembering the danger of not keeping her eyes on the man before her.

He shrugged negligently, but there was a gleam in his deep blue eyes and a dangerous set to his chiseled features. "Nothing too extraordinary, I assure you. I merely wish to stay in this room for the night."

"Neither of us wanted to room together *before* you knew my gender. Now that you know I am a female, surely you can see the impropriety?"

"The impropriety exists now, where it didn't exist before?"

"No. Yes. You know to what I refer!"

He leaned against the bedpost. "I don't believe I do. Enlighten me."

"If you were a gentleman, you would see the dilemma."

"Ah, but I never claimed to be a gentleman."

She narrowed her eyes and swiped the ceramic pitcher from the floor. "Surely anyone as *discerning* as yourself could tell that you are anything other than what you claim."

His eyes narrowed, and she congratulated herself on wiping the arrogance from his face.

"And just what do you mean by that statement?"

"Goodness, sir, who dressed *you*? The black-smith's apprentice?"

She gave him credit. He didn't so much as peer down at his clothes.

"*You* mock *my* clothes?"

"Those aren't your clothes."

"I'm wearing them, aren't I?"

"Badly."

His eyes narrowed further, and she thought she detected a hint of outrage. She would never have taken him for a dandy. Great, that was all she needed.

"I'll have you know, these clothes look fine. I even received a gracious offer from a rather lusty-looking blonde in this very establishment."

"Daisy? From what I'm to understand, you shouldn't feel quite so special about it."

Black smoothed down his shirt and cocked a brow. "Did you receive an offer, maiden?"

Kate blinked. "I'm just going to forget you asked me that. Now could you please just leave? Find somewhere else to stay?"

She nonchalantly tried to put the pitcher back in place, but it wobbled a bit.

His smile returned in force. Perfect white teeth, full lips, straight aristocratic nose, the corners of his eyes crinkled in amusement, dark rakishly arranged locks . . . she wasn't at all surprised Daisy had made an offer.

"No. I want to stay here with you. If nothing else, you will prove amusing."

Kate bristled, even though she knew she was fueling said amusement. "Mr. Black, or whatever *your* name is, you need to find somewhere else to stay. There will be no further discussion."

A self-satisfied smile appeared. "You are correct, unless you want me to tell dear Mr. Wicket and his staff that you are not *Mr.* Kaden after all."

Kate went cold. "You wouldn't."

"And why wouldn't I? You are denying me a

place to sleep, after all. And you did suggest I was anything but a gentleman."

Kate swallowed. "Fine. Take the room then. I'll find somewhere else to stay. Perhaps with one of the servants." But she knew that was not an option. The staff had been doubled up and even tripled because of the additional servants the guests had brought with them. The small post town was overflowing for the holidays. The Wickets' nine-guest-room inn was packed to the brim.

"No need to do that, maiden." His smile wasn't quite conciliatory, but it wasn't as self-satisfied as it had been. "I'm going to remain in the tap-room most of the evening. Other than requiring a few hours' sleep, you won't even realize I'm around."

She highly doubted that. But she nodded. She would nap while he was downstairs, then stay awake the rest of the night. Something in the soft-ening of his eyes after her obvious distress told her that he could be trusted—to an extent.

And he obviously wasn't pining for female attention—his looks if nothing else would guaran-tee that. His breed of arrogance was a siren call to those of her gender. Kate was determined to keep cotton stuffed in her ears to resist his lure.

No, Black wasn't the strong-arm type. He was a cajoler, a seducer, a charmer. She could readily fend off those tactics.

There was no way she was opening herself up to the type of scorn she would experience. A man like that wanted perfection, he wanted—

Wait a moment. Why was her stomach fluttering, and why was she worrying about him seducing her? He was more likely to prefer a romp with the willing, voluptuous Daisy. Actually she could probably put money on it.

"Then we are agreed, maiden?"

Having convinced herself that she had been experiencing a bad case of nerves, she nodded. "Yes, but stop calling me that."

"What is your real name?"

"Kate," she admitted grudgingly.

"Kate Kaden? How awful." She stiffened. "Ah, so Kaden isn't your real last name. Quite clever of you. Much easier to respond to a new name when it sounds so similar to the old one."

Well, Kate had thought herself clever. But now she just felt mocked.

"Are we through, Mr. Black?" She stressed his last name.

He gave her that charming, teeth-gnashing smile that caused her toes to curl in her ill-fitting

41

boots. "Yes we are, Kate. And you may call me Christian."

A name less suited to a person, she had yet to hear.

"I'm honored."

"I know."

She attempted a smile, but it was forced. With teeth clenched, she barely restrained a hiss.

"See you after supper, Kate."

"You could only wish," she muttered to his retreating back as he sauntered to the door. "And don't call me that!"

Christian barely suppressed a real smile as he descended the winding stairs, hugging the railing to avoid the squeaky seventh step. If he had known having a roommate would be such fun, he'd have taken one sooner.

Christian walked into the smoky taproom and seated himself on a hard chair in the back corner. It was an ideal place to observe everyone entering and exiting the taproom, the dining room, and the inn itself. As soon as Freewater entered for dinner or a drink, Christian would slip upstairs, rifle through his room, find the journal, then spend a few hopefully memorable hours trying to coax his new roommate into spending the time pleasurably.

He'd need at least a few hours to work on such a feisty one.

Daisy sidled up to his table and gave him a saucy smile. "Whatcha havin', handsome?"

He cocked a brow. "What do you recommend?"

She leaned forward, raising her brows invitingly. "There are so many choices."

Christian caught a flurry of brown moving through the room, and saw Kate shooting him a look of annoyance before shaking her head and disappearing into the hall. She had every right to be irritated with him after being outmaneuvered.

Disapproval was a normal response to his actions, and generally he was able to shrug it off. But for some reason he felt the unreasonable urge to drag her back into the room. Irritation vied with amusement. Perhaps he had finally reached his limit.

Christian turned to Daisy. "A pint of your winter ale will be fine. For now." He winked, though it took some effort.

Daisy gave him a saucy grin and sauntered off.

It took everything Christian had to return her look. He internally shook his head. Within his reach was an experienced wench, ready to be tossed for a few coins, or even for just the pleasure, yet his mind was on a fey child-woman pretending to be a man.

He had never been able to resist a challenge.

His time was too short, though. Better to take pleasure with the lass already primed for action. He tried to picture Daisy, breasts and blond locks bouncing while she vigorously rode him, but the image faded and was replaced with Kate's lithe body, fiery blue eyes, and disapproving glare. The urge to bury his face between Daisy's ample assets was replaced with the urge to run his fingers through Kate's short, silky curls. In fact, he'd be more than willing to look for short curls in other places on her body as well. Maybe not as silky, but no less interesting, to be sure.

His body began to respond.

Damn. His presence at the inn was a challenge itself, he didn't need another. But the image of Kate slithered through his mind, taunting him. He rarely backed down from a task, and had a well-earned reputation for tenacity. Other than accepting challenges, only solving puzzles interested him more. Kate was a very nice-looking combination of the two.

As he shifted uncomfortably in his chair, he guessed he really did need that country respite Anthony had been advocating. It was easy enough for Anthony to suggest, since his friend was chasing a skirt while leaving Christian to clean up his mess.

"I just need you to pick up the journal, Christian. Won't take but ten minutes," Christian mimicked.

Daisy reappeared with his ale and a suggestive wink, then headed to a booth across the room to serve another patron.

He took a swig and let the tankard drop to the table with a thud, women forgotten for the moment. Ten minutes had turned into ten days of trailing Frederick Freewater around the Midlands.

Anthony, in all his carelessness, had left his journal and travel cases at his aunt's home when he had run off to chase his ladylove in the middle of the night after a lovers' spat. Even after ascending to his title, Anthony still did a lot of stupid things. Then again, like two peas in a pod, Christian and he were such good friends for a reason.

Freewater had been working with Anthony's dotty aunt to publish her husband's memoirs. Apparently she had given Freewater carte blanche to search the entire house and take anything that would help. Freewater had done just that. He hadn't even waited to finish the old man's memoirs before offering Anthony's aunt a feeble excuse to leave and hightailing it off the property.

To a publisher like Freewater, Anthony's journal must have been a godsend. The damn man had probably heard the blasted angels playing as he opened the first page.

After Christian had spoken with the dotty lady and discovered the journal missing, it hadn't been hard to connect the dots. The only saving grace was that Freewater seemed to be making his way to London slowly and haphazardly. He was probably trying to avoid Anthony while he made notes and composed a forward to Anthony's unauthorized "memoirs." More like Anthony's sinful confessions of every married woman, widow, and harlot he had ever tossed. Detailed ones, if what Anthony hinted was true.

Tracking Freewater's disjointed path had been more than painful. Christian had been in a state of gritted teeth and painful smiles ever since leaving Anthony's aunt. He wasn't sure if he shouldn't just kill Anthony before his friend had the chance to kill *him* for losing the journal.

Hell, it wasn't Christian's fault that Anthony's aunt had involuntarily given it away. So, yes, he *had* arrived at her house a day late due to a hangover and extenuating circumstances involving long, shapely legs wrapped around his, but he hadn't been *that* late. Not late enough to anticipate that someone would *steal* the damn thing before he got there. What had Anthony been thinking to leave the journal with his crazy aunt? A voice in his head that sounded remarkably like his father's asked, What had Anthony been thinking of to give Christian the task of appropriating something of such obvious value?

Christian pushed the voice away with a snarl and a second swig of bitter ale. Great. That was all he needed, the sound of his father's condescending voice echoing in the void. He'd just visit his father at Rosewood Manor if he felt like punishing himself.

Christian watched a scuffle break out among the patrons at two of the large benched tables in the middle of the room. One of the men lunged, and a brawl began in earnest. Probably a fight over some woman or someone's pride or honor.

The fight mirrored his sudden change in mood.

He leaned back, shifting to keep the front of the hard chair from digging into his backside. He had at least an hour or two more before Freewater would show for supper. Plenty of time to drink a few pints and indulge in a bit of mischief if he wanted to join the fray or banter with his room-mate.

A swatch of brown caught his attention. His eyes followed Kate as she picked up two empty mugs on a table. It still amazed him that no one seemed to realize she was female. She blended into the background so well that most of the pa-trons barely spared her a glance.

What did she look like beneath the oversized men's garments? He wanted to strip her of her outer coverings and get rid of that damn cap and head wrap thing. She would never be a showy beauty, but she had a quiet prettiness. And there was a spark to her that vied with her demure looks. A zest—the real kind, not the type expertly faked by a courtesan trying to catch a man's eye.

Yes, a tumble between the sheets with the fey lady would be quite an adventure. More so than with some practiced barmaid, no matter how lus-ciously endowed. Now if only he could get past the outrage and propriety she had shown. All it took was the right phrase or words of encourage-ment to get most women beyond proper . . . and properly out of their clothes.

He was on a time constraint, but that only made it more of a challenge. Kate bent over to assist a man on the floor, providing Christian with an excellent view of her backside. Yes, the challenge was definitely going to be worth the effort. Now to figure out how to remove those nicely clinging breeches . . .

Stuck in his musings over Kate's shapely backside, Christian barely had time to register the fist flying toward his face.

Chapter 4

I don't care if your brother hit you first. I'm sure you deserved it.

The Marquess of Penderdale
to Christian, age six

Christian ducked just in time to avoid a burly fist headed straight for his nose. The fist connected with the mortared wall behind him and a howl of pain issued forth from its owner. Christian half rose and used the man's forward momentum to thrust his head into the wall as well. The fighter crumpled like a wet rag to the floor, and Christian stood to join the melee.

After everything that had happened to him during the past week, a bit of exercise might go a long way in releasing some pent-up tension. From experience he knew it would be only a matter of moments before another person tried to engage him in a fight.

Benches and chairs overturned, tables jostled, and liquid splashed as mugs were thrown. Off to his side a flash of wide blue eyes and a brown cap caught his attention. What the devil was Kate still doing in here? Christian stepped forward, grabbed her wrist, and unceremoniously pulled her behind him, pushing her shapely backside into the protected wall.

She made a slight mew of protest that barely registered over the din of angry words, bones crushing bones, and bodies hitting the floor. But she didn't resist.

She was such a tiny thing that one flying elbow would take her down. A dark blur entered his vision on the right, close to Kate. A wave of fury swept through him at the image.

Christian moved in front of her and allowed the man's fist to glance off his jaw. The movement left the man's entire side unprotected. Christian dropped him with a sharp blow to the gut, white-hot anger flowing through his veins. The man groaned and hit the floor a few feet away.

Christian reached back and grabbed a section of

Kate's shirt without taking his eyes from the man on the ground or the ongoing brawl. Her squawk told him she was fine, and he let go. A small hand came up to rest lightly in the middle of his back. He pressed against it, warmed by the contact.

The man on the floor had been bent on hitting her. Christian looked down at the crumpled figure and considered kicking him for good measure.

Mr. Wicket bustled into the taproom wielding a broom and yelling, "Stop! Stop!" then promptly slipped on a wet patch of the now slick wooden floor. Flailing his arms, he tried to maintain his balance, but dropped the broom and toppled onto his back. Moments later a whoosh of air issued from his throat as a brute landed on his prominent belly.

Christian looked from the pile to the dark-haired bastard he had felled moments before. The man was rising with a grimace, but with a no less determined expression. "No one hits me. I'll beat you to a pulp, you cur."

The man started forward, his fists flying. The hand on Christian's back knotted into his jacket.

Christian lifted his foot and indulged his urge to kick, aiming straight for the man's knees. The strike wasn't as hard as it could have been, but tears welled in the man's eyes as he fell bellowing to the floor once again.

Two bruisers mopped up the fighters across the room, while two blond-haired men grappled in front of the fireplace.

A well-built, expensively dressed man casually sipped his drink in the corner, seemingly unbothered by anything or anyone else in the room. The man turned and tipped his head to Christian, an amused smirk on his face, no fear or wariness in his gaze. The bruisers must have belonged to him. Either that or he was one peg short like Nicodemus Nickford upstairs.

Kate's hand released the death grip on his jacket and she stepped closer, her shoulder brushing the back of his arm as she peered around him. The bottom edge of her coat brushed his hand. He ran the thick fabric through his fingers, wondering when the rougher material had become more interesting than silk.

The bruisers joined the lounging man at his table. Groans issued from the six, no seven, bodies on the floor and several draped over the tables.

As if on cue, a rawboned woman came screeching into the room.

"Aiiieeee!"

Belying her scrawny frame, the woman pulled the only two still grappling men apart by the ears and hauled the blonds to one of the few benches that had remained upright.

"Lawrence Lake, Julius Janson, you should be ashamed! What have you done to my inn?" She gave both men an evil glare. "Well, Mr. Lake? I'm waiting."

Lawrence Lake's brown eyes narrowed dangerously upon Julius Janson's self-satisfied face. Lake, the leaner of the two, wiped the back of his sleeve across his torn lip. Blood was running freely from the wound. "Ask Janson."

Janson shrugged. "Lake is just bitter about being such a half-arsed cricket player."

"Why you—" Lake lunged for Janson. The expensively dressed man in the corner tipped his head, and one of his two bruisers gripped Lake's shoulder and shoved him unceremoniously back in his seat.

The innkeeper's wife narrowed her eyes at the large man, but refocused on Lake. "Mr. Lake, I must *insist* you behave yourself or you will be asked to leave. I may ask you to leave in any case."

Lake's mouth opened, then abruptly shut as he looked toward the door. Christian turned and saw a number of servants scrunched in the doorway watching. The innkeeper's daughter Mary, the epitome of the healthy country lass, was in front, her brows drawn together. Christian glanced back to see Lake's pained expression. Ah, so that was the way the wind blew.

Julius Janson's smirk grew. His green eyes took on a malicious glow. "Lake is a sore loser. Can't measure up in any way, as a player, as a fighter, or as a man."

Lake's eyes darted to Mary again before turning to her mother. "Mr. Janson made a few rather obnoxious comments about . . . some things . . . and the fight broke out. You can ask the other members of my team."

He pointed at a number of downed players, none of whom looked coherent enough to confirm or deny his statement.

Janson laughed, his expression hard and resentful. "Ask any of the members of *our* team, Mr. and Mrs. Wicket, and you'll find the story to be much different. Just ask Donald." He pointed to the man who was pushing himself up from where Christian had laid him out twice.

Kate's small hand returned to rest comfortingly on Christian's back.

Christian's kicking instinct quieted. Donald Desmond. He thought he had heard someone call out the name earlier. The man had dark hair and dark eyes and looked to be on par with his bully friend, Janson. Desmond shot Christian a hard, cold look that promised retribution. He was obviously not the kind of man who took well to being beaten.

Unfortunately for him, his look of retribution, especially after being soundly thrashed, just made him look silly.

"Julius made a casual comment and Lake lunged across the table, much as he did just a few seconds ago," Desmond sneeringly corroborated. He sent a calculating look toward Mary. "Very violent man, Mr. Lake. One can never be too careful around him."

Christian sensed Lake's deepening anger. The man seemed to be holding himself by a thread. Perhaps it was outrage over the two men's statements combined with the glaring fact that if he continued to fight it would just lend credence to their arguments. The bruiser also seemed to realize that sheer will alone was holding Lake from pouncing, and the hand on Lake's shoulder tightened.

"Mr. Lake, you will come with me." The innkeeper's wife turned and wagged her finger. "And you, Julius, should know better!"

Julius assumed a hangdog expression. "Yes, ma'am, I'm terribly ashamed."

The innkeeper huffed next to his wife. "There now, Julius is full of spirit. I know sometimes the mood strikes. Just not in the taproom, man!"

"Yes, sir, Mr. Wicket, sir."

Mr. Wicket smiled. "Can't have our best player injured. Mary would be devastated, of course."

All heads turned to the doorway to look for confirmation, but Mary had disappeared.

The innkeeper puttered around the room chastising the men for fighting and possibly hurting themselves so close to cricket season. Christian raised a brow. Cricket season was a good five months away.

The small, comforting hand dropped from his back. Kate stepped forward and gave Christian an unreadable look, then frowned in disgust at the combatants, who were in various states of awareness.

Daisy came breezing in to help clean up the mess. "I can't believe how men love to fight. Just look at them." The men were sheepish as they began to sort themselves out. "The blacksmith, the cobbler, and the cobbler's son all in a pile."

"Yeah, and I'm the baker," groaned the man who had taken a wild swing at Christian earlier and then ended up attached to the wall. He was looking sheepish as he apologized profusely to Christian and the innkeeper.

"So what do those two do for a living?" Christian asked, nodding to Desmond and Janson.

"Not much, I hear," Kate muttered under her breath.

Daisy picked up a mug. "Donald Desmond's the son of a well-to-do family, and Julius Janson is the squire's son."

The hierarchy was soon apparent as the combatants tidied up. Janson ruled their side of the cricket divide, with Desmond sneering next to him.

Christian turned to Kate as Daisy moved away. "And you, Mr. Kaden? What were you doing in this fine taproom while a fight ensued?"

"Some of us have to earn our way. We can't just be inveterate gamblers and taproom brawlers, Mr. Black," she said primly, although the effect was rather ruined by the splashed ale on her shirt and the smudge on her nose.

"So you were, what? Sewing in the corner?"

"I was helping Daisy clear mugs from the tables. Which is what I should be doing now."

"Helpful of you. Next time try to follow Daisy's lead and beat a hasty retreat from the room when a fight breaks out."

Her chin rose. She started to say something, gritted her teeth, and then repeated the sequence several times before finally saying, "Thank you for helping me during the fight."

The sentence was torn from her, but Christian just smiled. The hand on his back had said it already. Maybe, just maybe he could stay an extra night at the inn after retrieving the journal. He had a feeling that seducing Kate would be worth it. And his feelings about women seldom led him astray. "You're welcome, Kate."

Kate glanced around quickly, her shoulders relaxing as she saw the others had congregated in the center of the room to discuss matters, too far away to hear his soft statement of her name. She gave Christian an unreadable look, muttered something about helping in the kitchen since Mr. Wicket was making the men clean up, and hurried off.

He watched her go. Yes, the night was shaping up to be interesting indeed.

The tables were soon righted and the mess cleaned. Some men drifted into the open dining room, while others ordered another round. Christian noticed that the new round of drinks tasted substantially weaker than the previous one, no doubt watered down to prevent another brawl.

"Mr. Tiegs, Mr. Black, my apologies about the mess. You are both unhurt?"

Christian and the well-dressed man who had stayed out of the fight nodded, their gazes resting on each other rather than on the innkeeper. Christian had a feeling he was looking at the most dangerous man in the room.

"Good, good. Julius, help me with this heavy bench? Wouldn't want to trip Mr. Tiegs."

Julius winced infinitesimally as he looked at Tiegs. So there was someone Julius obviously deferred to and/or feared. Interesting.

Christian leaned back in his chair, lifted his new mug, and watched the door for Freewater and the damn journal. He also decided to keep an eye on Tiegs. Two bodyguards? And why had he ordered his lackey to stop Lake from hitting Janson? Janson, with all his bravado, was obviously cowed by Tiegs.

Christian shook his head. No sense in speculating. He wouldn't be at the inn long enough to sort through the layers of politics and maneuverings motivating the room's occupants. His primary focus was on snatching Anthony's journal.

As much as he wanted to strangle his friend, he really would do anything for him. Meeting and befriending Anthony at Eton had changed his life and taken him from the dark shadow of his family. If the journal was as damaging to Anthony as he had led Christian to believe, then Christian had to get it out of Freewater's possession as soon as possible.

Nothing would stop him.

Hours later, Christian wearily made his way upstairs. Nothing would stop him except Freewater never leaving his damn room. He was going to resort to knocking on the man's door and hitting him with a fireplace poker if he didn't cooperate soon.

He gave Freewater's door a disgusted glance and reached for the knob on his own door, only to find it locked. Light knocking did no good, so he pounded on the grainy wood. Moments later Kate stuck her head out, looking disgruntled, her cap and head wrap slightly askew. She made a hasty check of the hallway before dragging him inside.

"What are you doing?" she hissed as she began to gather up a pile of clothing laid out for mending. She had obviously taken a nap, if her rumpled clothing and skewed headgear were anything to go by.

"I'm returning to my room."

She straightened and placed her hands on her

hips. "You said you were going to stay in the tap-room most of the night."

"I changed my mind."

A muffled bang came from the connecting wall. Freewater was obviously doing something in there. Christian wished the irritating man would grow discouraged with whatever it was and fetch something to eat.

"Maid!"

Or maybe not.

Kate gave the wall a disgusted glance. "He's been calling for things all night. Refuses to get up and fetch them for himself."

"Yes, most annoying," Christian muttered. At least next door to the man he would be able to hear if Freewater moved.

"Let's get back to you being here. You can't just change your mind. We had an agreement."

"Too true. Our agreement was to share a room."

"You said you would stay in the taproom all night."

"You are repeating yourself, Kate."

"Don't call me that," she huffed, while obviously waiting for him to leave. "Fine. I will go then."

The first rule in handling skittish women was to keep them on their toes about whether you were really trying to seduce them.

He shrugged negligently. "More room for me." He plopped on the bed and watched as a delicate pink fanned her cheeks and then burst into a beautiful rose. His trousers tightened at the sight. "You are starting to resemble an overly ripe tomato, Kate. An out-of-season one, of course."

His body disagreed vehemently.

Her eyes narrowed and she stomped over, tugged on a large jacket, and gathered the mending. "Good evening, Mr. Black."

"You mean Christian," he reminded her breezily as she slammed the door.

He smiled and reclined on the bed, then lifted his legs to scoot toward the wall. She'd be back soon and as feisty as ever.

He might as well make use of his time until she did. What would it take to get the journal if he couldn't steal it back from Freewater? Blackmail? Extortion? He hadn't had time to hire someone to check into Freewater's background. He had instead jumped right into following the man. After all, how hard could getting the journal back be?

He snorted at his initial assumption. After chasing the man for over a week he was reasonably sure that nothing short of an Act of Parliament was likely to make Freewater relinquish his grip.

The journal had hooks into nearly everyone in the ton. Webs and relationships. Too many prominent people connected to one another in lewd or ill-advised arrangements. Husbands would be calling for blood, women would be forced into seclusion. Anthony had acknowledged that anyone who had frequented illicit house parties, taverns, and brothels where he was present was mentioned.

Unless Anthony had deliberately left him out, Christian was likely mentioned in a number of those entries. He had committed many a debauchery alongside his friend. Not that it mattered if he was named. It wasn't as if he had the respect of his family to lose. He had made his own way in society, and it would withstand scrutiny. Hell, the "good" ton that would be implicated would overshadow any of Christian's exploits.

No doubt Freewater had already read Anthony's journal, so the entries were already compromised, but the damage would be much greater if the actual document was released to the public in all its glory. Anthony would either be strung from society's rafters or be the most notorious man to survive a hundred duels.

That was if he survived his ladylove leaving him over the exposure.

No, Christian would take the journal back. And he didn't much care how he had to do it.

Christian pressed his ear to the wall, listening as Freewater again started yelling for a maid.

As she exited the room, Kate ran into Sally. The maid was on her way to answer Mr. Freewater's summons.

"Pardon me, Sally, I wasn't watching where I was stepping."

The maid's eyes remained downcast. "It was my fault, sir."

"No it wasn't. Do you need help with Mr. Freewater?"

Sally shook her head and looked at the poker in her hand. "I was just on my way to stoke the fire in the common room."

Kate shifted the garments and reached for the poker. "Here, allow me. I need a distraction."

Sally looked at her questioningly, but handed her the implement. "Thank you, sir."

"Think nothing of it. Have a good night, Sally."

Sally smiled. "Good night, sir."

Kate headed for the common room, stooping momentarily in the hall to pick up a linen handkerchief. Freewater bellowed again from his chambers as Sally knocked on his door. Raised voices, muffled but still audible, came from the common room. Curiosity made Kate walk more softly.

"The bitch won't touch you now."

Kate abruptly stopped outside the door.

"Don't call her that!" Lawrence Lake's angry voice echoed from within the room.

"I can call her anything I want." Kate leaned in closer to hear Julius Janson's lowered words. "Soon we'll be married and she'll be my bitch to do with whatever I want."

"I'll kill you before that happens."

"Yeah, let's see you attempt it. Can't differentiate a pistol cock from the wee one attached between your legs."

"Why doesn't anyone else see what you are?" Lake asked, a tad desperately.

Kate peered around the door to see Janson lean into Lake's face. "What, that I'm a real man? That you will always be second best? At bat, in the field, to me." He shot a cocky grin. "Now I need to go find my future wife and feel those curvy hips, silky and smooth."

"You won't touch her."

"She likes it when I touch her, Lake. She whispers my name in her dreams. When she touches herself in the bath. Screaming with her head thrown back as I pound into her."

Lake's fists knotted. "Go to the devil, Janson. I'd send you there now if I knew I wouldn't be thrown out of here and unable to keep an eye on you."

"Tut, tut, Lake. Hiding behind the Wickets again like the pansy you are. Make sure to change your nappy before the next match."

Janson sauntered out onto the balcony, leaving a raging Lake to punch the hardwood wall Janson's head had been leaning against moments before.

Kate waited a few moments before entering the common room. "Good evening."

Lake looked up from rubbing his knuckles and issued a distracted greeting in return, his lip still swollen from the taproom fight.

Kate added a log and quickly stoked the fire, hoping to leave before the emotional pressure in the room exploded.

"What is it about beastly men that women bloody love?"

Kate blinked. "Pardon me?"

"You look like a nice enough man, but I'll bet women don't look at you twice."

Kate didn't know whether to be insulted or amused. Christian had commented earlier about Daisy not noticing her as a man. Really, if she maintained this line of thought, she might as well grow some chest hair and add a cocky swagger to her step.

The devastated look on Lake's face caused sympathy to bloom instead. "I can honestly say that most women do not look at me twice, you are correct." Kate decided to find the humor in the situation.

He shook his head. "No one notices a monster in their midst when they don't choose to. Not if he is the team hero or the worshipped man about town."

Kate felt the bloom grow. He obviously held a tendre for Mary, who was promised to Janson. The innkeeper clearly thought Janson a right sporting fellow, and couldn't look past his hero status in cricket. She wondered how Mary felt. Her face, happy and kind like her father's, became unreadable around Janson and Lake. Maybe Mary saw more than people credited.

"If it would make you feel better, if I were a female, I wouldn't go for the likes of Julius Janson."

"Too bad you aren't a female."

"Er, yes, too bad." Kate replaced the poker next to the fireplace grate. "Don't let a man like Julius Janson get to you, Mr. Lake. It is what he wants above all other things. Even more than the girl you fight over."

Lake's mouth dropped in surprise, but before he could respond, Mr. Tiegs entered the room. The two large men who shadowed him were nowhere to be seen.

"Rough night, Mr. Lake?" he asked, swinging a pocket fob. An aura of power emanated from his every word. He was quite attractive in a rough way.

Lake's eyes narrowed before they clouded over. "One of the longest nights of the year."

Kate grabbed the opportunity to leave. "If you two gentlemen would excuse me." Kate nodded at both men.

"Have a pleasant evening, Mr. Kaden," Tiegs drawled.

Kate paused. She didn't know how Tiegs knew her name; she was beneath most people's notice in her disguise. There was something very disquieting about the man. There was something disquieting about Christian too, but they were disparate feelings, as if the two men both held power, but in different ways.

"You too, Mr. Tiegs. Mr. Lake."

Kate let her thoughts wander as she trooped downstairs with the items she had mended. Men lingered in the taproom, and a few women had joined them, including the vivacious widow Olivia

Trent, dressed in green satin. Her quieter companion, Francine, complemented her in blue. They created a splash of color amid the dully clothed men. Mrs. Wicket had looked upon them both with a measure of disdain, so Kate could only speculate as to their reputations.

She dropped off the mending in the office, grabbed something to eat in the kitchen, and after a quick gab with Bess, the cook, Kate headed for the stairs.

She had barely reached the first step when the hall clock started to sing. Kate's breath became shallow and started coming out in pants. One, two. She pressed herself against the wall and closed her eyes as the chimes continued. Five, six. She should have been in her room for the midnight chimes. On the other hand, she would rather break down in the stairwell than in front of Christian Black. Nine, ten. She put a hand to her damaged ear. She couldn't breathe. Twelve. The bell pealed and echoed the last strike in a parody of a farewell.

Kate forced open her eyes, thankful no one had happened upon her. She took a shaky step up, then another, and another, turning right when she reached the landing to go out to the gallery for some air.

Opening the door, she was assailed by pungent

cigar smoke. Memories of home overwhelmed her. This was not the full-bodied, mellow scent of her father's expensive imported Spanish leaf, but the sharp, cheap version her brother and his cronies preferred.

In the dark, all she could see was a pinpoint of a burning ember and the glowing outline of Janson puffing on a cigar. The frigid air hit her face and she shivered, her breath creating puffs big enough to put the cigar smoke to shame. The sweat that had beaded her brow froze in the cool blast. The weather had definitely changed from the morning. The locals believed they were due for a snowstorm, and she was inclined to agree.

Janson gave her little notice as she walked around him toward the other end of the balcony. She leaned over, resting her elbows against the cold wooden railing and cradling her cheeks. Would her fright response over the chimes ever cease?

If her father were here he'd laugh with her and tell her she was acting like a ninny. But her father wasn't here, and she had never missed him more. There was no one here for her now. No friends to fuss with over ribbons in the village, no one to giggle with over a dashing man passing through town, no beaus to flirt with, no one to read with on a lazy Sunday afternoon. Those times were long past, although they had occurred less than six weeks ago. That life was all but closed, and unless she could arrive in London at the right moment, all would be for naught. She would be without family and without a penny to her name.

And even then she would have a long way to go before she could gain back a smidgeon of the careless verve of her youth. While all her old friends from the village might still laugh and cajole the men in their midst, Kate had lost the will for the art. She touched her covered left ear. No dashing young man would even want her now. The derogatory peals of her brother's and Connor's words rang in her ears like the chimes of the clock.

Two large dark tabbies yowled below. Well, at least the cats had companionship tonight. She turned to lean back against the railing and tucked her arms into her chest.

Of the four rooms with direct access to the gallery, only Janson's and Olivia Trent's were lit. The Crescents had long since retired, and Desmond was still in the taproom probably waiting for Janson to return. Kate tried to catch her breath in the cold air, but she only succeeded in coughing.

She dropped her arms, her fingers skimming the cold wood railing as she glanced inside the common room to see Lake and Tiegs talking. Tiegs ran his fingers along the chain of his pocket watch, while Lake intensely watched the movements. She wondered what they were discussing. What kind of information could a man like Tiegs have for a man like Lake?

She shivered again. Now that the chimes were done, she could try and get some sleep. If only she could get rid of Black. She was still unnerved from the taproom. Who would have thought him the chivalrous type? And the way his muscles corded beneath her fingers, even through the jacket he wore. She could have stayed in that position all night, and wasn't that just a frightening thought.

Perhaps his gallantry was a ploy to get her between the sheets. But a man like Christian Black could do far better than a damaged girl like Kate.

With that depressing thought she walked past Janson again and into the warm hallway.

She opened the door to her room, intent on having it out with Christian again. Perhaps she could revive the seed of chivalry. Yes, better to concentrate on that than on what lay beneath his clothing.

She stepped inside and froze.

Golden skin and rippling muscles stared back.

She couldn't stop the thought that perhaps chivalry was overvalued as Christian stood shirtless by the bed, with his fingers lingering on the buttons of his trousers.

Chapter 5

What type of sorcery did you employ this time? I won't
have it, and your denials mean nothing, just like you.

The Marquess of Penderdale
to Christian, age fifteen

Her bottom hit the door, and it closed with a
clack. She jumped at the sound, and her
hand rose to her chest to still her racing heart.

"Wh-what are you doing?"

"I'm taking off my trousers."

"I see that," she snapped, heat licking her cheeks.
"Why are you removing your trousers?"

"They restrict me when I'm sleeping." He moved
his fingers over a button and quirked a brow.

"You aren't sleeping!"

"Not at the moment."

She rubbed her suddenly moist hands against the rough cotton weave of her breeches and said a bit desperately, "B-but, you can't sleep here."

"Tsk, tsk, Kate. You're stuttering, and I thought we'd already been through this." He shook his head in mock resignation.

"We have. Multiple times, if you will recall."

"Buck up, Kate. I'll toast up the bed for you. No need to fear I'll leave you cold." He smiled devilishly and undid the last fastening.

She examined the knotty floorboards with interest, waiting for the thud of heavy cloth striking wood.

As the silence stretched on, she risked a glance upward to see him still standing motionless before her, bare-chested, with his thumbs hooked into the top of his trousers, buttons redone. If Daisy were here she would surely be in euphoria by now. Kate had just overheard Daisy talking to Bess, the cook, about chests and big hands.

She peered at Christian. He did have large hands, capable, although more graceful than utilitarian. What had Daisy said about chests? That she loved it when men had large, capable hands to handle a well-developed chest. Well, Christian certainly had capable hands.

Heat licked her skin again as her thoughts caught up to her. She noticed his predatory smile and realized she'd been staring like a starving woman.

She lifted her chin and marched to the bed, snatched the counterpane, and dragged it to the rickety pine chair in the corner. She pulled the spread around her shoulders and cocooned herself in it, then plopped onto the hard, uncomfortable chair.

"Honey, what are you doing?"

"Don't call me honey. My name is Kate Simon. Mr. Kaden to you."

He sighed. "Kate, get into the bed."

"No. I'm not sleeping with you."

"I'm not going to steal your virtue. Not when I could relieve you of it so easily," he drawled.

She gasped in outrage. "You are a blackguard."

He shrugged, an easy smile played at the corners of his mouth. "Not much fun to be anything else."

"What's wrong with being a gentleman?"

"Dull, dull, dull."

"I'll have you know that gentlemen deserve the utmost respect. And they treat ladies in kind."

"Never knew a lady who dressed like a lad." His voice grew sly.

Angry heat stole into her cheeks, and she wondered if it would be a permanent condition for the night. "And I never knew a gentleman who would say such a thing."

He leaned back against the bedpost and crossed his bare forearms. He was an artist's delight—a tall, lean, muscular Adonis. Blast him, why couldn't he just put on his shirt?

"And how many times do I have to tell you that I'm not a gentleman." He shuddered. "Dead boring. Now get into this bed."

He unfolded his arms and reached for a plain white shirt, the muscles in his stomach stretching beneath the golden light of the lamp as he did so.

Kate swallowed, and it took her a moment to remember what they were arguing about.

"You just claimed you weren't a gentleman. Why would I climb into bed with you?"

He smoothed the shirt down over his chest, and she swore she could still make out the definition beneath. "Because all the ladies like to bow and curtsy and trade staid witticisms with gentlemen, but none of them want one in their bed."

"Of all th—"

"It's true." He leaned his head back against the post, peering at her lazily from under half-closed eyelids. "Ask the widow downstairs. Or ask her companion. Even the dour Mrs. Wicket could probably tell you that Mr. Wicket is a jolly underachiever between the sheets."

"This conversation is finished."

"Are you a prude, Kate? How depressing."

"I'm not a prude, I'm just not a . . . not a trollop." She jerked the counterpane higher.

"You don't have to be a trollop to enjoy the pleasures of the flesh, Kate. You merely have to have the passion and fire to *revel* in it."

The word all but dripped from his tongue. If her face and body were going to remain this heated, perhaps she wouldn't require the coverlet after all. "Well, there will be no reveling tonight."

"It's a damn shame, that."

"Good night, Mr. Black."

He sighed. "Kate, get into the bed."

"No."

"I'll carry you over here and deposit you myself."

"You wouldn't dare."

He lifted a brow.

All right, so perhaps challenging him hadn't been the smartest rejoinder.

"I wish to sleep in this chair."

"No you don't."

"I don't wish to sleep with you, Mr. Black, no matter what charms you think you possess."

Or what her body thought otherwise.

"I have no use for unwilling or contrary females, Kate. Until you choose to *revel*, you are quite safe."

"Hardly reassuring."

"You will freeze in that chair."

"Quite possibly."

He tapped a rhythm against the post with his finger. "Looks quite uncomfortable. You'll end up in the bed sooner or later."

"I highly doubt that. Now leave me be."

"Fine. But you're going to get a stiff neck and Lord knows what else. When you relent, feel free to crawl right in." He motioned to the bed magnanimously and then pointed to her bare feet. "I'll even let you warm your pinkies on me."

Kate tucked the traitorous digits into the coverlet. "Lovely. I assure you I'd as soon be knocked dead as to warm my feet on you."

"Interesting. And here I thought—"

Whatever he thought was cut short by a shout of rage coming from the room behind Kate. A shuffling knock from the wall behind Christian indicated that Freewater had heard the shout as well and was likely pressing his ear to the boards.

"Do you know who is occupying that room?" Christian's voice was low as he pointed toward the wall behind her.

She matched his whispering tone. "Lawrence Lake, I believe."

"The man who started the fight in the taproom?"

Kate nodded. "He and Janson have more between them than just an unfriendly cricket rivalry."

"That much seems obvious."

Another bellow of rage echoed through the walls, followed by the tinkling of glass shattering against the floorboards.

Heavy footsteps pounded across the floor above. A small section of the innkeeper's room was directly above theirs, the rest of it located above Mr. Freewater's room.

Sure enough, footsteps treaded heavily on the stairs and someone pounded on the door next to theirs moments later.

They heard the door creak open and a voice boomed, "Mr. Lake, I warned you earlier."

"How can you stand it, Mrs. Wicket? Janson must be stopped. He's an animal unfit for society."

"Mr. Lake! Do not speak about Mr. Janson that way. It is no business of yours."

"Deep inside everyone must know what kind of man he is."

"Mr. Janson is a passionate man. Headstrong and competitive. And furthermore, he is a guest here at the inn, as are you, although how much longer you remain is yet to be determined. I expect you to clean up that glass; I won't be sending Sally to sweep up this mess as she has other tasks occupying her."

There was a pause. "Sorry, ma'am," Lake said in a voice that could only be described as defeated.

Mrs. Wicket's voice dropped and Kate had to strain to hear. "No more of this, do you hear me, Mr. Lake? I thought we had straightened this out earlier. You remember what we discussed?"

"Yes." Lake's voice was subdued.

"Very well. Good night, Mr. Lake."

"Good night, Mrs. Wicket."

The door shut and footsteps treaded back upstairs.

Christian gazed at the wall thoughtfully, before looking back toward the Freewater wall. The room seemed to chill momentarily.

"Good night, Kate."

Kate blinked, unsure what had occurred to change his mind. He wasn't going to argue anymore? She really didn't want to sleep in a chair, but the alternative was . . . unacceptable. Much too dangerous. Sharing a room with a man who was obviously of a rakish stamp was a danger by itself. Sharing a bed? She'd be lucky to leave without an extra mouth to feed nine months down the road.

"Good night, Mr. Black."

Kate watched him slip under the bedcovers and scoot up against the wall, his body facing Freewater's room. She didn't know why he wanted to listen to Freewater, who seemed dull in the extreme. Other than the occasional swearing, the only things to be heard were shuffled papers, slammed books, and squeaky bedsprings. If Freewater didn't keep making little noises every few minutes, she would forget him completely.

Kate watched Christian settle in. His dark locks contrasted sharply with the white embroidered pillowcase, like a demon who had taken advantage of an angel's fluffy cloud.

She blew out the candle on the small table between her chair and the bed, then buried her head into the surprisingly soft counterpane and closed her eyes. It was going to be a long, uncomfortable night.

Kate woke at the one o'clock chime and again at two. She automatically looked to the shadows and didn't see the lump she had expected. Where had her roommate gone? A loud snore came from Freewater's room, and she could hear the steady beat of Lake's leg as he bounced it up and down on the floor.

The door opened and Christian was silhouetted in the low light of the hall. He looked weary.

"Where have you been?" she asked tiredly.

He shut the door and walked toward the bed. "Nowhere interesting. Pretty curious for someone who is not sharing my bed. You ready to give up your chair?"

She was more than ready to give up the chair.

"No."

"You are going to be cramped by morning."

That was probably true. And she could use a trip to the common room's chamber pot. There was no way she was using one in front of Christian.

Making sure her head wrap was in place, she stood and hobbled to the door. Christian's chuckle followed her. "A bit stiff, Kate?"

Although pins and needles stung her feet and she thought she could hear her knees creaking, she ignored him and ambled to the common room at the end of the hall. Smug, irritating man. Thought he knew everything.

No one was in the room so she ducked behind the privacy screen and quickly took care of things.

On her return she noticed two figures standing on the gallery; one looked like Janson, but she couldn't be sure from the distance. Shrugging, she hurried back to their room and slid inside.

"Where did you go, Kate?"

"Nowhere interesting. Pretty curious for someone who is not sharing my chair."

There was a pause. "I could be, you know. There is plenty of room for the both of us to get off."

"Why would you get on a chair if you were only planning on getting right back off?"

A snort was her only answer. "Good night again, Kate."

When Kate next opened her eyes it was to find them inches from another pair, a dark blue pair calmly studying her.

Shrieking, she pushed backward and promptly fell on the floor, the covers tangled around her.

Christian leaned over. "Graceful too, I see."

"What are you doing in my bed?"

He raised a brow.

"What am I doing in the bed?" she amended at a lower volume.

"You were moaning and I figured if you were

going to be moaning that sexily, you might as well do it in bed so that I could get maximum enjoyment from it as well."

"What?!"

"Quite a deep tenor you have when you moan." He winked down at her. "Not quite the same as a man's though, to the pity of your disguise, but not to my ears. Quite the sexy sounds you make when you sleep, Kate. Passion veritably lashing at its bindings."

Kate's mouth worked in silent starts, her legs still wrapped tightly in the bedcovers. Sometime during the night Christian had removed his shirt and was lounging half naked on the bed, idly tapping a finger on the sheet and lazily inspecting her.

She took a deep breath. "Let me repeat my question. What am I doing in this bed?"

"Seems to me you are on the floor. And have taken most of the bedcovers with you. Not very hospitable."

The edges of the covers remained tucked under the mattress, while the rest were either draped over the edge of the bed or wrapped tightly around her body. She tugged at the covers on the bed, attempting to unwrap herself, but Christian grabbed them before she could complete the task.

She tugged again. "Let go."

"No." He smiled, his teeth even and white in the morning light.

"Why did you move me?"

"You don't believe you wandered over here and curled against my lovely body on your own? I'm wounded."

"I'll just bet you are."

He flopped on his back, staring toward the ceiling, one arm covering his face. "Crushed."

"Black!"

"Irreparably damaged."

"Christian!"

"Yes, sweetest?" He turned over, propped his head on his elbow, and peered down at her, the same lazy, heavy-lidded gaze in place.

"You are the biggest blackguard imaginable."

"Why, thank you. Although I'm not sure you should grant me that title yet. There are plenty of blackguards you have yet to meet. But that you think of me that way . . . well, it is an honor."

"I'll bet," she muttered, finally slithering out from between the twined sheet and blankets, but remaining on the floor. "Now would you explain why I was in the unfortunate position of being in bed with you?"

"You fancy me, of course."

"I assure you, I most definitely do not." She focused on the insipid watercolor above his head again. It seemed a prudent place to stare. His eyes were too intense and his skin too, too *uncovered* in the bright light.

"Maybe you just aren't quite aware of it yet."

"May that never happen then. Now answer the question."

She unwisely met his eyes, and the blue deepened to midnight.

"You were moaning most deliciously, until you started screaming around three. Yes, it was most definitely three. I remember the chimes."

Kate maintained a blank expression as she straightened her shirt and touched her hair, sighing in profound relief to find her wrap still in place. She couldn't believe she had forgotten to check immediately. The man had completely muddled her brain.

"And?"

"And we couldn't very well have Mrs. Wicket rushing down here to investigate the noise, now could we? Could expose your whole ruse."

She narrowed her eyes. "Why would you care?"

"Inconvenient, that. Might toss me out too."

Kate snorted. He probably did think that. Yet it would be easy enough for Christian to claim he hadn't known she was a female. Since he was a paying customer and a man, the Wickets wouldn't throw him out. And Kate had a feeling that Christian knew it too.

"So you, what? Carried me to bed to shut me up?"

"Course. You were most willing too. Snuggled right up against me. Lovely flashes of skin too. You should really wear less to bed." He reached out a finger and traced it down her forehead and off her nose.

Kate automatically withdrew and touched her still hidden ear. He hadn't seen it then. Not that she would care, she told herself in a voice that was too defensive by far. He was a devilishly handsome man and no doubt a connoisseur of beautiful women. It would sting to hear disgust and condescension from anyone, but doubly so from this type of man. It had been only two weeks since Connor had destroyed a few of her more naïve views. She still needed to work on building up her defenses.

"That was it? We just slept?"

"That was all. Unfortunately. I even let you have all the covers while I slept on top of the sheet."

Kate noticed that he was indeed on top, pinning it down—part of the reason she had become so entangled.

Christian grabbed his shirt, seemingly bored with the conversation all of a sudden. "I'm going down to the dining room. Coming?"

Kate narrowed her eyes at his abrupt change in attitude, but nodded. She checked the clock. It was nearly eight. Why hadn't the sounds from the carriages, the post, and the bustle of the early morning country folk awakened her?

"You go ahead. I'll be down after I dress."

"I could help you dress." His smirk grew at her frown. "No? I'll just wait in the hall then."

As the door closed, Kate bounced off the bed. She completed her toilette in record time, not wanting to press her luck and have Christian saunter back in midway through.

Stepping into the hall and walking toward the stairs, Kate was stunned to see snow, heavy and thick, piled on the furthest section of the covered gallery walkway, as if the winds had distributed the entire clump in one area.

Christian followed her gaze. "Snowed all night. Seems the storm the farmers have been expecting finally materialized."

They walked into the dining room, where only Tiegs and his two cronies had congregated. Kate sat at a small table, and Christian sank into the seat across from her.

She gave him a pointed stare. "You are aware that our sharing a room does not necessitate sitting together?"

He smiled. "Why would I want to sit with anyone else?"

She shook her head, but her words held no real bite. "I cannot be rid of you soon enough."

"I'm afraid that won't be possible."

Kate turned to see Mr. Wicket wringing his hands on his apron.

"Snowed in. Completely snowed in. Received word that the roads are all blocked. A blizzard stormed across the lowlands. Earliest estimate for the roads to be cleared is a week. The south road from Sherringate will be particularly troublesome, didn't you know? The coaches will get stuck in the drifts if they run too soon. Even the Haywood would be hard-pressed to make the trip. Oh, and I had some new supplies scheduled to arrive. The winter ale needs replenishing."

Kate stared at the man, her mind not quite getting past the "week" portion of his words. "A week?"

"At the least."

"But I need to be in London by Monday next."

"Reduced room rate, Mr. Kaden. Sure as sure that you would not get that in London. I suppose that is a good thing. Our inn full of guests for the week. I expect that Misters Janson, Desmond, and Lake may choose to leave, as they are locals, but the rest, yes, good business."

The innkeeper hurried off, leaving Kate stunned in his wake. She turned to see Christian smirking.

"What are you so jolly about?"

"Nothing. Nothing at all."

As guests arrived in the dining room, they were informed of the dismal conditions. They responded to the news that they would be forced to stay for another week with varying degrees of dismay (the Crescents), or joy (Nickford).

By nine o'clock everyone was gathered except Janson and Freewater. Mr. Wicket clapped his hands to gain everyone's attention.

"I have a few announcements to make. Oh, now, where are Julius and Mr. Freewater?"

No one said a word.

"Mary, dear, fetch them, will you?"

Kate watched Lake's eyes narrow, but he said nothing as Mary walked from the room.

Freewater appeared in the dining room a few minutes later, looking disgruntled and muttering to himself. He chose a seat at a table by himself and glared at everyone whose eyes he met.

Mr. Wicket fiddled with some papers until Mary returned with a strange look on her face. "Mr. Janson doesn't appear to be in his room. I knocked loudly and called out, but he didn't respond."

Mr. Wicket's brows drew together. "Elias, take the key and wake Julius."

Elias did as he was told, only to return with a strange expression as well. "Mr. Janson is not in his room, nor are his belongings."

Mr. Wicket twitched. "Not like Julius to dash off without paying. A lively lad, Julius, but not inconsiderate."

Kate held back a snort. From what she had seen, Janson was a blackguard in the truest sense. At least Christian was the harmless type unless a woman did something foolish like love the man. Everyone knew that men like Christian flitted from one thing or person to another, leaving only unhappiness in their wake. Men like Janson, however, caused much worse damage. Physical scars, even. Kate had no idea why the Wickets didn't see what was in store for their own daughter. Kate was inclined to agree with Lake's assessment.

"Well, we'll just have to wait until—"

The side door burst open and a stocky man fell inside along with a drift of snow.

"Gordon! What are you doing, man? You're letting in the snow and wind. Get inside and close that door."

"Mr. Wicket, sir. There's a dead body in the stables. Julius Janson's been murdered."

Chapter 6

Always look beneath the surface, my girl.

George Simon
to Kate, age twelve

Kate stopped breathing. Had he just said—
"Murdered? What do you mean, Gordon?"

"I found Mr. Janson facedown in the stables. Under a pile of straw."

"Good God, man, did you check to see if he was hurt?"

Nearly every eye turned to stare incredulously at Mr. Wicket after his rather odd statement. Gordon had a dazed expression, but even his brows knit as he gaped at the innkeeper. "His head was bashed in. Don't think he's going to need a doctor, Mr. Wicket."

The shock on the innkeeper's face might have been amusing in another situation. However, in this instance it was decidedly not. Shock seemed to be just one of many reactions around the room. Lake's eyes were narrowed. Desmond looked furious. Tiegs appeared thoughtful. Olivia Trent blinked nervously. And Mary . . . Kate wasn't sure what emotion was on her face . . . horror . . . or relief.

"Here now, Mr. Wicket, when are the coaches to arrive? The snow's piled waist-high and I have to be somewhere on the morrow."

Every eye turned to Freewater, who was impatiently tapping a foot.

"Mr. Freewater, a man was found dead. His murderer perhaps still in our midst, and you are concerned about where you have to be tomorrow?" Olivia Trent's companion, Francine, asked.

"None of my concern."

"Trying to get away from the scene of your crime, Freewater?" Mr. Crescent raised his chin above his somewhat old-fashioned but nevertheless well-tailored jacket, his similarly styled wife stalwartly nodding in agreement.

Donald Desmond's dark eyes sparked as he stood. "Trying to get away with murdering my friend."

"Now wait a moment—" Freewater blubbered.

Kate held out her hand to fend off further accusations. "Oh, for goodness' sakes, just because the man is grossly inconsiderate does not make him a murderer. I know for certain that Mr. Freewater was in his room last night. I could hear him swearing and pacing."

Desmond glared at her and took a step forward. "Maybe it was you then, boy."

Christian pushed his cup across the table. The rattling china echoed in the room as the cup stopped at the edge. "Stop right there. I can vouch for Mr. Kaden's whereabouts."

"Maybe you were in on it together!" Desmond's face purpled as he turned hateful eyes on Christian. His fists clenched. "You knocked me down with a lucky shot yesterday, care to try again?"

"Perhaps your accusations and outrage are an attempt to draw attention away from you," Christian said in a rather lazy manner.

Everyone started to argue. Their voices grew angry and increasingly accusatory.

Kate watched the volley of finger pointing through dazed eyes. Christian nudged her with his foot under the table, an unreadable look on his face.

Mr. Crescent peered from one guest to another until his eyes finally rested on Lake. "Heard about the brawl last night," he said above the din, the rest of the conversations coming to a sudden halt. "That was you and Janson, wasn't it Lake?"

Lake nodded stiffly.

"That's right! It was Lake who wanted to kill Janson," someone shouted.

Lake stood defensively. "I didn't kill anyone."

"Whoa there, Lake. You keep your murdering paws away from the rest of us," Crescent declared, tugging his wife behind him.

"When are the carriages arriving?" Freewater demanded, more impatiently this time.

"There he goes again, asking for a way out."

"Don't you think we should find the constable?"

Mr. Wicket seemed to recover from his shock. "Old Freddy is the parish constable this month. But last night he left town to visit family. He won't be back for a week. And Julius's parents are in London while their manor is being remodeled. Julius was staying here on and off while the construction took place. What will we tell the squire?"

"Why the devil won't the constable be back? There—"

"Language, Freewater! How dare you swear in front of my wife!" Mr. Crescent shook his fist.

"How dare you interrupt me, sir. I won't have it!"

Kate felt an oncoming megrim. Christian nudged her foot once more, and her attention snapped back to the quarrel.

"Choose another constable—"

"What we need is—"

"I won't have it!"

"Murdered!"

"Do you think—"

"Julius is dead? Really dead?"

"Deserved it, lousy bastard."

"You did this!"

"—he was really murdered?"

"Why the fuss?"

"QUIET!"

"—a Bow Street Runner." Mrs. Crescent's voice trailed off in the ensuing silence. Everyone stared at her. Her chin rose imperiously. "Well, it would help, wouldn't it? Someone to take notes and search all the rooms and do whatever it is a Runner does?"

Kate saw Christian tense.

"And where are we going to find a Runner this far from London and in the middle of a snowstorm no less?" Francine scoffed.

"Right here."

All eyes focused on Christian as he tipped his chair back against the wall. Kate blinked, but when she opened her eyes, she saw the same mocking grin and calculating air.

"You?" Freewater cocked a brow. "I don't believe it."

"Believe it, Mr. Freewater. And under Section Two Hundred Seventy-one of the Runner's Code, I think I'll search your room first." Christian smirked.

"Don't you think you should take a look at the body first," Kate whispered, in disbelief at the turn of events.

"Yes, of course," Christian replied smoothly. "But I think the first room will be Freewater's." He crossed his arms. "If only for his gross insolence, disregard for the dead, and questioning of my authority."

That seemed to shut up both Desmond and Crescent. Tiegs appeared amused, almost cheerful, if a man could look jovial under the circumstances.

There was no way Christian Black was a Runner. It was too fantastic, and besides, Kate had never expected Runners to be so, well, virile.

"How are we to believe you?" Freewater asked,

his tone a bit more respectful, and Kate marveled at the authority that Christian suddenly seemed to wield.

"I'm here on another case. I had to stay at the inn incognito, as Mr. Wicket can attest. A veritable frenzy it was to stay yesterday. But necessary. Right, Mr. Wicket? Crazy happenings yesterday."

Mr. Wicket nodded, but from the man's befuddled expression, Kate had to wonder if the innkeeper even knew to what he was agreeing.

"Then what is your other case?" Freewater demanded suspiciously, although the innkeeper's nod had dampened his distrustful gaze somewhat.

"Sensitive case. I'm not at liberty to divulge the particulars. Has to do with *delicate* matters."

The men seemed to understand what he meant, and they nodded knowledgeably. Mrs. Crescent appeared confused. Kate took that to mean it had something to do with a male indiscretion.

Indiscretions seemed to be right in line with Christian's character.

"Well then, Mr. Black. How do you intend to proceed? What would you have us do?"

Thirteen pairs of eyes shifted to Christian—ten guests, two bodyguards, a valet, a maid, and twelve employees from the inn.

"Everyone shall remain here in the inn while I take a look at the body with—Gordon, was it?"

Gordon nodded.

"And Mr. Kaden will take notes."

Kate blinked at him.

"Come, Mr. Kaden. You offered to help with my other case, did you not?"

She gazed around to see the others peering at her and resisted the urge to shrink into the shadows. The unwanted attention was not helping her charade in the least.

She looked at Christian. His eyes were shuttered as he awaited her response. She could say that she hadn't offered to help him—she hadn't the slightest notion what he was talking about or why he was including her. He must know that she could destroy his ruse with a few words. Could even claim he was the murderer. Donald Desmond looked ready to string up anyone whose name was put forth.

And she could have her room back all to herself.

"Of course I'll help, Mr. Black." The voice seemed to come from far away and it took her a moment to realize it was hers.

The mischievous twinkle reappeared in Christian's eye as he shook her hand to seal the deal. He rose and motioned Gordon toward the door. Kate hastily pushed back her chair and grabbed her workman's cloak from a hook inside the entrance hall. Just as Gordon opened the outer door, a strong, cold gust of wind swirled inside.

Christian turned abruptly. "Everyone stays here until we return. No venturing outside or returning to your rooms. Meals can be served, but everyone needs to remain together here on the main floor, understood? Anyone leaving the inn will be arrested immediately. And don't allow anyone else to enter. Turn away any villagers and don't breathe a word of the murder, or I'll prosecute you under Section Eleven, understood?"

A nod from Mr. Wicket seemed to satisfy Christian. Kate wondered where the indomitable Mrs. Wicket was, but then spied her leaning weakly against a back bench, Mary holding her up.

Christian's cloak whipped around the corner of the door. She admired the dramatic exit, especially after his last statement. He didn't have the presence of a down-and-out gambler, but a Runner?

Kate slipped through the door. She staggered as the cold swirling snow stung her cheeks. Overnight the world had transformed. A deep sea of white blanketed the ground.

The Dragon's Tale sign creaked in the howling

wind as Christian grabbed her arm and whispered in her ear, "Follow close behind me, Kate. Gordon and I will cut a path."

Kate nodded, but was feeling disoriented. She didn't know what had prompted Christian to say that she was helping. Perhaps it was the little devil that seemed to reside permanently inside, peeking through his vivid eyes and purring with his silk-smooth tongue. There was no arguing that Christian Black had her full attention whenever he was in the same room. She doubted the same was true in return. Christian was honey to bees. She was just a dandelion.

In any case, despite the dangerous attention working with him would bring to her, her curiosity was piqued. As if there weren't enough things that were strange about Christian Black, he didn't look or act like any Bow Street Runner she had ever imagined or read about.

They trudged slowly across the courtyard. The thirty or forty steps that they would normally have walked were doubled due to the difficulty of moving through the high drifts. Snow clung to the legs of her breeches. A narrow path had been somewhat cleared, but visibility was so poor that moving in a straight line was impossible.

Halfway there, Kate yelled over the blowing

wind. "Were you the one to clear this path, Gordon?"

Gordon turned and nodded yes.

"So there were no other tracks?"

He pulled his muffler down. "No, why do you ask?"

Her brother might be a thieving maggot, but he was a damn good hunter and a braggart to boot. He made sure everyone knew of his successes and how smart he was. She had picked up more than one tracking tip from his glorified stories.

"It would show that someone else had been here," she yelled. "Perhaps dragging Janson's body from the inn to the stables."

Wait. She was going to look at a *body*. A dead body. She shivered, not entirely due to the cold.

She hadn't thought through what she was agreeing to. She had always been fond of puzzles, and solving a mystery had sounded interesting. Solving the mystery that was Christian Black even more so. It just hadn't connected in her brain that this puzzle involved *murder*.

Then again, maybe it was a freak accident. She was intimately familiar with those. And she could badly do with closure on *something*. She desperately wanted some level of peace.

She just wasn't sure she deserved it.

They trudged on several more steps when Gordon stopped again and turned.

"Don't know nothing about dragging bodies or the like. There were a few tracks out here though."

"I thought you said there weren't?"

"I said I made the path."

Seemed like quibbling to her, and again there was that pause in Gordon's answers. Or was it just a matter of him catching his breath in the cold?

Kate was breathless when they finally reached the stables. Gordon led them inside the middle door of the large brick and stucco building.

"What kind of tracks?" Christian asked.

"Funny tracks. Like someone had been . . . dragged. Yes, you may be right."

Kate felt a queer sensation in her chest as they walked toward the body. The straw had been cleared away. Janson's leg was bent at a weird angle, and so was his neck. The back of his head had been bashed in.

She looked away, nausea rising and the vision of her father's body appearing before her.

Chapter 7

It could be right under your nose, and you wouldn't notice a thing.

The Marquess of Penderdale
to Christian, age eight

Christian watched Kate pale and stepped in front of her, blocking her view of Janson's body.

"When did you find him?"

Gordon gave him a look edged with suspicion. "Just a few moments before I ran into the inn."

He had to think like a Bow Street Runner. However that was. If he could get through this, he would have a legitimate excuse to search

Freewater's room—barrier free. He could already feel the leather-bound journal in his grasp.

"Were you in this part of the stables before you found him?"

"Yeah, I do rounds at dawn and get the horses warmed up for the road."

"And you didn't notice the body then?"

"That's what I told you. I found the body when I began mucking out the stables and pitching hay."

Christian searched the ground close to Janson's body. He could see no bloody weapon nearby. He straightened, glancing at the tack hanging from the walls and rails, lots of potential weapons here. The stable was remarkably neat and clean. Well-cared-for saddles, harnesses, bits, bridles, and blankets were neatly stacked. Nothing seemed amiss or bloodstained.

Christian walked the long, brick-lined path between the stalls, speaking softly to the horses as he passed. They were restless and didn't look exercised in the least. Kate seemed more than happy to follow behind and away from Janson's body. Her light eyes were creased near the edges. The urge to smooth the worry lines from her face rushed through him.

He licked suddenly dry lips and turned to Gordon. "You took the horses out?"

"We were going to, but we were already snowed in at that point. Nowhere to take them."

Of course they hadn't taken the horses out. It had been a stupid question—Mr. Wicket must be rubbing off on him. It couldn't be nerves. Christian hadn't had a case of nerves since he had stopped caring.

"You said 'we.' Who else was here?"

"Me and Tom."

"Did Tom discover the body with you?"

"No, he was in the inn with the rest of you."

Tom must have been the square, bulky man near the door. "So how many times did you enter this building?"

"What difference does it make?"

"We need to ascertain what you were doing."

"I told you what I was doing." Gordon looked a bit shifty as he stared at the ground. "I did my work and found Janson, poor bloody bastard."

"So you didn't like Janson?"

"What? No. The man was an ass," he said bluntly.

"Did you ever feel like murdering him?"

"What? No!"

"Your account of the events seems awfully suspicious, Gordon. You haven't answered the question of how many times you were in here this morning."

"Cuz it makes no difference." Gordon kicked a stray piece of hay.

"You couldn't be more wrong. Runner's Code Number Thirty—determine the whereabouts of the person who discovered the body."

From the corner of his eye he saw Kate react, but he ignored her for the moment. Gordon seemed to believe him, and he noted a thin film of sweat had formed on the man's brow.

"I entered the barn twice, but until a bit ago never to this section. Don't know nothing else."

"Was anyone else in here?" Kate asked quietly as they walked back to the body.

"Just Tom. He won't know nothing neither. He lives on the upper floor over the stable office. Uses the straight stairs at the other end. Janson probably got drunk, grabbed his things, wandered outside, and bashed his head into the wall."

Christian looked dubiously at the body with its broken leg and bashed skull. "Are you saying that he somehow managed to bury himself beneath the straw too? A talent, that."

He watched Kate inhale deeply before crouching

down beside the body. She tried unsuccessfully to turn Janson over.

"He's stiff, Mr. Kaden. No use you trying to do anything with him."

Kate ignored Gordon and continued to examine Janson. Christian didn't know what she thought she would find—she was less an investigator than he was. She gave him a pointed look, and he crouched down next to her.

He poked through the man's pockets. A pocket watch and two quid were inside one, a letter in another. Kate seemed to be engrossed in examining rips on the front of Janson's shirt, so Christian tried to assist her by moving Janson's stiff right arm. It didn't budge. Pushing to the left, the corpse shifted, and Christian was nearly struck by Janson's stiff left arm.

Beaten by a dead guy. He was sure he would never have lived that down.

Something in Janson's fisted hand caught his attention. A swatch of green was clutched in his fingers.

Kate watched intently as Christian pried the slip of cloth from Janson's hand. He caught her eye, and she shrugged in bafflement.

"Gordon, does this look familiar?"

The servant peered at the cloth. "No."

Christian handed the cloth to Kate, lightly brushing her fingers. She shivered, shook her head, and stuffed the cloth into her pocket.

A search through his scattered belongings turned up a snuffbox, some extra clothes, but little else. Christian sat back on his heels.

"I think it's time to search the rooms." He was anxious to get into Freewater's, and had little notion of what else to do about Janson.

"Don't you think we should move the body back to the inn?"

"Why? I don't think he's going anywhere, and we don't want the body to warm and decompose."

"What if the killer comes back to dispose of it? We may need it later."

"Need it for what? The man's dead."

"To find the killer."

Christian glanced at Gordon, who was observing their exchange with interest.

"Um, I know you are new to this, Mr. Kaden, but Section Fourteen of the Runner's Code states that the body should not be moved. We'll just have to leave Gordon to guard it."

Gordon's eyes went wide. "What?"

Christian stood from his crouched position. "Don't worry, my good man. We will send one of the maids with food and something warm to drink." He patted Gordon on the shoulder as the man sputtered.

"Surely you aren't going to leave me here with . . . with him?" he said, pointing to Janson.

"Well, you and the boys do need to care for the horses, don't you?"

"But there's a dead body in here!"

"He won't hurt you. But don't lose him. Section Fourteen A says you can be held responsible for the loss of the body. Must keep away the body thieves."

"Body thieves?"

"Very dangerous, you know. But I'm sure you're up to the task. And the snow should keep them at bay for a few days. Good luck, Gordon. We'll be by to check on you later. Oh, and don't move the body. Thanks."

Christian walked out the door, Kate scampering after.

"What are you doing?" she hissed.

"Solving the murder, of course."

"You think this is all a joke."

"Of course I don't."

"You do. It is evident in every syllable you utter. Every statement you make." She poked him in the arm, the tip of her finger barely making a dent in the heavy coat.

"I'm just going by the Runner's Code."

"The Runner's what? I've never heard of such a thing."

"Are you a Runner?"

"No."

"Well, there you go."

"I think neither are *you*."

"Course I am. Wouldn't know the Runner's Code otherwise, now would I?" He waved a hand as they neared the inn door.

"You struck me as a charlatan yesterday, and nothing has yet to change my impression."

"I'm wounded, Kate."

"Don't call me that!" She was starting to remind him of a cat—cute, cuddly, and with hair bristling in every direction.

"If you stop calling me a charlatan, I may remember not to call you Kate."

She paused with her hand above the knob. "Duly noted."

They walked back into the inn, a crowd of anxious faces greeting their return.

"What did you find?"

"How'd he die?"

"Who did it?"

* * *

Kate looked across the sea of faces and shivered as she removed her coat. Christian held up a hand to silence the crowd.

"Folks, please calm down. We are all stuck in the inn for today and tomorrow at the very least. I'm sure Mr. Wicket would be more than happy to accommodate anyone in the taproom. Billiards, cards, dice, backgammon, and refreshments will be available. I'm going to begin a room-to-room search, and it would be better to have everyone down here."

"Why?" Mr. Desmond demanded. "What do you hope to find?"

"Well, isn't it obvious? Someone murdered Julius Janson. We need to determine if one of you did it."

"Now see here—"

"I ain't murdered nobody—"

"Not having some two-bit Runner go through—"

"We're trapped with a murderer?"

"What happened to Julius?"

"Will I still get to test my invention?"

Everyone turned to Nickford, who smiled brightly.

Christian looked unnerved for a moment. "Er, if we rule you out as the murderer, yes." He cast a glance around the room. "Right, then, I'll start the search and Mr. Kaden can take statements."

Desmond looked irritated and Lake's expression was unreadable.

"Hold a minute. Shouldn't you take statements too?" someone asked.

"Yes, send the boy to search the first rooms, I want to talk to you," Mr. Crescent said importantly.

"What if the boy goes up there to poach our things?"

"Too true. Send the Runner."

"What if the Runner poaches our things?"

Christian had the gall to look affronted. "I'll have you know, Runners don't poach."

"But how're *we* to know?"

"You need to have faith in your law enforcement."

Kate's brows drew together. "We *should* really have someone else with us when we search, at least until everyone can return to their rooms. That way people can be relieved of their concerns."

"Capital idea, boy!"

Christian looked irritated. "I assure you, that's not neces—"

"Send the boy and someone from the inn with the Runner."

Christian glared at Mr. Crescent, who, Kate noticed, had the presence of mind to back up a step.

"If you say one more word about this investigation, Mr. Crescent, I can assure you that things will not be pleasant."

But it was too late, as others murmured their agreement with Crescent's plan. Christian scowled and searched the crowd. "You, boy, over here."

Kate watched as a wide-eyed Benji, a twenty-year-old servant who was standing with Mary, Sally, Bess, Daisy, and several male servants, shuffled forward. "Yes, sir?"

"You will be assisting us." Christian turned to the innkeeper, authority underscoring his voice. "Keys, Mr. Wicket?"

"Should I be going with you as well, Mr. Black?"

Christian waved off the innkeeper. "No, no, this fine lad will do. In the meantime, you've the inn to run and people to tend. Just remember my instructions from earlier—no one is allowed in or out of the inn. I trust you to find a good excuse if someone outside should ask."

Mr. Wicket quickly handed over the key ring.

Christian walked from the room, with Kate hurrying to catch up, and Benji trailing awkwardly behind.

"What is the plan?" she asked.

"First we are going to change out of these wet

clothes, and then we will search Mr. Freewater's room," he responded, climbing the stairs.

"Why his room? We know he was there all night."

"Do we? I, for one, do not."

"The man was making enough racket to wake the dead."

"Or make the dead." He flashed a brilliant toothy grin, his eyes crinkling at the corners.

She frowned. "This isn't funny."

"I know. I've gone and ruined my boots." He made a production out of examining them before searching for the room key.

"You aren't a Runner. I know you aren't. You could get into a lot of trouble posing as one." She glanced over her shoulder as he opened the room, but Benji was lagging behind and had just reached the top of the stairs.

"Benji, is it? Could you get us some paper and ink while we change?" Christian asked.

The young man nodded and hurried away, seemingly very glad to be leaving.

Christian entered their room. "Who said I wasn't a Runner? And if you don't want to be involved, don't be. I don't remember inviting you along to search rooms. That fool Crescent did."

She shot him a dirty look. "You are the one who

brought me into this by making me a scribe for your mad scheme, whatever it is. And besides, unlike you, I want to know what happened."

"Why?" He was already stepping out of his clothes. Kate quickly turned her back, caught off guard by both the question and his state of undress.

Why *did* she care? Perhaps because last night she might have seen the murderer with Janson on the balcony. That gave her cause. But she cared little about Janson himself, so that was not reason enough. Justice? She had always been a proponent, but had never involved herself in its workings before. Was it because Christian had gotten involved? She firmly pushed that thought away. Irritating man.

Or perhaps her motivation was to put closure to some element of her life, as she had thought earlier? She shut her eyes. She just wanted to feel happy again. She just needed some spark to keep her going.

She finally responded. "Someone has to care."

He snorted. "No, someone does not. Have you ever been to London? There's an entire town full of people who don't care."

"Oh, really, that is quite a ridiculous statement."

"You can turn around now, Kate. And that

would be a no to my question. You would think otherwise had you been there."

"I've been to London," she scoffed, moving from one foot to another to try and avoid the snow turned to slush that sloshed in the bottom of her boots.

"Really." It was a sardonic statement instead of a question.

"More than once."

"Mmm-hmmm."

"I have! My aunt rents a house for the season. I have visited her there several times." She gave up and hastily removed her wet boots and rummaged through her portmanteau for some extra hose.

"Part of the ton, is she?" he asked casually while pulling on a dry pair of boots.

Kate found a pair of hose and wished Christian to the other side of the inn so that she could put them on. "She attends some events. She spends a week there during the holidays as well, before returning to the country."

"Going to meet her in London, were you?"

Christian didn't look up, so she gaped at the top of his head instead. "How'd you know?"

He shrugged. "I didn't. But you are on the coaching road to London, traveling in disguise. What, did your father want you to marry the gnarled vicar?"

"My father is dead," she said stiffly.

He straightened, his eyes boring into hers, unreadable. "My sympathies."

His face was closed and she couldn't detect from his tone of voice if he was being sincere. "Please wait outside while I dress."

He rose, and she was startled to see his features change abruptly, a flippant mask sliding into place. "No chance for a quick tumble to warm our blood?"

"No. Out."

He gave her a lazy smile as he left. She stared at the door, unnerved for a few moments, before gathering her clothing together.

She changed quickly and walked into the room next door to find Christian already rifling through scattered books and papers. Freewater's room was a mess.

"What are you doing?"

Christian stopped probing through the bureau drawers and looked up. "Freewater is a member of a less than reputable publishing press in London. I'm trying to ascertain if he is up to anything beastly."

His voice was full of disdain, and she blinked. "What difference does that make?"

He muttered something she couldn't quite

catch. She decided to ignore him for the moment as she picked through a few belongings on the side table.

"So what are we looking for? A weapon, a motive?"

"Oh, anything that might prove incriminating. You don't happen to see any journals other than these, do you?"

She gazed around the room. There were dozens of journals. She absently opened one. "What does Freewater need all of these for? Is he a writer?"

He shrugged carelessly, although there was an underlying tension to the action. "Perhaps. See if you can find any more."

She complied. If nothing else, perhaps humoring Christian and his obsession with Freewater might expedite their search of the man's room and move them into another sooner. She was certain that Freewater hadn't done it.

Benji finally returned with ink and paper, and Christian set him to searching floorboards and walls as well. It was a bit cramped with the three of them, and as this was one of the larger rooms, she had little doubt that when they reached the smaller ones their searching strategies would have to change.

She was interested to see how Christian would proceed with the investigation.

She searched under the bed and said casually, "I saw two people on the balcony last night around two. One looked like Janson."

Christian's head shot up and his voice held a spark of interest. "Can you describe the other person?"

"It was a man, taller than the one I thought was Janson. I couldn't see very well."

"Well, Janson wasn't very tall, so there are three or four men here at the inn who would fit—Desmond, Lake, Tiegs . . . Perhaps Gordon or that other servant, Elias. Could have been a servant bringing him something."

Kate was reluctantly pleased by his assessment. Although his attitude might be suspect, Christian's intelligence seemed quick.

"Hmmm . . . could have been."

"Benji, what is the other male servant's name? The one Gordon said lives above the stables?"

"You mean Tom, sir?"

"Thank you. You and Tom are too short, so you're off the hook for now."

Christian give Benji a teasing smile, but Benji was wide-eyed and looked horrified. She felt a stab of pity for the poor man.

"Benji, do you know if anyone on the staff served Janson last night out on the gallery?" Christian asked.

"No, sir. Perhaps you should ask Mrs. Wicket."

"I will. The man could have been Lake. Man was out for blood last night."

Kate bit her lip. "I heard them arguing prior to going to bed."

Christian narrowed his eyes as he flipped through the pages in each journal. "What about?"

Kate caught Christian's gaze and looked at Benji's bent head. It was going to be quite awkward talking about certain topics in front of one of the servants.

Christian nodded his understanding. "Benji, do you think you might ask Mrs. Wicket if she sent any of the servants to Janson while he was on the gallery? Especially around two in the morning?"

"Of course, sir." Benji withdrew from the room. She heard his footsteps disappear downstairs.

"They were fighting about Mary."

Christian looked unsurprised. "They fought over her like two cocks. That's what precipitated the fight in the taproom. Could be that Lake finally saw his chance."

"Julius Janson was not the nicest of fellows."

"Most of us aren't."

Kate was uncomfortable thinking about the conversation between the two men. "Lake threatened him after he said some . . . rather awful things about Mary."

A warm hand squeezed her shoulder. "The man was a right bastard, so I can only imagine. There's a difference between wit and crudeness. Also differing levels of bastardy. Can't imagine the man had many friends."

"The Wickets seem—seemed—awfully fond of him, though."

"The innkeeper is not the brightest of men." He let his gaze wash over her boy's clothing in a pointed fashion.

Kate swallowed at the look in his eyes as they locked back onto hers. "Don't you think we should search another room? Freewater is not exactly suspect."

Christian turned to glare at the knobby desk in the corner. "There's nothing else here," he muttered, irritation in every crease of his face.

"What did you expect?"

He waved her off. "We need to search the people too."

She stared at him, her mouth dropping slightly. "You think the murderer just brought the weapon he used down to breakfast?"

Christian shrugged. "You never know."

Benji huffed back through the door. "Mrs. Wicket said that no one was sent to Janson after midnight."

"Thanks, Benji. What is the atmosphere in the dining room? Anyone getting anxious?"

Benji looked uncertain. "Mr. Crescent was particularly interested in what was happening up here. Mary said he had cornered Mr. Freewater earlier and badgered him about something. And of course Mr. Desmond is especially upset."

Christian's face became pensive. Benji watched him anxiously, and even Kate held her breath, though why she was holding her breath she couldn't say.

"We should search the Crescents' room next."

Surprise ran through Kate. She had little doubt they would find anything more than drab yet officious clothing.

Sure enough, between the three of them they discovered nothing of interest in the Crescents' room. Christian appeared agitated. He hadn't even made an inappropriate remark in the past hour, and that said something about his state. Surely he hadn't expected to find anything of value?

"Benji, are you sure you lowoked under the tick?

Mattresses make excellent hiding places. No heavy poles or crops? Not even, perhaps, a journal?"

"Mr. Black." Kate gave him a pointed stare. "We have searched this room three times. We searched through Freewater's nigh on five times. I don't know what you expect to find. A loose floorboard? A sign proclaiming where the weapon is hidden?"

Christian cast a speculative glance at the floor and Kate threw her hands up. She was tired of his single-mindedness. She would never have guessed the man would be so thorough. It would be a good trait if expressed in any way other than his obsession with the two rooms they had searched . . . two rooms at the very bottom of the suspect pool.

She marched forward to tell him so, but a knock at the door stopped her in place.

"Enter," Christian called out.

Sally opened the door, and Kate's eyebrows rose as color flooded Benji's cheeks. The inn was turning into a veritable feast of potential lovebirds. "Pardon me, Mr. Black, Mr. Kaden, Benji, but Mr. Wicket would like to know when the patrons can return to their rooms."

Christian gave the floorboards one last frustrated glance. "Tell Mr. Wicket that we will be down in ten minutes. Thank you, Sally. Benji, you can go with Sally. Please report what we talked about to the Wickets. Thank you for helping."

Benji was hot on Sally's heels, as he hightailed it from the room.

Christian leaned his head against the wall. "Well, we should get downstairs and search Freewater and Crescent to make sure they aren't hiding anything."

"They aren't hiding anything, Mr. Black."

His brows rose at the irritation clear in her voice. "How do you know, Mr. Kaden?"

"It doesn't make any sense. You are just making things difficult for them because they are miserable men you obviously dislike."

"If that were true, Desmond's room would be upside down by now."

"Desmond is a much more likely suspect."

Christian's full lips thinned. "Perhaps. Let's go downstairs, search a few people, and call it a day."

"What?" Kate felt cold. All of the positive traits she had recently attributed to Christian Black withered under the growing storm of anger, something that never seemed to be in short supply for her lately. The man was an utter cad, just as she had first suspected.

"Search a few people, then give up and do something else?" She felt the need to clarify.

He winked, his façade once more in place. She was far, far from being amused.

"I knew you weren't a Bow Street Runner, but I didn't realize what a charlatan you really were," she said evenly and firmly pushed her disappointment aside.

He raised a brow. "What is your point, *Mr. Kaden*?"

She raised her chin at the jab. "Fine. Search a few people and then be on your merry way. I will solve this on my own. Good day, Mr. Black. Please have the courtesy to keep your merry way far from mine."

His eyes narrowed. "You think you can solve Janson's murder on your own?"

"I *will* solve it."

"Why do you even care? And don't give me that drivel about how someone has to care. I could give you plenty of instances of that statement being utterly false."

She noted the bitterness in his voice, but it was drowned by the earlier thoughts of why she wanted to find out what happened to Janson.

"I want to see justice done."

He snorted. "Justice probably was done. We both agreed that Janson wasn't exactly a pillar of the community."

Kate ignored him and marched to the door. Solace wasn't going to be found in this room. Perhaps it wasn't even to be found at this inn. But she would find it. And she would find out what happened to Janson.

"Wait, Kate—"

She yanked open the door so hard it crashed into the wall and recoiled, barely missing her. She was brimming with too much emotion to care. Too much anger, at both herself for allowing accidents to happen, and at the world for punishing her. She marched toward the stairs without a backward glance.

She could hear Christian swearing as he ran to catch her. He hopped in front of her, blocking the way, his left arm against the banister.

"Kate, you can't just walk down there and start making things up."

She gave him a pointed look. "No, that would be wrong, wouldn't it?"

He brushed her comment aside. "They won't believe you."

"Why, because I'm not the charming Christian Black, Bow Street Runner, founder of the ludicrous Runner's Code?"

He glanced over his shoulder. "Shhh. No, because you have no credentials."

"Neither do you. Now if you'll excuse me."

She ducked under his arm and marched determinedly down the stairs, through the hallway, and into the dining room.

Chapter 8

◈◈◈

Have no fear. There is nothing you can't do if you put your mind to it.

George Simon
to Kate, age sixteen

Everyone turned as she entered, their chair legs scraping the hard floor.

"Good people. You may return to your rooms if you like, but I may be coming by to ask a few questions. Please continue to enjoy your stay."

The patrons exchanged glances, but didn't seem inclined to go back to their drinks or conversations.

"Did you find anything? Are you still searching?"

Kate tugged her head wrap, her anger converting into nerves as she realized that her actions were putting her directly into attention's path. She straightened her shoulders resolutely. Looking out over the sea of faces, she knew no one else would take the helm. She caught Desmond's sneer. Well, at least no one without an agenda. She would just have to deal with the consequences of being center stage.

"We haven't found anything conclusive yet. And I can't divulge any part of the investigation, I'm sure you understand." She remembered her village constable, who had held the position more or less permanently, saying something equally pompous when a villager had lost a few sheep and blamed his neighbor.

"No, I don't understand at all." Desmond gave her a calculating look. "Why don't you tell everyone what is going on?"

"I'm afraid Mr. Kaden can't do that. He's under strict orders. If you have issues, take them up with me."

Kate stiffened as the smooth voice curled the hairs at the back of her neck. Desmond looked sour, but backed down under Christian's authoritarian tone.

"We will be creating a plan and going over it

with Mr. Wicket later. We will let you know what we can. We're not holding you hostage, the storm is doing that."

He gave one of his too charming smiles, and Kate gritted her teeth as he received a few in return.

"You may ask us questions this evening."

And with that, Christian nudged the middle of her back and they settled in at the only empty table, near the front of the room, slightly apart from the others. Daisy immediately appeared with a fruit and cheese plate.

"What are you doing?" Kate hissed to Christian after the barmaid left.

"Helping." He popped a piece of cheese in his mouth, as if he once more hadn't a care in the world.

"I thought you wanted to search a few people and then call it quits?"

"Couldn't let you have all the fun, Mr. Kaden."

She huffed and leaned against the back of her chair. "I don't need your help."

He played with another piece of cheese, rolling it end over end. Finally he looked up, his eyes growing serious. "Maybe not, but I'm offering it."

She blinked, her remaining ire draining away amid his sober demeanor and accommodating words.

"Do you mean that?"

His eyes shadowed, but he responded in an even tone. "I may not say the right things all the time, and it may not be what anyone wants to hear, but sometimes even I mean what I say."

She saw truth in his eyes. A strange thing, really.

"But you said earlier that you were going to find the killer and then you seemed to give up when your search of Freewater's room didn't yield whatever it was you wanted."

He picked up a piece of bread. "I said I was going to take a look at the body and search a few rooms. I did that."

"Under a false identity," she whispered.

"How do you know I'm not a Runner?" He winked, the earlier shadows dissipating as if they had never been.

She shook her head. She didn't know if she felt up to the task of unraveling the intricacies of the man in front of her. Somehow it seemed a more difficult task than discovering what had happened to Janson. But she was more relieved than she allowed herself to let on that he was once more on the job.

They could help each other. It had nothing to do with wanting to strangle him one minute and let him do to her whatever his eyes kept promising the next.

"I could use the help," she said tentatively, looking around to make sure they weren't being overheard. "I don't actually know what I'm doing."

He smiled. "I've been in enough trouble. I think I can handle the authority aspects without too much difficulty."

She didn't know whether to return the smile, or frown.

Daisy appeared with two plates of beef and two bowls of stew, all balanced perfectly. "Here you go, sweet cheeks." She gave Christian a saucy smile and winked at Kate. Kate forced a smile and dug into her stew. It was flavorful, the meat and vegetables tender and perfectly cooked.

Kate ignored the stares from the other patrons. Even the walls of the room appeared shadowed, as if reflecting the edgy and nervous feelings of the occupants.

"We should probably devise a plan, just like you suggested. We don't even really know what we are searching for," Kate said as she mopped up the last of her stew.

"Whatever he was murdered with, I suppose."

"Any ideas?"

"Something heavy."

Amusement and annoyance had never fit together as well as they did with Christian Black.

"Any more ideas?"

"Something wielded with force, judging by Janson's head, but then too he *could* have sustained the damage from a fall off the gallery."

"But you don't believe that."

He shook his head and played with his spoon, clinking it against the side of the bowl. "No. The broken leg is probably a result of the fall, but it's just not that high for the type of damage he sustained to the back of his skull."

"Perhaps the green cloth we found belongs to the killer. Caught in the scuffle?"

"Perhaps." He gave her a smile that she automatically returned for once. "And we have those other things that we found."

"Do tell what you've found, Black." Desmond appeared at their table and sat down imperiously, his dark hair ruffling as he tossed his head.

Christian's eyes narrowed. "You'll know when everyone else does, Desmond."

"Everyone knows that Lake did it, the jealous bastard. When are you going to arrest him?" Desmond drummed his fingers on the table.

"There's no evidence that Lake did it."

"You are the only ones that refuse to see the truth. Pretty obvious, even for a simpleton." He gave Christian a once-over. "Or maybe you don't know what you're doing after all. I'm going to be a barrister. Perhaps I should take over this investigation."

Kate watched, fascinated, as Christian relaxed against the back of his chair.

"No, you won't. I'll have you strung up under Section Three of the Runner's Code—for interfering with an investigation. Nasty business being prosecuted for Section Three, don't you agree, Mr. Kaden?"

Kate nodded, trying to keep the bemusement from her face. She had no idea where Christan was going with his comments, but she didn't much like Desmond. He seemed to have taken up Janson's vendetta against Lake, and most likely all of Janson's less appealing characteristics now that the man was no longer his leader. Lake, on the other hand, seemed like a nice enough man, if somewhat unlucky.

"Ever see a man hanged on a gibbet, Desmond? His eyes bulging, lips quivering, his last thoughts of his god and mama shown clearly on his face? Happened to Ronnie McTiernay for fighting old man Creeper, best Runner around. McTiernay barely had time to make out his will before they had him swinging. Creeper's a friend of mine. A good friend. No, a great friend."

Desmond shoved away from the table. "I've got my eyes on you, Black."

"Well, best get them off me. I have plenty better offers already."

Desmond shot him a disgusted look and slunk off to the darkened corners of the taproom.

Kate clutched her spoon. "Do you think it wise to make an enemy of him? After this is over, he may come after you."

Christian smirked. "I'd like to see him try."

"He could hurt you."

"Why, Kate, I didn't know you cared. Besides, if he tried anything, he'd be swinging before the week is out."

"Shhh!" She looked around wildly to see if anyone had caught his use of her name. Only Olivia, Francine, and Freewater were left in the room, the others having returned to their rooms or gone to the taproom. Christian kept sending irritated glances Freewater's way. "And you don't really believe your own tripe, do you? Next you'll be telling everyone you are a peer of the realm."

"The Earl of Canley, at your service." He gave a short bow, smirking the entire time.

She dropped her spoon and threw up her hands. "Fine. Let's get back to Julius Janson. What are we searching for, other than the weapon and the garment that may have produced the fabric swatch in his hand? How about where the murder was committed?"

His brows knit, the smirk fading from his face as easily as peeling the outer skin from an onion.

"Somewhere near the gallery most likely in order for someone to toss him over."

Kate nodded. "Why don't we quickly search the rooms on this floor and then the gallery. I saw him standing out there last night, and his room leads directly onto it. It makes the most sense."

Christian nodded and pushed away from the table, once again sending a look Freewater's way. "Hold on for a moment, Kate." He walked over to Freewater, and she followed in curiosity.

"Mr. Freewater, we finished searching your room. Do you mind turning out your pockets, so that we can eliminate you from our list of suspects?"

Freewater looked annoyed and huffed as he complied with the order. Kate watched with interest as the man's face went completely white while patting an inner pocket. "What? Where?"

The man became frantic, and Kate watched Christian's eyes narrow in speculation. "Have you lost something, Mr. Freewater?"

A bead of sweat ran down Freewater's forehead. "No, no. Here, here is what is in my pocket."

He held out a few pounds and a handkerchief. Christian made a point of examining the articles and then waved him off. "Thank you, Freewater. After seeing this, we may have further questions."

"Yes, yes, as you will." The man was already darting around the table and out of the room. Christian's face looked torn between frustration and glee, neither of which she understood.

He turned toward her. "Shall we?"

They searched the kitchen, storage rooms, and private dining areas, but didn't find anything interesting. The guests had started to return to their rooms, so Christian and Kate were surprised upon entering the upstairs gallery to see Nickford scraping at the railing.

"What are you doing, Mr. Nickford?"

"Gathering samples."

Christian and Kate exchanged glances. "Samples for what?" she asked.

"For my experiment."

"What experiment are you running?"

He scraped a few slivers into a small glass container. "I'm going to test to see if the spirits took Mr. Janson."

Kate gaped and could see Christian's eyebrows rise almost to his hairline. "The spirits?"

"Devilish things. They have been plaguing the inn for the last few days. Mr. Wicket said so. He said, 'Nickford, didn't you know, the spirits have been acting up?' I, of course, determined to discover what was happening. Poor Mrs. Wicket has had a hard time sleeping lately. Always up and about roaming around with the dead."

Kate would never have guessed Nickford could get any stranger.

"Er, wouldn't you be taking away her company then, by ridding the inn of the, um, spirits?"

Christian sent her an amused glance.

"No, no. The spirits are most likely calling to her. Get rid of them and she'll sleep peaceful-like again. Heard them calling last night, and then her up and roaming outside my room."

Kate frowned. "She was roaming outside your room last night."

"Oh yes. Heard a thud and a loud moan. Knew it had to be the spirits fussing with Mrs. Wicket again."

Christian and Kate exchanged glances, and Christian finally leaned forward to stop Nickford from gathering more "evidence."

"When did you hear this thud?"

"Round about half past two, I'd say."

"Did you look out your door?"

"No, already knew what it was, didn't I? But I set up a specter thingamajiggy. Should catch it tonight or tomorrow."

Christian nodded absently, but Nickford looked expectant.

"I'm sure you will catch it, Mr. Nickford," Kate said.

"Right good of you to say so, Mr. Kaden. Well, looks like I'm done here. Good evening."

Kate examined the spot on the railing as soon as Nickford disappeared. It had been scraped clean. Christian bent below and examined the slats.

"Look." He pointed to a spot on one of the slats.

Kate peered below and saw a darkened spot, as if blood had formed a small puddle there. "You think Nickford cleaned up the rest of the evidence? That these are bloodstains and this is the spot?"

She looked over the railing and saw that the snow below was slightly indented. Nothing too obvious, as the newly fallen flakes had covered the indentation. Still, it looked as if something might have landed there and been dragged away.

"The new trail Gordon made covered the tracks, but I'll bet that is where the body landed and was dragged."

"Nice work, Mr. Black." Kate gave him an admiring glance, a real one, and he smiled back, a real smile in return.

"Oh, I think we make a good team, Kate."

He didn't move toward her, but the air felt a bit warmer, as if his body had suddenly grown closer. The air pricked her exposed skin as warmth caressed her less exposed areas.

She stumbled back into the railing and nicked her hand on one of the splinters created by Nickford's tests. She jerked her hand away from the railing and was relieved to see the splintered edge was a few inches from the bloodstains.

"Kate?"

She waved him off and peered at her hand under the fading light. "Just a splinter from the rail."

"Here, allow me."

Before she could protest, Christian lifted her hand to inspect it. "Hmmm, looks like there is a sliver of wood in there. I should remove it."

And with that she could only watch in shock as he took the side of her hand into his mouth, which was hot and wet and indescribable. His tongue looped around the underside and a shiver racked her body as he gently began to suck.

Chapter 9

Can't do a damn thing right, boy. Might as well replace you with one of the scullery servants. At least in the trade I would get a son with half a brain.

The Marquess of Penderdale
to Christian, age ten

For Kate, splinter removal had always involved a needle and some painful poking. Who knew that all it took was a warm, talented mouth to get the job done?

Christian Black obviously had the right idea.

His teeth grazed the side of her palm, and she rose slightly onto her toes as her breath caught. Was that his tongue? What was he *doing*?

Heat shot through her body and her breath

released in little pants as he continued to suck and lick and *kiss* the sensitive side of her hand. Unfamiliar sensations tingled across her skin and down her spine, spiraling somewhere near her middle.

Desire. She couldn't stop her head from tilting back or her mouth from falling open as he held her gaze and nipped her hand. His blue eyes, dark and intense, were unrelenting as he licked and sucked and *bit*. She felt desirable for the first time in so many long weeks.

What would it be like to kiss this man?

Somehow her pinkie ended up in his mouth and she couldn't withhold a moan as he slowly withdrew it with a pop.

He leaned forward, pressing her against the wood railing, his unshaved jaw lightly brushing her smooth cheek. He buried his head in her hair. He smelled like cinnamon.

He leaned back and removed something from his tongue. He winked as he held up the splinter and then flicked it over the railing. Before she could regain her thoughts, he spun her around, reversing their positions, so he was leaning back against the rail and she was nestled against him.

"Wouldn't want you to get a splinter in a more delicate location, Kate." His face was full of supreme male self-satisfaction. She didn't have the presence of mind to say anything witty in return.

He pulled her body closer, and the heat curled in her middle moved farther south. His mouth was a hairsbreadth away from her own.

"Unless of course, you want me to remove another splinter? I would be happy to chase them all over your body."

His voice was husky; his warm cinnamon breath caressed her lips as his hovered millimeters over hers.

"I . . ."

Her eyes were focused on his lips, waiting for them to connect with hers, but they curled upward instead.

He pushed away from the rail, hot and hard against her. His lips brushed the lobe of her good ear. "Perhaps later, then? Hmmm?"

"Perhaps," she whispered, her mouth developing a mind of its own.

"Excellent." His jaw brushed against her cheek again and he straightened. "Come. While Nickford is downstairs, let's search his room."

Kate nodded, trying to organize her muddled thoughts. A thread of delight filtered through her. He wanted her. Poor, damaged Kate.

Her temporary delight shriveled back to the shadows. He had no idea that she was scarred, and when he did, how would he express his revulsion? Connor had treated her well until she had removed her head covering. After she had removed it, things . . . things hadn't gone so well.

Christian tugged her hand, releasing it as they entered the common room.

For emotional survival, Kate had to keep the relationship with Christian strictly geared toward the investigation. No more personal involvement or physical innuendos.

She couldn't afford the rejection.

For whatever reason, whether it was the hazardous situation, the high possibility for rejection, or just Christian himself, seductive and worldly, Kate felt more was at stake than with any previous suitor or flirtation. Her feelings were more intense toward Christian Black than she had ever felt toward another.

She couldn't let him hurt her. She would reject him first.

Christian inserted the key in the lock and they stepped inside Nickford's room. It was in chaos, just as it had been the night before. A mountain of clothes was heaped across a chair. Empty dishes and leftover food were stacked on a table. Journals and equipment littered the makeshift workspaces and bed. The pallet sat innocuously on the floor.

She nervously touched the knotty wood wall. As soon as he made a move toward her, she would reject him. It was for the best. No matter that her body screamed otherwise. No matter that a tendril of happiness had been stirred, the first in so long.

She waited as Christian started flipping through journals. Wasn't he going to continue his seduction? He had said later, but she didn't think he was the type to employ self-control. Any minute now he would make his move.

She had known the man for merely two days, and there was little evidence to prove he wasn't the scoundrel ninety percent of his gestures claimed him.

He stepped in front of you, guarded you in the taproom fight.

She scoffed. He would have done it for Daisy.

But doesn't that mean he isn't a complete scoundrel?

It meant he looked out for his own interests. He was probably waiting to make a final move on her, deliberately laying the groundwork piece by piece to keep her off balance.

Or maybe he isn't quite as interested in you as you are in him.

She grudgingly admitted that her feminine side

most definitely wanted his attention. Christian was a very handsome and charming man. Dashing. Most women would feel flattered to be the center of his focus. But that was just it. He was the type of man to concentrate intensely on one woman, only to drop her and be off as soon as his attention wavered to the next bit of muslin. Or as soon as he saw her scars.

Not all charmers have ill intent.

The annoying little voice in her head needed to stop playing devil's advocate.

Some rogues turned out to be quite the catch. The most infamous rascal in their county being Joshua McShaver, the rakish cobbler, who rivaled anyone in the Midland villages in his number of sheer conquests. Then one summer afternoon he met Caroline Travis, a woman who had just moved to their village. Within a week he had chased, caught, and married her, surprising everyone in the district and causing massive sums of money to exchange hands in lost bets.

Joshua was an utterly devoted husband, and the look in his eyes when he gazed on his wife made more than one woman sigh dreamily. Something about Caroline Travis had ensnared him as no other woman within fifty miles had been able to accomplish.

Kate didn't quite see herself as the Caroline to Christian's Joshua though. Christian seemed to be more worldly, for one, and more cynical for another.

She covertly studied him. She had known him only two days. But then Caroline and Joshua had known each other only ten minutes before he began the chase, and look how that relationship had turned out.

Will you deny the happiness you so desperately seek because of fear?

She scoffed. She didn't fear rejection. She just awaited it with all the trepidation of the hangman's noose.

Oh, all right, fine. She feared it. She just wished the bothersome voice in her head would pick a side and stick with it.

Kate left Christian to the journals, which he was meticulously opening, examining, and discarding. She picked through the items nearest the door. The vial of bloodstained slivers was there, as was a stained handkerchief and a stamp with red wax adhering to the edges. The image on the stamp was a leaping lion. Kate made a mental note of the items, and looked up to see Christian muttering disgustedly as he closed the last journal and tossed it in the pile.

"What?"

He waved her off. Working through the rest of the room, they examined the catapult Nickford had been working on the day before. There was little else of interest until Christian reached under the bed and pulled out a metal pipe. He hefted it and looked speculatively at the pile near the door.

"A good murder weapon, no?"

Kate lifted her brows. "Wouldn't there be dried blood on it?"

"Not if he wiped it on that handkerchief."

He pointed to the handkerchief she had found. She looked back to the pile with the slivers and the stamp. "The red stains could be from the sealing wax."

Christian smiled. "We'll make a Runner of you yet."

She rolled her eyes, trying to ignore the pleasurable tingles his genuine smile elicited. She took the pipe and rolled it in her hands. It looked clean, though again they couldn't be sure it hadn't been wiped clean the night before.

Kate took a last gander around the room. "Do you think we should move on to another room?"

Christian appeared to consider their alternatives. "Sure, let's visit Lake's next."

Kate nodded, conflicted on the temporary

reprieve from returning to their room. He touched her hand lightly as he locked Nickford's room, and she wondered if it was by accident or design. He gestured for her to lead the way. No teasing smile anywhere on his face, just a certain watchfulness.

Kate's mind whirled as she walked to Lake's room. That look. The one that Joshua had given Caroline when he wasn't sure if he was moving too fast and was very concerned with the result.

Was it just her imagination desperately conjuring the images she wished to see?

Kate snapped to attention as Christian nudged her with his hip. She had just been staring at Lake's door—daydreaming. How mortifying. That had happened far too frequently of late. She knocked. No one answered, so Christian inserted the key and unlocked the door.

If they had thought Nickford's room was messy, Lake's was a sty. Clothes were strewn everywhere, as if thrown in a jealous rage. Perhaps during the breakage the night before. Sure enough, there was shattered glass in one corner that had been poorly swept to the side.

Kate knelt by the glass shards, touched the discoloration, and brought her fingers to her nose. Judging by the smell, the liquid had been from an oil lamp.

"Does Lake want to burn down the inn?" she asked.

"Wouldn't be a very good way to woo a woman by burning down her family's business."

"I wouldn't think so, no."

They searched through the rubble, shifting things from one pile to another.

"Look at this, Christian." Kate held up a cricket bat. Various colors and stains decorated the surface, but one most definitely looked like blood.

Christian reached for the bat. "That would surely make a dent."

"And there appears to be dried blood on it."

"You think Lake bludgeoned Janson with his cricket bat? Seems a fitting weapon, actually, since they were rivals."

She nodded.

He looked distracted. "There was an indentation in the wood railing. Let me check something, I'll be right back."

Christian walked from the room, leaving Kate alone with the bat in hand. Something twinkled in the corner and she walked over to examine it. Broken glass, but not the same quality or kind as the glass from the lamp. This was darker in color. She turned it over in her hand, wondering what it was from.

Another oil lamp? Lawrence Lake seemed prone to smashing glass.

"Good evening, Mr. Kaden."

Kate whipped around, startled to see Lake standing in the doorway, staring intently at the bat in her hand. His expression grew sinister as he lifted his eyes to hers, stepped inside the room, and closed the door.

Chapter 10

Trust is something that is hard to define. Much like love.

George Simon
to Kate, age seventeen

Kate panicked. How had he slipped in so quietly? Most of the inn's doors squeaked. It was almost as if Lake had oiled his . . .

"I see you found my bat, Mr. Kaden."

He moved toward her. When he wasn't breaking things, Lake seemed like such a nice, nonthreatening man. But now as he stalked toward her . . . candlelight flickered, casting eerie shadows across his features.

Kate backed up a step, taking a firm grip on the

bat. "Mr. Lake, I'd like you to stay where you are."

"Why is that, Mr. Kaden?"

"You are making me nervous."

Lake stopped a few steps in front of her, and Kate gripped the bat more tightly. He held his hand out, reaching for it.

"May I have my bat, Mr. Kaden? After that, perhaps we can discuss matters."

A tight voice interrupted. "The only thing we are going to discuss, Lake, is you stepping the hell away from Ka— Mr. Kaden."

Lake stiffened, but turned to the door where Christian stood. Christian shut the door and walked over to Kate, stepping in front of her, close enough to Lake to make him back up a step.

"What is going on here?" Christian's voice was low and menacing.

"I was simply asking Mr. Kaden to hand over my bat."

"We are searching your room, Lake. Mr. Kaden doesn't have to hand anything back to you. And I must say things aren't looking so good for you. Gone into a rage lately, have we?"

Lake raised his chin. "I apologized for my bad behavior yesterday."

"Indeed. And now threatening my partner?"

Lake appeared affronted. "I was not threatening Mr. Kaden. Was I, Mr. Kaden?"

Kate had felt threatened, that was for sure, but now that Christian was back, Lake looked harmless, and she felt silly. She shrugged uncomfortably.

Lake's eyes widened.

Christian's eyes narrowed. "Did you kill Janson?"

Lake's expression returned to the bland, slightly unfocused one he had sported before. "I would have dearly liked to. Even Kaden here can tell you I didn't like the man. But no, I didn't kill him. Would like to shake the hand of the person who did, but it wasn't me."

"That's a bit morbid, Mr. Lake," Kate said.

Lake stared at her, and his head tipped a bit to the side. "Yes, it is. But Janson was the worst kind of man, and he would have made Mary's life hell. One of these days it would have been her, lying dead in the cold. I'm not sad the rotter is gone."

Kate wasn't quite sure how to respond to his declaration. Christian didn't seem as affected.

"Who do you think murdered him then?"

"Don't know." Lake shrugged carelessly. "Don't much care, other than to offer the man a thanks and a pint."

"Talk like that is going to get you in trouble, Lake."

Kate smelled alcohol as Lake carefully, too carefully, maneuvered to the bed and flopped onto the covers. He was drunk, although hiding it well. That explained his earlier expressions a bit more.

"Do those thoughts make me a bad man, Mr. Black? That I want to protect the woman I love? That I am glad she didn't end up with a man who would likely have beaten or raped her."

"Why do—did—the Wickets like him so much then?"

Lake ran a hand over his face roughly. "Mr. Wicket sees what he wants. Janson put on a good show when he chose to. Mary's father refused to see the bad side of his personality and kept pushing Mary to accept him. I have to believe that Mr. Wicket would have opened his eyes and come to his senses before it was too late. Most of the other servants knew what Janson was really like. I don't think they would have allowed her to marry him. I think they were ready to confront her father."

Christian reached for the bat.

"What about the blood on this bat?"

"That's from a match fight a few weeks ago. It's my blood actually. I wiped it from my face and inadvertently transferred it to the bat when Janson came after me."

"Fighting with Janson?"

"We fought all the time."

"And you think Mary Wicket will be safer in your company?"

Kate expected Lake to react vehemently to Christian's words. Perhaps to charge at him or yell; instead he merely shrugged.

"I'd never hurt Mary. Never hurt any woman. Truth is I haven't had the desire to hurt anyone except Julius Janson."

"Not a stunning defense against an accusation of murder," Christian pointed out.

"You can ask anyone. I've only ever fought with Janson."

"Even in bar fights or fights on the field?"

"As if you have never fought in a bar fight, Mr. Black?" Lake's face was full of disbelief. "I meant that I never had any urge to fight with anyone but Janson. I have been in a few tumbles, and in each of those, Janson has been on the opposing side."

Kate signaled to Christian. This was getting them nowhere and they needed to move on.

"We'll be back to talk to you later, Lake, understand?"

He nodded and his eyes closed. He'd probably be asleep in minutes. Christian propped the bat against the wall as he and Kate exited the room.

"We need to talk," Kate said as she preceded Christian to their room.

When their door was shut, she said, "Lake didn't do it."

"I know."

She blinked. "You do? You seemed to be questioning him pretty fiercely."

"Just wanted to see if he really did have violent tendencies."

"And does he?"

"When I attacked him verbally, his first response, even being half drunk, was not to attack me physically. Something that would definitely not have been true of Janson. Did you notice that Lake seemed genuinely upset to be labeled as violent? For the most part, he seems to deal with accusations appropriately."

"Except with Janson."

Christian smirked. "I thought you said he didn't do it?"

She swatted his arm.

"Oh, now look who is being violent."

"Should we search other rooms tonight?"

He shook his head. "Most of the guests were

retiring when I was in the hall. Desmond is still demanding to know what we've discovered."

"Now there's someone who is volatile. He also seems overly curious."

Christian shrugged. "He was a friend of Janson's, two peas in a pod. Wants revenge on Lake even if he can't prove he did it. Desmond is an idiot."

"So what will we do for the rest of the night?"

He raised his eyebrows suggestively, but said, "Well, what have we learned so far?"

"Lake and Janson fought last night, both with words and fists. We also know that Tiegs talked to Lake after his verbal fight with Janson?"

"Yes."

"Hold on a moment. I'll be right back."

Kate watched as Christian fairly skipped from the room in excitement. He returned a few minutes later with an inkpot, quill, and some paper.

"How is your handwriting?"

"Fair."

"Good, have a seat, because mine is barely legible. Or at least so my father tells me." A quick cloud passed over his features, nearly too quick for her to detect if she hadn't been observing him closely.

"You are lucky to still have your father."

"Oh, lucky doesn't begin to describe the feeling."

His carefree manner returned, brighter than before. Brighter . . . and most definitely more false.

He gestured to the paper. "Let's write down everything we know. See if something doesn't all of a sudden make more sense."

"You are really getting into this investigation, aren't you?"

His smile was brittle. "I used to want to be a constable. Thought that the position would allow me to have justice. I mean, bring justice to others, of course. Mentioned it to my father once, and as a result was relegated to eating alone for an entire month."

Kate's mouth opened and closed wordlessly, not knowing how to respond to that piece of information. Finally she said, "Was that because you are a gentleman and he thought the position beneath you?"

"Oh, come now, Kate. You and I both know I'm not a gentleman. No, my biggest sin was killing my mother when I was born. Nothing after that could wipe away the murder my father claimed I had committed."

"Your mother died in childbirth?"

He picked up the quill and handed it to her with obvious intent to close the thread of conversation.

"You do know it was not your fault, right?"

His face was expressionless. "Of course. Shall we begin our lists?"

She uncapped the inkpot and dipped the edge of the quill into the dark liquid. She felt a tendril of connection. They were both motherless, although her father had been loving and kind, when his was obviously anything but.

She switched back to a safe subject. "You seem much more excited this evening."

"I have a few theories. Plus, think of what a boon it would be to catch the killer." She detected a hint of relief in his tone at the subject change.

"I thought men in your profession apprehended criminals all the time," she said dryly, knowing without a shadow of a doubt that he was not a Runner.

He waved aside her sarcasm. "I've always loved puzzles. Though I was reminded regularly that being a dab hand at puzzles did me little good."

She grasped the personal information that he had all of a sudden begun to dole out to her. Prior to this he had hidden behind false smiles and careless comments. Now those seemingly carelessly tossed comments actually contained kernels. Here he was admitting to a vulnerability plain as day, or as plain as he ever seemed to get. Some hidden insight of which she had previously thought him incapable.

Then again, everyone had some measure of depth, including Julius Janson. And Christian Black. And Joshua McShaver, who dearly loved his wife.

She shook her head to dislodge the suddenly romantic thoughts. "After we compile our list, perhaps we should discuss the motives for murdering Julius Janson."

"Seems pretty obvious."

Hidden depths or not, the man was irritating.

"So how should we proceed?"

"Title the list 'Facts.'"

Kate dragged the quill across and down to form the F, the scratch of the tip leaving a trail of ink as she finished the uppercase letter with a flourish. Scratching out the other four letters more neatly, she looked up to see Christian give a satisfied nod. He reached down and placed his hand over hers, drawing a line under the word, his fingers trailing off hers at the end of the stroke.

Kate's breath lodged somewhere in her chest, and she busied herself with dipping the quill in the inkpot. The quill hit the edge of the opening before she steadied herself enough to successfully dip it. She took extra time tapping the excess ink onto the pot's throat before glancing up.

Christian was staring at her, but his gaze wasn't entirely focused, as if he were in deep thought. The lamp flickered golden light onto his already handsome features, playing with his cheekbones and straight nose. After a moment he shook his head as though to clear it.

"Let's think through the sequence of events. Lake and Janson started a brawl in the taproom, presumably over Mary. They were reprimanded by the Wickets. Soon afterward, you heard the two of them arguing in the common room, this argument also concerning Mary. Janson then left. Tiegs, who is already suspicious at best, entered and approached Janson. They conversed about a topic which remains a mystery, but could have possibly concerned his problems with Janson. Tiegs did something with a pocket watch, but what that was we don't know. This was all around midnight, and Janson was still alive. Correct so far?"

"Yes." She wrote down his dictation, trying to keep pace and trying not to stare at the way the light from the lamp caressed his skin.

"Next you came back to the room. Lake got

angry and threw the lamp. Mrs. Wicket stormed down to reprimand him. Around two, you left the room and observed two men on the balcony. One looked like Janson. We will assume for the moment it was he. Janson was still alive at two, because the snow had just started to fall and by the impression left in the snow, we can assume that it had been snowing awhile before the body was cast over the balcony, yet it had to have been well before the snow stopped falling. Gordon stated the snow had stopped by six o'clock when he made his rounds. So we can deduce that Janson was murdered between two and six, probably closer to a time between two and four."

Kate had stopped scratching, mesmerized by his account.

"That is quite a deduction." She was impressed despite herself. "Maybe you should consider thumbing your nose at your father and becoming a constable or investigator anyway."

"Kate, you say the sweetest things." He ran a hand over the back of her neck, massaging the muscles and skin. "And of course, how could I forget; at three you started moaning, and I captured you between the sheets."

The mortification that Kate would have experienced had he said something like that earlier was strangely absent while he continued doing sinfully wonderful things to her shoulders and neck.

"I do remember someone's footsteps treading down the hall at that time. Not loudly, but as if the person were checking that all was well. Possibly Mrs. Wicket, as Nickford claimed earlier. He said he heard a thud and moan about half past two."

"Which he blamed on his ghost." Her eyes slid shut as he pushed gently against the top of her spine. A sound of satisfaction escaped.

"Mmm . . . Kate, if you continue to make those sounds, you'll have to let me take you instead of you taking notes."

His whisper brushed the hairs at the back of her neck. She jerked open her eyes to see the tip of the quill halfway down the page, a jagged line in its wake.

She cleared her throat, trying to regain some semblance of dignity, and tapped the quill against the inkpot. She had to remember her resolve. She was going to be the one in charge. She'd do the rejecting. "Whoever was walking around last night should have been quite tired this morning."

"Everyone looked tired this morning, unfortunately."

"Except Nickford."

"I don't think that man belongs in normal company."

"Possibly not. Should we compile a list of the people staying in the inn, as well as possible suspects?"

His fingers ghosted the nape of her neck, playing with the tendrils there. "Excellent idea, Kate."

She would not let his charm wash over her. She would not.

His hand brushed her arm.

"What are you doing?"

His body leaned over hers, his face next to hers, cheek to cheek.

"I'm listing the names of the guests for you."

She focused on the paper and not the tingles zipping through her body.

"Don't forget to list the servants, although I don't know the names of those who are traveling with the guests."

He cocked his head toward her, the edge of his lip lightly brushing hers. "Servants? What do you mean? Why should we list the servants?"

She was so distracted that she could barely focus on the conversation—his lips were a breath away, the heat of his body scorched hers. "They are staying in the inn too."

"But servants . . . serve." His full lower lip grazed her cheek.

"And they don't commit crimes?" she whispered.

He reached down and rested a hand on her thigh, tugging the durable fabric in the same way he was pulling her reactions. "Well, I suppose the odd trouser theft here and there. Father always claimed the servants were not to be trusted. I suppose that's why I always want to trust them."

She disengaged herself and turned to look him full in the face.

"Christian." She paused, committing to memory all the remarks about his father so she could surreptitiously question him about them at a later time. His statement also confirmed that he was wellborn and that he had had servants at some point. "It's not that your father was right, but the servants have just as much reason to commit a crime as anyone."

"Gordon did act might shifty when he was talking to us at the stables." Christian straightened, tapping his chin, and suddenly Kate was unsure if he was having her on or not.

Her eyes narrowed suspiciously, but she decided to go along with the conversation in case he was serious. "There you go."

"On the other hand, Gordon reported the body. Why report it? Better to leave it hidden instead. Mr. Wicket was willing to write off Janson as leaving early."

"There is that." She missed the heat of his body and cursed herself for the thought.

"What about Mr. Wicket then? Awfully convenient. Perhaps he found out what a churl Janson really was."

"And then objected to his daughter being involved?"

Christian nodded, then shook his head. The man was nearly impossible to read. When he was feigning carelessness he might be dead serious, and when he acted serious he might just be having her on.

"Wicket just doesn't strike me as a very good fabricator. I think he truly thought, or hoped, that Janson was a right fine bloke."

"But remember, not everyone held that sentiment. Lake seems to believe that many of the servants shared his disdain for Janson. Mary was very close-faced whenever Janson was around, and Janson made no bones about his feelings for both Lake and Mary. If he had, I wouldn't have overheard them. Lake was incensed."

"So that brings us back to Lake."

"Everything does seem to circle back to him."

"Wouldn't we have heard him leave his room?"

She raised a brow. "Didn't I use that argument about Freewater, to no avail?"

"I can't seem to recall." His eyes were wide and innocent.

"I bet you can't," she muttered. "But in any case, Lake's door was well oiled. He startled me when he silently entered the room today. And you slipped in unnoticed as well."

Christian absently nodded. "There is that. And Lake could have hired Tiegs or one of his bodyguards."

He paused.

"Or Tiegs could have done it on his own. He seemed to know Janson, and Janson appeared intimidated by him, even frightened."

"We should probably search Tiegs's room next."

"I agree."

Kate finished the list, writing down servants' names or descriptions if she didn't know their names. The Crescents had brought a maid and valet.

Just as she was writing out the last name, the chimes struck midnight. Twelve strikes of sheer helplessness. The quill wrenched across the page, creating a second jagged line in its path. Two, three, four. Kate closed her eyes and leaned forward, determined not to let Christian see her reaction. Seven, eight, nine. The quill snapped and she felt strong fingers pry open her grip and remove the broken pieces. Twelve.

She inhaled deeply and after a few moments forced herself to look up. Christian was staring at her, an unreadable look on his face. His fingers turned the broken quill pieces, staining the edges of his finger pads.

Christian tilted his head, his eyes intently watching hers for something—just as they had earlier, watching for something she didn't understand.

"What now?" she forced herself to say.

"Now we go to bed."

Kate reached for the counterpane. There was no way she could continue their dance after all of Christian's touches and the unwanted memories from the chimes.

Christian stayed her hand. "Kate, I'll sleep on top of the sheet. Just . . . just don't argue."

She was about to do just that, but fatigue set in. She might as well share the bed, his bed. It wasn't as if her reputation would be any worse if someone discovered her ruse. They would assume the worst anyway.

She hadn't slept well last night or during the

previous month. And as he looked at her, she saw comfort and something else in his eyes. Something she needed.

She nodded and slipped between the covers, fully clothed, and nestled up against the wall. Christian, true to his word, arranged the covers so that he lay on top of the sheet, and in contrast to the night before, stayed fully clothed. He maintained a respectful distance, but she could still feel the heat from his body seeping through the thin sheet and into her own. Tomorrow she'd figure out all the conflicting emotions. For now she'd sleep.

She awakened three hours later, thrashing in the throes of another nightmare. But comforting arms pulled her closer, and she calmed in the warmth and safety of the embrace.

A vague alarm sounded as gentle fingers caressed the hair at the nape of her neck. But the concern was buried between layers of bliss. Skillful fingers stroked her skin, and warmth lulled her to a peaceful sleep.

Chapter 11

It should have been you lying there dead, not your brothers.

The Marquess of Penderdale
to Christian, age nineteen

Christian propped his chin on his hand as he halfheartedly stirred his dark tea.

It had been a long morning. They had risen and checked all around the outside of the inn, into the nooks and crannies, retracing steps and examining angles from the gallery to the ground. The winds had stopped blowing and the villagers had gotten to work sweeping and clearing the roads and opening everything back up for business. Christian had been forced to let Mr. Wicket allow the villagers to come in for a spot of tea or bowl of stew, as was normal. Luckily they were on the outskirts of town, and only a few had ventured in, people still sticking close to home due to the drifts.

The male servants had been drafted into clearing the roads so that the post could get back running. Christian had tersely threatened them about revealing information on Janson, his death or the investigation. The eyes of the servants had been too knowing for his piece of mind and sleep-weary brain.

It had been a long, restless night.

From across the table, he watched Kate sip her sugared tea. He didn't know what to think about her nightmares last night and the night before, but it was obvious that she didn't want to talk about them.

Kate had thrashed every hour on the hour. Finally, at three, he had given in to his instincts by pulling her against him and holding her. Never having been consoled himself, he had been quite unsure how to go about soothing someone else. Kate's back had been damp with sweat, but her skin had been cold, even under the layers of clothes and covers.

Ever since he had laid eyes on her two days ago something had been calling to him. But what?

She wasn't his usual style. Not at all. She was entirely too forthright and uninterested in playing games. But for once he found that playing games with a female was the last thing on his mind. The only problem was he wasn't sure what he was supposed to do *instead*.

He had looked at her that first night wearing her boy's garb and head wrap, a slightly lost look in her eyes backed by steel determination, and had been unable to look away since.

Loss and determination were emotions with which he was intimately acquainted, so perhaps that was part of the reason.

What he *did* know was that he wanted to discover what was wrong with her. Why she was experiencing such dreadful nightmares. What the devil she was hiding. Where she was going after leaving the inn. *And how she tasted.*

Yes, he definitely wanted to know the answer to that last one.

There were so many unanswered questions, but first he needed to gain her trust. And to make her his. And to fix her problems. Not necessarily in that order. Anthony had always said a burden shared was a burden partially relieved. He didn't know, as he had never taken the advice himself.

He might be a careless bastard—no, unfortunately for his family not a bastard; perhaps a careless rotter was a better description—but he wasn't a hypocrite. At least he had liked to think so. Therefore, he had never forced or coaxed anyone into sharing their problems. There were much more pleasant ways to spend an evening, after all.

He watched her clutch her cup in both hands, a grayish cast to her skin. On second thought . . .

"Found anything useful, Black?" a caustic, unwelcome voice asked.

Christian didn't take his eyes from Kate as he answered. "Found out you are the cock of the company, Desmond. Other than that, we are still sorting things out."

Desmond's hand smacked the table with a loud thud, and Christian turned, not impressed in the least.

Desmond's eyes narrowed dangerously. "What did you call me?"

"The cock of the company, Desmond. Aren't you supposed to be the one who is heading to London for a prominent job? Better brush up on your vocabulary skills. You are a weak shill who wishes he were the cock of the walk, but instead are merely a trifling fool."

That mottled red color did nothing to enhance

Desmond's complexion, and Christian couldn't help pointing it out.

"You should watch what you say, Black. Could be that accidents happen twice."

"Are you threatening me? You wouldn't be that much of an idiot, would you, Desmond?"

Desmond pushed his hands off the table, rattling it. "On your feet, Black."

Christian leaned back against the wall, a well-chosen spot to sit in any room, the dining room being no exception. "Now really, Desmond, wouldn't want you to hurt yourself again."

Desmond's hands clenched at his sides as he lurched toward Christian. Kate stood and blocked his way, putting a hand against Desmond's chest with surprising force. She glared at Christian, undoubtedly for encouraging Desmond's behavior. He found himself thinking that even that expression looked cute on her pixieish face.

She turned toward the idiot. "Now, Mr. Desmond, we are in the middle of an investigation. You can't attack a Runner. Best to just ignore him."

"Get out of my way, pissant."

Kate's eyes narrowed, but she held her ground. "Mr. Desmond, get hold of your emotions."

"Get out of the way. We all know Lake killed Julius. It's only this bastard who claims otherwise.

For some reason, he's dragging out this investigation." He pointed a knobby finger at Christian.

"That is not true, Mr. Desmond. I too have doubts about Lake's culpability, as do others."

Desmond roughly grabbed her arm and Christian pushed away from the wall, all humor extinguished.

"Well then, you must be in cahoots with him too, you feeble excuse for a man." Desmond shoved her roughly aside.

Christian was on his feet before Desmond's hand left Kate's arm. Kate stumbled, but braced herself on the table. Christian grabbed Desmond's outstretched hand and twisted. The man squawked, dropped to his knees, and tried to evade the crushing grip. Christian could feel skin, muscle, and bone shifting beneath his grasp. With a mere twist he could snap Desmond's wrist and break his arm.

Desmond was making inaudible gasping sounds. He was looking at the hand Christian held, tears leaking down his cheeks.

Just another twist. That's all, his father would say.

A slim hand appeared on his sleeve. It didn't tug or encourage. It just rested on top. Just another twist.

Christian let Desmond's arm go with a snarl of disgust.

Desmond sank back on his heels, grasping his arm and staring at Christian with utter hatred in his tear-glazed eyes.

"Here now, what's going on?" Mr. Wicket came bustling over to their table.

Kate rallied. "Mr. Desmond had some questions about the investigation."

Mr. Wicket's eyes darted nervously between Christian's scowl and Desmond's bowed head and clutched arm. Desmond struggled from the floor to a bench.

"Everything answered now?" the innkeeper asked.

Desmond grunted while Christian settled on a terse nod.

"Good, good. Now, Mr. Kaden, I know you no longer need to work for me since you are aiding Mr. Black, but I need your assistance to draw that map you requested earlier."

Kate nodded and lifted her hand from Christian's sleeve. She gave him a searching glance, and Christian returned a careless grin. They were always easiest when he was angry.

She frowned. "Perhaps you would like to accompany us, Mr. Black?"

181

Christian looked at Desmond's bowed head. "An excellent idea, do excuse us, Desmond." He patted him on the head as he passed.

Kate frowned more sharply as she turned and followed the innkeeper.

But really, what did she expect from him? Desmond was a maggot.

Once they were in Wicket's office the man drew a rough sketch of the first-floor rooms where the guests were lodged.

"And the guests' names?"

Wicket nodded and began to pen in the names. The common room stretched across the entire south end of the structure, and Christian could picture someone chasing Janson through the room with a bat in hand. Continuing along the west corridor were rooms occupied by Nickford, Tiegs, and Freewater, two of which they had searched the previous day. Christian mentally checked them off while trying to figure out how to search Freewater's room again without raising undue suspicion. He had been gleeful at first when Freewater had reacted as if he had lost the journal, but if it hadn't been on his person, then where would it be? The blasted thing had to be in his room somewhere.

Wicket penned in Black and Kaden in the first

full north-facing room, and Lake's name into the adjacent room to the east. The Crescents' name was written on the north- and eastern-facing room, the largest in the inn, and the first of the gallery-accessible rooms. Other than the thought that Free-water could have passed the journal to Crescent, their room had held little interest, just like the couple themselves.

Christian would bet their lovemaking—no, copulation sessions—never lasted beyond five minutes, and never took place without the lights being fully extinguished. Of course, they would skip nights with full moons. Imagine the horror.

He caught Kate looking at him peculiarly and realized he had been grinning—a real grin. He quickly replaced it with a lazy smile. With brows drawn together, she turned from him. He momentarily regretted his action, then stiffened. No, he wasn't going to regret anything. He didn't need to pass some kind of acceptability test for anyone anymore.

She smiled at Mr. Wicket as he asked a question. Her eyes crinkled in the corners and her mouth quirked a bit to the left. He wanted that smile aimed at him. He wanted her to look at him as she had last night before they went to sleep. With a genuine smile, her eyes lit from within.

Damn it. Damn it! He didn't want to rely on anyone else's good opinion. He had long since stamped out the need for approval. He had, damn it.

"Mr. Black?"

"What?" His tone was a bit sharper than he intended, and Mr. Wicket looked unsure for a moment.

"I was just telling Mr. Kaden about the improvements to the gallery. Did you hear me?"

"Yes, of course I did. Please continue."

He had no idea what they had been talking about, but he tried to concentrate as the innkeeper drew Desmond's south-facing room as the L-shaped inn curved clockwise around the staircase to Olivia and Francine's room. Christian tried not to notice the small lock of hair that peeked out from under Kate's cap when she tilted her head *just so*.

The innkeeper grew more agitated as he labeled Julius Janson's room, connecting it back to the common room, both having gallery access.

Kate's head tilted back as a ray of sun pierced through the window and hit her cheek, caressing the rose and cream skin. One bright ray in an otherwise cloudy and stormy day.

Her mouth was moving. Perfect rosebuds. How

was she fooling anyone with this masquerade as a boy?

He shook himself as he realized the innkeeper and Kate had continued the conversation while he had been daydreaming like an infatuated fool. Bloody hell. Might as well call him Lawrence Lake and be done with it.

"What about the ground floor and workers' quarters?" Kate asked.

Mr. Wicket looked at her oddly, but sketched out both the ground floor and second floor. Christian examined the drawing of the servants' quarters with interest, thankful to be looking at anything other than Kate. It was a square floor positioned on top of the northwest section of the inn. The Wickets were located directly over the northwest portion above their room and Freewater's. To the south of the innkeepers' lodgings was a room in which three names were written.

"Benji, Elias, and Mr. Crescent's valet stay here?" Christian pointed to the square on the makeshift map.

Wicket nodded. Christian traced his finger to the east of the innkeeper's room. There were two rooms labeled. Daisy and Bess, the serving wench and cook, respectively, were listed with Mrs. Crescent's maid, while Mary and Sally's names were written on the easternmost room. Marks indicating a staircase were located in the southeast corner.

"And Tom and Gordon stay in the stables?" he clarified.

"Yes, usually."

"Thank you, Mr. Wicket. This will be most useful," Kate said, gathering up the papers.

"I only hope you two will catch the fiend who murdered Julius. He was a good man, didn't you know?"

Christian didn't, but he refrained from saying so.

"Such a loss. Was hoping that Mary would accept his suit. He approached me about pressing it."

"When did he do that, Mr. Wicket?" Kate asked.

Mr. Wicket looked surprised, but answered, "The night before last, actually. Right before the taproom fight. I was going to talk to Mary about it the next day, um, yesterday."

"Mary didn't know?"

"I think she suspected. Shy girl, my Mary. Think she liked Julius though." Mr. Wicket looked wistful. "Fine cricket player, Julius was, not sure what we will do without him."

"I'm sure the team will rally in his fine memory."

"Good bunch of men, our team. Very spirited. Julius and Donald are two of our best. Now we will lose both."

"Both?" Kate asked and glanced at a stoic Christian. He must have forgotten to tell her about Desmond.

"Donald is taking a position in London with a barrister. Some connection through his family."

"Maybe you should recruit Lake for your team. I hear he is a fine player as well," Christian said smoothly. His sudden concern and identification with Lake was irritating, so he ignored it.

Mr. Wicket's brows drew together. "Something would have to cause Mr. Lake to move from Lehigh. He is a good player. Not as talented as Julius. Or as spirited. But better than Donald. Always drives Donald something fierce."

Kate raised her brows. "I thought the rivalry was between Janson and Lake, not Desmond and Lake."

"Lake's rival has always been Julius, and vice versa. Donald, as Julius's friend, has always focused on Lake, but the reverse hasn't been true. Something occurred last year that really sparked the rivalry between Julius and Lake. I was hoping things would settle down for Mary's eighteenth birthday celebration next month."

Wicket really was blind if he didn't understand. Mary was a pretty girl, curvy and natural. A year ago she had probably blossomed into the woman she was now. Christian shook his head.

Mr. Wicket continued on, blithely unaware. "Lake expressed interest in attending. Nice to have some crosstown interaction, even if he is on the opposing team." Mr. Wicket chuckled at his own joke.

Christian and Kate excused themselves minutes later and headed back to the dining room. Lake was speaking earnestly to Mary. The girl was blushing. Desmond was at a table across the room with a scowl on his face.

"It all comes back to Lake, doesn't it?" Kate muttered.

Christian shook his head as he watched Lake and Mary and noted minute gestures of affection between them, gestures he had in the past avoided like the plague. "No, it all comes back to Mary."

Kate looked at him sharply, and he could see her mind start to churn. Before she could question him, Freewater scuttled over to them from his corner.

"I want to participate in your search of the rooms."

"What?" Kate looked incredulous.

"I want to help you search the rooms."

Christian narrowed his eyes as fierce triumph and irritation warred within him.

Kate shook her head. "I'm sorry, sir, but that is just not—"

"Why do you want to help?"

Kate looked at Christian in shock as he abruptly cut off her explanation. He was staring at Freewater, his gaze shrewd. After hearing his contemplative thought about Mary, Kate's mind was in turmoil. That Freewater should suddenly pop up like a child's toy was disconcerting.

Freewater straightened importantly. "I want to help your investigation."

"No you don't." Christian's tone was moderate, as if talking about the weather.

"What do you mean, no I don't?" Freewater blustered.

"I mean exactly what I said; you don't want to help investigate Janson's murder."

"Why else would I offer to help?"

"Did you lose something, Freewater?" Christian purred. Kate stared at him. His eyes were mocking, but there was something fierce and narrow behind the mocking.

"Didn't lose anything. There's just nothing to do in this blasted inn while we wait to be set free."

Christian examined his nails. "You can play cards or gossip with the others. You could hide away in your room as you did before, doing who knows what. We can't help you, Freewater, if you don't help us." He continued to examine his nails, his voice idle.

Freewater clenched his lips, his face turning purple. "Fine. A journal was stolen from me."

"Stolen?" Christian's eyes grabbed Freewater's. "Why would someone steal your journal?"

Freewater hesitated before answering. He seemed to be waging an internal battle. "Because the journal was valuable. Priceless."

"Oh yes? What did the journal contain?"

"It was a private account."

"A gentleman's account? Why would that be valuable, or *priceless*, as you say?"

Freewater gritted his teeth. "The gentleman has a lot to lose should the journal fall into the wrong hands."

"Sounds like the journal already did." Christian's eyes were icy, and Kate, already feeling as if she was missing something, grew more suspicious.

Christian seemed to notice her reaction, even though his eyes never left Freewater's. He gave a small negative gesture with his hand and she stayed silent.

"The journal was given to me," Freewater sniffed.

"By the owner?"

"Yes," he said, but Kate noticed Freewater's left eye twitch.

"Describe it."

"Dark brown leather, about a fingernail thick, gold embossed."

"What name is engraved?"

"Darton." The name was ripped from Freewater's throat. Kate thought it sounded vaguely familiar, but couldn't place it. She watched Christian's eyes turn hard, and she had a feeling that while she might not be able to place the name, Christian certainly could.

"Hmmm . . . we haven't come across a journal of that description so far, have we, Mr. Kaden?"

She shook her head.

"That is why I should be involved as well," Freewater said.

"We can't have you involved in the investigation, Mr. Freewater."

"But—"

191

"It would compromise the entire process. It's against Runner's Code Section Forty-one. Firm statute, that one."

Kate had no idea what Christian was talking about, and she thought Christian probably didn't either. He seemed quite capable of making things up on the spot, however.

"I need that journal!"

"We will see if we can't find your missing journal, Freewater. We will, of course, inform you, should we find it."

Kate thought that from the look on Christian's face and the tone of his voice that was very unlikely, but Freewater tersely nodded.

"I will pay handsomely for its safe return."

"Excellent. That will encourage faster results."

Freewater seemed to think that it would too, since he nodded.

He shuffled off to his dark corner and Christian smirked.

"What was that about?" she hissed.

"Why, nothing, nothing at all. We'll attempt to find Freewater's journal, just as I said we would."

"But what do you know of it?"

"Tut, tut, Kate, so suspicious. I know only what you do, that Freewater lost a journal that really belongs to someone else."

Daisy approached with a bean stew that smelled as tasty as the beef from the day before. Kate picked small slivers of the table's wood from her nails as Daisy touched and cooed over Christian. She curled her nails into her palms instead.

After an unbearably long time in which Kate shredded her bread to crumbs and nearly cracked her bowl with the force of her spoon thrust, Daisy finally swaggered off.

Ready to deliver a scathing comment, Kate pointed her spoon at Christian, whose eyes were smoothly mocking. "I really don't think—"

"Ladies and gentlemen, may I have your attention?" Mr. Wicket interrupted, waving his stubby arms.

"You really don't think?" Christian mock whispered to Kate's half-delivered invective.

Kate glared as Mr. Wicket finally gained the attention of the room.

"I have just received an update from the men clearing the roads. Coaches and carriages may be running as early as tomorrow afternoon." Someone gave a little cheer. "Mr. Black will be continuing his investigation, searching rooms, and speaking to each of you, so please be polite and forthcoming so you can all be on your way tomorrow."

The little innkeeper was such a contradiction. On one hand he seemed to understand his patrons; on the other he seemed not to notice anything in his own household and village.

She glanced over to see Christian looking thoughtful and determined. They would be able to leave tomorrow, and that meant Christian Black would saunter right out of her life the same way he had sauntered in.

She swallowed.

They had the rest of the day and night and maybe tomorrow morning to discover the killer's identity; after that, the murderer might go free. A chill went through her, followed by steely resolve. She couldn't let that happen. This was something she could control, unlike all the other things in her life. She was finally doing something constructive. Justice could be served here, and she intended to see it happen.

Chapter 12

Keep your wits about you. Your instincts will never lead you astray.

George Simon
to Kate, age fourteen

They searched Tiegs's room first, even though at this point they were looking less for actual evidence, which had most likely been hidden or destroyed, and more for indicators about the people and clues to the puzzle. When Christian had told Tiegs that his room was the next they would search, the man had given them a nonchalant wave of his hand. Kate had thought it odd, as secretive as Tiegs seemed.

One of his two bruisers followed them upstairs

and watched intently as they searched through Tiegs's belongings.

With the big man standing at the door, arms crossed, hairless head gleaming in the firelight, Kate was less inclined to search than she had been at first. Christian seemed to take the behemoth's presence in stride, even going so far as to ask if the man was nervous that they might find his lace undergarments.

The man hadn't been amused.

"Look at this."

Kate glanced up to see Christian holding a bat. Crossing over, she touched the bat, and could see stains on the end. They appeared to be old stains, and the wood was nicked and chipped.

"Is Mr. Tiegs a cricket player?"

The bruiser grunted.

"I'll take that as a yes then."

"Perhaps that was why Tiegs was talking to Lake?" Kate murmured. No use giving the bruiser information for Tiegs to use in case he was the guilty party.

"It could also explain how Janson knew him."

"I'll ask Mr. Wicket."

Christian nodded.

She found a pocket watch next and showed it to Christian and whispered, "I was hoping the pocket watch we found on Janson's body would be the one I saw that night, but I think this is the one I saw. This chain looks similar, even seeing it from a distance."

Christian just nodded his head.

Their search turned up a small arsenal of weaponry packed in a large trunk. Three rifles, four pistols, and a sword.

Kate thought she might give Tiegs a wider berth than she already had.

The bruiser remained in the room even as Christian and Kate proceeded across the hall to Olivia and Francine's room. Christian knocked lightly on the door.

"Oh, Mr. Black," Olivia purred as she wrapped one delicate hand around the oak frame. "I was wondering when you would make it to my room."

Kate gritted her teeth as Christian smiled brilliantly. "If it's not inconvenient, I was hoping to search your room? A mere formality, of course."

"Of course. Do come in now, but perhaps you would like to return later for a less formal search?" The woman's voice was smooth as satin, and Kate decided she hated that fabric.

"Perhaps," Christian replied easily.

Kate felt like throttling him. What was he thinking to flirt with one of their suspects? It's not as if she would normally *care*, but he was on this investigation with her, damn it. Least he could do was to act professionally.

"Do you mind if I watch you work? I have the utmost respect for you Runners. So strong, and brave, and *strong*." Kate saw the woman's fingertips run along the edge of Christian's arm, caressing his shirtsleeve. Wicked widow, indeed. Kate stumbled forward, and her flailing arm knocked the widow's hand off Christian's shirtsleeve.

"Oh, I'm terribly sorry, madam."

Olivia barely spared her a look, instead continuing to send smoldering glances in Christian's direction as she regained his arm and tucked hers under his. Olivia's dress swished as she strolled with him farther into the room. One would think they were at a ball and not in a room that was at most seven paces long. Irritating man.

"Do tell me what you are looking for, Mr. Black? You won't have to search us, will you?" She put her free hand to her bodice and fingered the delicate lace.

Kate blinked in shock, speechless.

"We just might have to at that, Mrs. Trent."

"Do call me Olivia."

"And you may call me Christian."

Olivia gave him a self-satisfied smile, and Kate

turned away to start rifling through the woman's belongings. She could feel a brief, distasteful glance at her back, but Olivia simply made a tutting sound and flirted shamelessly with Christian once more.

Kate stifled a gasp of shock at finding a rod with a thin leather tail. She shoved it back into the traveling case.

"Did you find something of interest, Mr. Kaden?" Christian's smooth voice sounded amused, and she just knew he had seen what had been uncovered in Olivia Trent's valise.

"Not yet." She cleared her throat. "Do carry on."

After sorting through several oils, unidentified implements, and a few perfectly identifiable implements, a red-faced Kate shoved the case back under the bed. If the murder weapon was in there, then happy hunting to Christian if he was going to avail himself of the merry widow later. Just like Connor, he was.

She checked under the mattress and searched through the nooks and crannies of the dresser. She was running out of places to search when Christian finally decided to do what they had originally come here to do.

"Olivia, was your first night at the inn the night that Mr. Janson was murdered?"

"Yes, Francine and I are traveling to London and our coach stopped here for the evening. We are taking in *all* the sights. It's been so long since I've been to Town properly."

After examining Mrs. Trent's case and watching her interact with Christian, Kate could just bet what those *sights* included. The shades were drawn and the lamps lit to cast Olivia in the best light.

"Did you hear anything odd the night Mr. Janson died?"

"I heard Mr. Lake yelling and glass shattering. Mr. Nickford was mucking about in the hall. I think Mrs. Wicket was down here twice, once to address the ruckus with Mr. Lake and a second time after."

Kate was intrigued, despite herself. "How do you know Nickford was in the hall?"

Olivia's gaze never left Christian. "I could hear him muttering. His voice is quite distinctive. Strange man, but rather well off, so I'm told."

"And Mrs. Wicket?"

"She tripped on something, I think, I heard her cry out."

"Cry out? Like she was hurt?"

"No. More like in shock. There was a bang like she hit the wall."

"And the gallery? Did you hear anything out there?" Christian entered the questioning.

"Two people were talking around two or three in the morning. The chimes sounded. There was a sound like a scuffle as well, but I was nearly asleep at that point."

Kate frowned. "Were you just falling asleep or had you been awakened by the scuffle?"

"Francine and I were talking. We had undressed and slipped under the covers."

"Talking about what?"

"What we were going to do in London, how glad we were to leave the country." Her look left Christian and she sent Kate a condescending glance. "Surely our conversation is of less interest to you than our toys."

Kate was unimpressed by the widow's patronizing glares and smug superiority. "I find you of very little interest actually, but we need to complete our investigation."

Olivia's eyes sparked and then narrowed.

"Did you notice anything else the night of Mr. Janson's death? Besides the common room, your room is the only one to share a wall with Janson's. Did you hear anything from his room?"

"Yes, I am quite aware of the layout, Mr. Kaden. Mr. Janson made a lot of noise until around two.

Quite drunk, I do believe. Wouldn't be surprised if in his drunken stupor he accidentally tossed himself over the railing."

Kate saw Christian's eyes narrow.

"Did you hear or see anything that could support that?" he asked.

"I wasn't spying on my neighbors, Christian." She looked up at him through half-lidded eyes. "I have much more pleasant ways of passing the time."

The hall clock began to chime and Kate shivered. Christian deftly disentangled himself from Olivia, who gave a moue of disappointment. He walked over to Kate, and his hand briefly brushed her side.

"Unfortunately, we still have several more rooms to search, Olivia. Will we see you at supper?"

"Most definitely," she purred.

Kate opened the door and walked from the room. She was irritated with Christian for flirting with a suspect and half surprised that he had walked away from the well-endowed widow to give her comfort. It made for a very aggravating and confusing state of mind.

Kate didn't wait for Christian to follow as she walked around the stairwell. She paused for a moment and looked around. Olivia Trent really did have the best room for hearing everything that went on. Centrally located, next to the stairs, opening onto the gallery, and adjacent to the victim's room. The only rooms that she would have trouble hearing conversations from would be the Crescents' and the common room.

Christian tapped her shoulder, his gaze once more unreadable. "Desmond's room next?"

She jerked her head in a nod and Christian strode forward and knocked. Desmond didn't answer, fortunately, and Christian unlocked the door. As soon as they were inside he turned to her.

"Why are you so irritable all of a sudden?"

"Oh, please. 'Christian, you are so strong and brave,'" she mimicked. "You did nothing to help in Olivia Trent's room!"

"I kept her occupied while you searched, didn't I?"

"You flirted shamelessly with her the entire time!"

He smirked. "Jealous?"

"No!"

He moved forward to flip open a book on top of the bed stand, his body touching hers. Before she could move, he leaned forward so his lips were barely brushing her half-exposed good ear. "There's no reason to be jealous, Kate."

Her voice caught somewhere in her throat, but her feet managed to move a step back.

"I'm not jealous, Black."

"We're suddenly back to last names, Kate? Seems I've made some progress after all."

"I have no idea what you are talking about." Unfortunately, she couldn't quite convince herself. His ability to unsettle her was reaching a new level that was a bit, well, unsettling.

Desmond's room was uninspiring, quite like the man himself. It was devoid of any personal objects, with his cricket gear stacked in the corner.

"I suppose that makes sense," Christian said. "He and Janson live nearby. They were staying at the inn for a night of celebration."

Kate frowned. That thought had been bothering her for days. "Why wouldn't they just leave to go home? Their other teammates did."

He shrugged. "Janson's home was being remodeled. His parents are still away; he likely was using the situation to his advantage. Wicket said he had that chat with Janson. He was attempting to woo Mary."

"But that doesn't explain why Desmond would also stay."

He shook his head. "Janson was the type who

needed someone else to back him. Someone standing behind his shoulder sneering."

"So you think that's why Desmond remained?"

"I think Desmond probably stayed because Janson asked him to." Christian picked through the cricket gear. "We will have to ask him though."

Kate looked under the bed. Nothing was there, not even a ball of dust. "Good housekeeping service here."

She turned to see Christian examine the cricket bat.

"There's no dearth of cricket bats in this inn, is there?"

Christian looked speculative. "Except Janson's. He played in the match the other day right along with Desmond and Lake. Yet I haven't seen his bat, have you?"

She shook her head, eyes wide. "You think he was killed by his own bat?"

"Why not?"

She watched him turn Desmond's bat. Unlike the others, Desmond's was clean and well kept. Christian saw her staring.

"Desmond's a mouthy one, not one to get dirty. The only reason he was even in the taproom fight was because he was assaulting people who weren't paying attention."

Christian placed the bat back on the chair and motioned to leave the room.

"You don't think it was Desmond."

Christian shrugged. "Could easily have been. A jealous rage, perhaps? Tired of being in Janson's shadow? Perhaps he wasn't as devoted a second as everyone seemed to think. Men like Desmond aspire to greatness, but are too petty to ever truly achieve it."

Christian somehow convinced her to search the Crescents' room again, since the couple was out. The room was probably very light and airy during the daytime hours, but the sun had already set, and Christian lit a lamp.

Other than a silver-handled cane, there was little of interest. The room was well-appointed, with three casement windows and direct access to the gallery.

Kate watched Christian look through the desk and raised a brow as he swore.

"You didn't see anything resembling the journal that Freewater mentioned, did you?"

"No. Why are you so single-minded about trying to get your hands on Freewater's journal? It's the first thing you search for in every room. I even saw you look under the mattress in Tiegs's room, don't think I didn't. That's what gave me the idea to do the same in Olivia Trent's room."

"Well, while we are searching, we might as well search for the journal too. We don't know what else we are looking for now, do we?" His voice was harsh.

"Let's look for Janson's bat. That was a splendid idea you had."

He gripped the desk. "But that still doesn't bring us closer to finding the journal."

Kate decided not to comment. There was obviously something special about the journal, but until he decided to share it with her, she would continue to keep her peace. Unless it impeded their investigation.

His grip on the desk gradually loosened, though there was a tiredness that remained in his eyes. "Fine. Let's search Janson's room. I know that the servants said it was completely bare, but we should still check it over to see if anything was left behind."

"Then we can go to supper. They should be serving soon."

"Fine." He nodded tightly as they exited the room and locked the door. Sally collided with them as they turned the hall corner at the stairwell. She murmured a quick apology and ducked her head after giving Kate a shy smile.

Christian waited for her to pass before leaning down to Kate. "Looks like you have an admirer after all, Mr. Kaden."

"You are mad. Have you seen the looks Sally gives Benji? Methinks you are blind if you haven't."

Christian started to whistle, and while she was glad his mood had improved, his mercurial nature still bothered her. She had determined sometime while in Olivia Trent's room that it wasn't Christian who was mercurial, but rather the façade he presented to everyone. The man had an ironclad persona that he seemed to don without a thought. She wondered why he felt the need to disguise his emotions so thoroughly.

Christian opened Janson's door. The servants had been correct; the room was completely clean.

"I wonder when Sally cleaned this room?" Christian asked.

"Elias and Mary did say there was nothing in the room just before Gordon found the body."

Christian frowned. "Mary didn't open the door. I think it was Elias."

Kate considered it. "You're right. Mary came down saying the door was locked and Janson wasn't responding. Wicket then sent Elias up. We should have probably examined this room first yesterday, but you were determined to search Free-water's."

She gave him a look that he chose to ignore.

There wasn't much furniture to search here either, but Christian checked under the mattress and Kate peered through the drapes and out onto the gallery. As she pulled the green drape closed, she noticed a bit of lighter green clinging to a sliver of wood. Curious, she leaned down and plucked up the few threads.

"Christian, is this the same color as the cloth we took from Janson's hand?"

He let the mattress fall and lifted the pieces up to examine them in the lamplight. "Well, the drapes are green. Could they be stray threads?"

"The drapes are a different fabric. The drapes are velvety; these cotton threads are similar to what we found in Janson's hand."

He grinned. "Excellent work, Kate."

She tried to wave it off, but a pleased heat spread through her.

They walked from the room and saw Nickford muttering to himself in the hallway.

"Good evening, Mr. Nickford," Kate said.

He looked up and blinked. "Ah, good evening, Mr. Kaden, Mr. Black. Good night for catching ghouls."

"Uh, sure, good luck, Mr. Nickford."

He gave a cheery wave.

"Nicked in the head," Christian muttered. Kate swatted his arm and he caught her hand, rubbing it between his bare fingers. His touch was light enough that small tingles radiated from the contact. She shivered.

He hadn't worn gloves since that first night. His smooth hands possessed a strength and firmness that echoed his personality. Smooth and shallow on the outside, but with a core of inner strength that sometimes peeked through. It was those glimpses that held her interest.

She reclaimed her hand, clasping the railing as they descended to the ground floor. Every new touch made her more nervous about what was happening between them. Or at least what was happening to her. He probably did this type of thing all the time.

As they entered the dining room, they could hear the general chatter.

". . . and he wasn't accounted for during that time. I know he did it!"

Kate stopped in mid-step. Mr. Crescent was gesturing wildly. He had discovered the murderer?

"And he's standing right there!"

He pointed directly at Christian.

Chapter 13

If you can't get it right the first time, you are a failure.

The Marquess of Penderdale
to Christian, age twelve

Christian wasn't sure why he froze. Perhaps it was the appalled look on Kate's face or the wild, accusing one on Crescent's, but he felt as if he had once again been accused of being a bad child when he hadn't done anything wrong.

"I didn't do it," he blurted out, the old feelings briefly resurfacing before he squashed them flat. "What are you on about, Crescent?" he said with his normal drawl.

He deliberately avoided looking at Kate. He was sure she wore the same look of disappointment that his father and brothers sported before he had escaped to Eton. Christian ruthlessly squashed those thoughts as well. And here he had thought he had shown that he could actually be of use for something besides witty repartee and debauchery. He should have known better.

A small hand tugged him to the side. He looked down to see Kate glaring at Crescent in confusion and horror. Horror directed at Crescent and not at him.

Something warm spread through him.

Crescent made an impatient motion with his hand. "Not you, Black, the man behind you!"

Christian turned to see Benji staring wide-eyed at Crescent. The male servants must have returned from working on the roads now that it was getting dark.

"You!"

Benji shrank back, and Christian felt his ire over his youthful demons redirected toward Crescent.

"Mr. Crescent, could you please explain what it is you are accusing Benji of?"

"He nicked my trousers!"

Christian's relief was so profound that he couldn't stifle the laughter that rose in his chest. He felt Kate shudder next to him and thought she too was snickering, but doing a better job of hiding it.

"This isn't funny, Black!"

Christian continued to grin. "No, not funny at all, Crescent."

"I demand he return my trousers at once!"

Christian let loose another snicker and a few of the other patrons couldn't hold in theirs as well. He noticed that Tom, who had returned with Benji after helping to clear the roads, was also standing in the doorway. He wasn't laughing. He was in fact shooting Crescent an extremely menacing glare.

Kate said out of the side of her mouth, "I guess you were right about the occasional trouser theft."

And with that he let go of his memories and the pain. Oh, they would return sometime in the future, they always did, but for now a true grin appeared. Kate surreptitiously squeezed his side.

Mr. Wicket waved his short arms to get everyone's attention. "Here now, what's this?"

Crescent's arm was trembling in rage. "He stole my trousers, I demand them back. It's not amusing!"

"Why do you think he stole your trousers, Mr. Crescent?" Kate asked.

"My valet, Bittens, said so."

Christian followed Tom's narrowed eyes to a man cowering in the corner. Bittens looked terrified.

"How does Bittens know?"

"He's staying in a room with him and some other fellow."

Mr. Wicket had said Elias, Benji, and Mr. Crescent's valet were sharing one of the second-floor rooms.

"Why would he steal your trousers, though? Doesn't it seem a bit obvious?"

Christian thought Kate's comment made excellent sense.

"Who knows why servants do what they do. Thieves and liars, the lot."

Christian's eyes narrowed. He sounded just like Christian's father. "A bold statement, Crescent. Especially seeing as you are outnumbered by those thieves and liars at the present moment."

"They wouldn't dare touch me," he blustered, though his eyes darted uncomfortably around the room. "I want those trousers returned or I'll hold the inn accountable." He wagged a finger at Mr. Wicket and then huffed out of the room.

The innkeeper wrung his hands, muttering something about better times and easier guests.

Daisy sauntered into the tense atmosphere, not missing a beat. "Supper will be served in five minutes."

Olivia Trent glided toward Christian. "Shall we sit together?"

Christian considered the offer. It had been so much fun to tweak Kate's jealousy earlier using Olivia, but he had a feeling that too much of that and he would lose her entirely. And he wasn't willing to let that happen yet.

As he opened his mouth to reply, Tiegs came swooping over. "Olivia, darling, didn't you say you'd like to join me for supper and cards?"

Olivia gave Tiegs's dangerous appearance and appealing expression a long, hard look, then stared back at Christian. She seemed to take the hint from Christian's less than enthusiastic response and closed expression and accepted Tiegs's arm and offer.

Tiegs shot Kate an amused look, then shifted it to Christian, his crooked smile growing broader. Christian had a feeling that Kate hadn't fooled this man for a second. Kate seemed to realize it too as she tensed next to him.

Christian prodded her to a seat, ready to pester and harry her throughout the meal.

A silent agreement was made and the visitors at the Dragon's Tale chose to discuss matters other than Janson's death. After a pleasant dinner, Kate and Christian went to the inn office to report to Mr. Wicket. The innkeeper seemed distressed to hear that Freewater's journal was missing (Christian wasn't happy with Kate for telling the innkeeper about the journal at all), and seemed to think that his inn was becoming a den of thievery, what with the recent trouser theft, didn't they know?

Christian listened to Kate reassure the innkeeper for at least fifteen minutes before he put a hand on her arm and tugged her toward the door.

"Gordon still in the stables?" he asked the innkeeper.

Mr. Wicket gave a distracted nod. "Should be. For some reason he's remained out there."

Christian ignored the censorious look Kate gave him and thanked the innkeeper as he pulled a coat from the peg and tossed it to her.

"Where are we going?"

"We are just stopping in to say hello to our friend Gordon and to search for Janson's bat."

Her mouth formed an O and she hurried her pace as they walked through the now well-trod path.

Gordon grimaced upon seeing them. "Back again, are you?"

"Gordon, you are doing an excellent job. You wouldn't have happened upon Mr. Janson's cricket bat, by chance?"

Gordon's brows drew together. "Can't say that I

have. Strange, that. He never went anywhere without it. Could be buried beneath the straw."

Christian nodded and walked to the stall where Janson's body and belongings lay.

They didn't find anything in the stall that they hadn't seen before. Janson's baggage had been as little as Desmond's—mostly cricket equipment, and a change of clothing. No bat. Kate tensed, and Christian followed her gaze to where Tom was leaning against the stall door, chewing on a stick. The man had moved silently, but could challenge Tiegs's bruisers for sheer bulk.

"Tom, is it? Did you hear or see anything the night of the murder?" Christian asked.

"Only that Janson got what 'e deserved."

Kate shot Christian a look.

"Didn't much like Julius Janson?"

"Nope."

"Do you know anything about Janson's death?"

"Nope."

The man's tone wasn't idle, nor was it menacing; it was simply implacable.

"Would you tell us if you did?"

Tom turned and walked away.

"Well that was strange," Kate murmured.

"Old Tom is always like that."

Christian turned to see Gordon staring at the stiff body.

"Where does Tom stay?"

"Out here with me usually. Sometimes we switch on and off in the extra bed in Benji and Elias's room."

"So he was out here the night Janson died?"

"We were taking care of the horses and getting them ready for the next day. Holy days are especially busy coaching days."

"Do you share a room? Did you see Tom leave?"

Gordon shrugged. "Tom does what Tom wants. Been with the inn since anyone can remember."

"Did he leave any time during the night?"

He shrugged again. "Could be. Lots of noises in the night. You learn to ignore some and awaken for others."

"But it snowed most of the early morning the night of Janson's death. Wouldn't that have muffled much of the outside noise, making it easier for you to know if Tom was out of bed?"

Gordon flushed and Christian went for the kill. "He was out of bed. You know he was. What are you trying to hide?"

"Nothing! I ain't trying to hide nothing. So Tom might have been out of bed for some of that time. Doesn't mean nothing. I was out of bed for part of the night too, and I didn't kill Janson. Tom didn't neither."

"I never said Tom did. But he may have helped. Someone dragged Janson's body into the stables. Someone strong—strong enough to drag a grown man's body through a snowbank. Tom is built like an ox."

Gordon's eyes went wide. Christian decided to leave him to think over that little tidbit.

"Come, Mr. Kaden. I think we found what we needed."

Kate hurried into the courtyard after him. "Brilliant, Christian. You think there were multiple people involved? That makes a lot of sense. One to murder him and throw him over the railing, one to hide the body."

Christian nodded. "We are still looking at two strong men working together. One or both must have panicked. It would have been wiser to leave the body where it landed. Would have looked like a drunken accident."

"I suppose there is always Lake," Kate said reluctantly. He had noticed Kate developing a soft spot for the man as the glances between Lake and Mary had started to change from shy to heated.

"Buck up, Kate. He may just be an innocent in this after all."

Christian stopped abruptly and pulled Kate to the side of the inn and behind one of the sentinel pines as the aforementioned Mr. Lake walked out, followed closely by Mary.

"I won't tell them what I heard."

"You heard nothing, Lawrence."

Lake stopped and put his fingers on her cheeks. "Mary, you were crying. I heard the sniffling."

"You heard no such thing." Mary didn't try to break away from Lake's caress.

"I want to know what he did to you. I know it is too late to avenge any other sins, but I still want to know. I love you, Mary."

Christian watched twin tears run down Mary's cheeks, only to be brushed away by Lake's thumbs. "Oh, Lawrence. What are we to do?"

"Shhh. There now, I'll take care of things. Let's go talk to Tom."

He wrapped an arm around her and led her to the stable.

Christian gave Kate a sardonic look. "They almost take the fun out of searching for the villain."

Kate appeared sad. "You think they did it? Threw the body over?"

Christian stared pensively after the couple's path. "Perhaps, but something just seems off."

"They do have a motive," Kate said reluctantly. "Should we follow them?"

"Probably. But I want to check with Freewater on the status of the journal. Somehow I don't think Lake and Mary are going to be talking to Tom for very long—more likely they will be indulging in other pastimes. I also don't think we would be able to spy on them without Tom or Gordon seeing us. I don't know about you, but I am terrible at keeping hidden. Several pranks nearly cost me dearly at E—" He cleared his throat. "In my village. I can't believe they didn't see us when they exited the inn. Save me from fools in love."

Kate gave him a dirty look.

He winked. "Not you, Kate. Feel free to fall in love with me at any time."

"I think not," she said tartly.

"You wound me, Kate, you really do."

He knew he looked anything but wounded as she prodded him toward the door, but something tightened in his chest.

"I'm not sure how you think we are going to solve this murder when you aren't willing to engage in a little eavesdropping."

"Oh, but we don't need to indulge in eavesdropping, Kate. Don't you know who the guilty parties are yet? It's quite simple. But on to the journal, now there's a puzzle."

She pushed him inside.

They found Freewater in the common room upstairs along with Nickford, Desmond, Tiegs, Olivia, and Francine. The last four were playing cards at the round table, and Freewater was furiously scribbling in a book at the maple desk. Nickford was puttering around the fireplace, alternately poking about with the tools and taking measurements of the courtesy screen. Kate had no idea what he was doing, but hoped that he didn't decide to abscond with the screen too. She was quite unlikely to keep her disguise if someone happened upon her using the chamber pot.

Tiegs's two thugs were nowhere to be seen.

Desmond shot Christian a poisonous glare as Christian headed straight for Freewater's corner.

She made it over in time to hear Christian ask so quietly that the other occupants in the room would have to strain to hear, "Have you recovered your journal, Freewater?"

Freewater looked up from his book, thoroughly distressed. "No, blast it. I haven't so much as seen a book nearing its description. I need that book."

His voice sounded desperate in the extreme.

"We are still looking for it. Hopefully we will have better news for you soon." Christian shrugged nonchalantly.

"You get your head straight from your arse yet, Black?"

Kate groaned as Desmond's narrowed eyes pierced Christian.

"Your mother was quite accommodating the other day with both, thanks Desmond."

Desmond lunged from his seat, and only Tiegs succeeded in holding him from Christian's throat.

Christian shook his head. "Tsk, tsk, such a temper. You should really rein it in. Wouldn't want to give someone the impression that you are capable of murder, would you?"

"I'll get you, Black! Just you wait! After I deal with that pansy Lake, it will be your head on the platter."

Christian lazily stretched his fingers. "Have a tendre for Mr. Lake, do you? I'm not sure he's interested in you, Desmond."

Desmond's struggles renewed with force. "I'll kill you! You're a dead man, Black."

"Oh, Desmond, promises, promises."

Christian strolled from the room, and Kate hurried after him until they were inside their own room.

"You really shouldn't bait him, Christian. I know you like to pretend you are a Runner and above the law, but he could really hurt you."

"Is that concern, Kate? I'm touched."

His acerbic tone set her off. "You are a rude, insufferable man. Why do you taunt him? You are no better than Janson, if you do!"

Christian looked like a bored nobleman, filled with ennui. "Donald Desmond talks and talks. That is the type of man he is. Will he actually do anything? No. He's all bluster and bravado. And as for being above the law, Desmond can't touch me."

"That is a silly statement."

"Most of my statements are."

She frowned at him. "What is wrong with you? You seem different all of a sudden."

"We should have found Freewater's journal by now. That should be my main priority." The last sentence was muttered, but she heard him clearly.

"What? You are concerned about Freewater's journal when a man was murdered?"

He waved a hand. "The servants did it. Does it really matter how and so forth? The reason why is quite clear."

Her mouth dropped. "So that's it? You are just going to—to let it be? Just be half—half-assed about it?"

He shrugged, his eyes dull. It made her angrier than she cared to reason why.

"Well, you can't. You promised me, and those people downstairs, that you would do this. Don't your promises mean anything?"

A dark look ran across his features. "Yes, that is exactly the point," he snapped.

"Well, you aren't very well proving it."

He pointed a finger at her. "I don't need this from you. I've had enough guilt and finger pointing to last a lifetime. Your opinion means nothing," he said viciously.

Her mouth dropped in shock. And hurt. She couldn't help the hurt, and her eyes lowered so that she could gather herself before meeting his again.

His face twisted. "Damn it to hell." He picked up a brush from the side table and threw it across the room. It smacked the wall and clattered to the floor. His back was to her. Deep breaths shuddered along his frame.

Kate was frozen in place.

He breathed harshly and slammed his palm against the tabletop. "He will never leave me in peace."

She stayed silent until he finally turned around and looked at her. He made no move to approach her, and for that she was glad.

His eyes were sad. "I'm sorry, Kate."

The words were given freely, but even so she had a feeling they were not often said.

"That was very bad-tempered of me. Ghosts from the past." His mouth curved into a far from amused smile. "Bad form of me to take them out on you."

She nodded, not knowing what to say, but feeling the icy grip of the past few minutes loosen around her heart.

"Apology accepted."

"I do value your opinion," he said softly. "Very much. I won't give up on solving Janson's death, though I think you will not like what we find."

"Why do you say that?" She sat down in her chair as he paced the floor, but without the restless agitation of before.

"Webs within webs. You are looking for justice. I don't think we will find it in the guilty parties."

"You do not believe we should seek justice and prosecute Janson's murderer or murderers?"

"I think it is more complicated than that. I know that you are involved in this hunt because you are compensating for something, Kate. I don't know what troubles you, but I'm familiar enough with the motive to notice it in another." He gave a self-deprecating smirk.

"My father always used to say that life is complicated," she muttered.

"Funny. Mine used to say failure was complicated. He was always very adamant that my life would be complicated."

A dark look passed across his face again, and she had the feeling that he wasn't completely happy to have shared that memory with her. She was thus surprised to find him taking the seat across from her at their small table and reaching across the top for her hand. Instead of his usual brash manner of taking her hand with a smirk and no apology, he waited for her. She moved her hand into his, and relief showed on his face.

Any remaining ice melted. That Christian was a bit brash was undeniable. That he was also smart enough to realize the consequences and modify his behavior was a relief. Father would have called him a hotheaded intellectual. His persona was cool and carefree, but the intense boiling underneath the crafted exterior was hot and seething. Kate had a feeling that not many people saw the molten lava flowing within.

She squeezed his fingers lightly and was

rewarded in return with a gentle stroke under her palm.

"I like to think that those things no longer bother me. I usually don't let them."

She nodded, but there wasn't much she could say. He hadn't confided in her about the journal, and she had only bare crumbs about what formed his shield. It was amazing how little she knew of him. She had no reason to trust him, and had no idea why she actually *did* trust him. But there it was.

"Sometimes it takes several attempts before you get something right," she said softly.

He smiled. It was a small grin, but genuine. "I suppose that is the crux of the problem. Second chances have always been quite rare."

She let him interlock their fingers. "You aren't a failure because of a setback; the important thing is to keep moving forward and not allow the tide to pull you under."

He looked at her strangely. "I thought you were from the Midlands?"

She nodded. "Father was originally from the seaside and into shipping when he was younger. Hence a lot of seaworthy sayings"—she leaned in—"and language."

He laughed, and she smiled in return. It felt

good. She hadn't talked of her father in weeks. She could barely make it past the chimes, although in the last few days she had been having increasingly better success during the day. She was only losing perspective at the noon and midnight chimes and when her mind shut down for sleep. Maybe she too was making progress.

Christian started to say something in response before abruptly stopping. He was looking over her shoulder, an odd expression on his face.

"What?" She looked over her shoulder, but only the burgundy-draped window was in view.

"The drapes."

"Yes?" she asked in confusion.

He squeezed her hand. "Do you remember what color the drapes were in Olivia Trent's room?"

Kate grimaced. "Blue drapes. Dark blue."

"And Desmond's?"

She racked her brain. They hadn't spent much time in his room. "Blue. Dark blue as well." Her eyes sharpened on his. "The Crescents also have dark blue drapes, as does the common room. All rooms with access to the gallery have dark blue drapes, except Janson's."

He stood up, bringing her with him. "Exactly. Julius Janson has dark green drapes. Why do you suppose that is?"

"Someone replaced the drapes."

Their eyes met. "Sally."

Kate hadn't seen the timid maid since they had passed her earlier in the hall, but she tended to pop up where needed with an uncanny sense of timing. The maid would definitely cover for Mary, her best friend, and probably for any of the other servants or guests. If someone told her to clean the room and keep her mouth shut, likely she would.

"Someone else may have switched the drapes. Any of the servants could have done it. Elias was absent with the keys for plenty of time that morning to make the switch."

"And servants are quite crafty; likely they all have keys to the rooms."

Christian lifted a brow as he led her to the door. "I'll have to remember that. Let's take a look at Janson's drapes, just to make sure."

They crossed the hall and exchanged greetings with a joyful Nickford, who looked more animated than usual as he took measurements in the hall.

Christian lifted their lamp, as they entered Janson's room and headed straight for the drapes. Dark green.

"Do you suppose the original drapes had blood-stains?"

He nodded. "I do."

"They were changed to hide the evidence. That means that Janson was killed in his room, not on the gallery."

"Exactly."

"I didn't see any other bloodstains. How is it that they all conveniently ended up on the drapes?"

Christian looked thoughtfully at the pristine bed. "What if he was murdered in bed? The counterpane could have been changed as well and any sheets."

They checked the bed, but could find no evidence of blood.

"Or he could have been knocked into the wall and drapes, dying in the process. The drapes could have fallen with the body. Olivia heard a thump. He could have been dragged out with the drapes and then tossed over the gallery, his head hitting the railing briefly and leaving the stains."

She sent him an admiring glance. "Yes, that sounds rather plausible, actually."

He bowed to her and picked up her hand for a formal kiss. "Thank you, my dear."

Warm air caressed her hand as he turned it palm up and placed a kiss in the very center. Shivers radiated from the spot, and Christian's eyes met hers in the soft glow of the lamplight.

Tinkling laughter interrupted the moment, and

Christian cocked his head. He blew out the lamp and peered through the drapes for a second and then pulled them back together, allowing just a sliver to remain open, a wicked grin on his moon-lit face.

"What are you doing?" she hissed.

"Shhh." He picked up her hand, the same one he had kissed, and tugged her to the edge of the drapes, in the right corner. The sliver of moonlight through the middle of the drape gave her just enough light to see the vague outline of where she was in the room. Christian pulled her in front of him, her back snug against his front, and opened the drape just enough so that she could see out without being seen in return.

Olivia and Tiegs were crushed together against the railing, her arms curled around him, his body curled around hers.

Kate jolted, and her body hit Christian's, causing her to jolt again.

"Kate," he whispered a little more harshly. "Stay still."

"What are you doing?"

"Watching our suspects, of course. Look over there in the stables, just out of view of Olivia and Tiegs."

Kate squinted and could see the unmistakable

forms of Mary and Lake standing close together, their heads bent toward each other as they too began to kiss.

"What are you doing? We are not going to watch them!" She turned her head slightly around to hiss at him.

"Oh, but Kate," he whispered into her ear. "You can learn so much just by watching your suspects."

He tilted her chin back toward the drapes, and his fingers brushed down her neck.

"We have the experienced lovers in blind lust, caring only for the mutual pleasure each can give the other. Look at the way they devour each other to achieve their own pleasure. And then we have the innocent romantics in love with their shy touches, smiles, and tentative kisses. They seek to affirm their affections and pleasure the other."

Kate shivered.

"Watch Lake as he runs his fingers reverently down Mary's face, as if her very skin holds the *essence* of silk and satin."

Christian's fingertips ghosted down the skin of her right cheek, and she forgot how to breathe.

"Light touches and small kisses."

His lips brushed right beneath her good ear,

and she couldn't help but tilt her head a bit to the left to allow him better access.

"Then look at Tiegs and Olivia."

Her eyes followed as if mesmerized.

"Bold strokes and needy hands, one of her legs wrapped around his waist pulling him closer. Closer to where the heat and lust pool."

He dragged his palm across her stomach and downward, his touch turning feather-light when it reached the area where the heat of his words had pulled her body's heat into a pool, just as he described. She unconsciously strained into his hand, wanting the touch to be exactly as he described instead of the teasing caress. She felt his lips touch her neck.

She started to turn around, but he nudged her back and lifted her arms so that her hands were pressed against the drapes, hitting the cool glass behind. She was sure Tiegs and Olivia had to have heard the sound and seen the pressed drapes, but they continued consuming each other against the railing.

"Keep watching, Kate." Her name rolled off his tongue, the T curling as if he were savoring a dessert. She had always thought her name somewhat harsh, but Christian made it sound delicious.

"Look at Mary, Kate." She looked to see Mary

lean into Lake. "Lake thinks she is more priceless than the finest china, more beautiful than the loveliest of roses."

Kate stiffened. Christian was running a finger up her jaw and toward her other ear. Her scarred ear, which was not like the finest china or more beautiful than the loveliest of roses.

"I'm not beautiful," she whispered.

"Why would you think that?" His lips pressed against her throat. "To me Mary is just a pretty lass. To Lake she is beauty personified. If I say you are beautiful, then who are you to tell me no?"

His fingers played with the cotton weave around her shirt, leaving trails of fire as they moved.

"Don't you trust me, Kate?"

His tone was light.

Did she trust him? Trust him not to hurt her when he did see that she wasn't beautiful after all? She badly wanted to continue their touches, to feel his heated glances. He made her *feel*. And she desperately wanted to continue despite her previous judgment that she should entrust no one with her heart.

Could she trust her own judgment?

"I want to trust you more than anything. I want to know who you really are." Her words were rough and needy.

He stilled his movements and she gave a quick look behind in distress, cursing her sudden honesty. There was an unreadable expression on his face. And then he slowly turned her so that she was facing him, put his hands lightly on the sides of her face and drew her forward.

His lips hovered a hairsbreadth over hers and he whispered against her lips, the smooth feel of strong silk against satin, "Be careful, Kate, or I'll never let you go."

And then he kissed her.

Chapter 14

Someday a deserving man will sweep you off your feet.
I only hope I am around to see it.

George Simon
to Kate, age seventeen

Panic, acceptance, eagerness, and desire pulsed through her as his lips touched hers. When she was fifteen and the squire's smooth son had helped her into a carriage, his eyes warmer than the summer sun, she hadn't known what the feeling in the pit of her stomach meant. When Connor had begun to pursue her, she hadn't known that the flurries in her stomach were desire.

But she knew it now. And those previous

feelings were nothing compared to what Christian stirred.

He reached for her hand and interlaced their fingers. Her heart increased its beat as her mind frantically fought to determine what to do. Her rational side lost as he pressed soft, strong lips to hers.

She had been kissed before. A few stolen kisses, terribly exciting due to the forbidden circumstances, but not very satisfying otherwise. Some had been exceedingly wet, others chapped and dry; some had made her stomach clench, others had left her completely unaffected. This one was like none of those, as Christian's lips skimmed hers lightly, allowing her to press forward or retreat.

She decided to press forward, only to be met with air as he pulled back. He tucked a strand of hair into her cap.

"Let's go back to our room."

They hastily made their way into the hall and into the safe haven of their room.

Christian softly closed the door and then walked toward her, his eyes dark and intense. She saw his intention as he leaned in, and instead of escaping, which he had given her plenty of time to do, she leaned forward as well. It was a sweet kiss, more along the lines of Lake's kiss to Mary, but with the promise of so much more. She let the promise overtake her.

He pressed a few light kisses to the corner of her mouth, the middle, the other corner, his hands moving into her hair and tugging on the wrap.

"The light," she breathed, wincing at her own cowardice.

Christian searched her gaze for a moment and then doused the light.

His fingers returned to her hair, removing the offending hair wrap, caressing the uncovered strands and tugging gently at the back of her head.

He was giving her a chance to stop. She threw caution and sense away and kissed him back, following the same pattern across his lips as he had done to her.

It felt heavenly, and Kate sank into him as their bodies drew closer and he pulled her onto his lap, straddling him. She had the fleeting thought that without trousers the entire maneuver would have been much more difficult.

Christian moved in the dark as if it were his natural habitat, and he pressed her to him.

The first chime of midnight sounded. She stiffened, but he kissed her more fiercely. She clung to him desperately as the second chime struck, and his fingers massaged the back of her neck as he continued to kiss her more deeply. The warmth of his body, lips, and hands contrasted with the chill of her memories—ghastly memories of the endless moments when she realized in a horrified haze that her father was dead and there was nothing she could do, and the clock continued its relentless knell, its toll that life cruelly continued on as her father lay lifeless.

Christian kissed her forehead and her eyes in the darkness before she even realized she was crying, and he held her to him, repeating comforting phrases, resting her head against his shoulder.

When she had regained a modicum of calm, he lifted her chin in the dark.

"Tell me, Kate. Why do you fear the chimes?"

Kate felt it all rush from her, the memories, the fear.

"The chandelier fell. An accident, they said. Crushed my father and hit me as well." She touched her ear. "The hall chandelier. It was old, but Father loved it. We were bickering in the entrance hall, I didn't want to go to the village. If only I hadn't said anything. Hadn't paused to argue with him. If only we had just gone to the village."

"If you hadn't paused, both of you might have died."

"Or my father would still be alive." She felt tears curl down her cheeks.

"You don't know that." He seemed to sense her tears and he brushed the wetness away with two swipes of his finger. "Why the chimes?"

"The chandelier fell and we both went down. I panicked; my head was on fire and there was so much blood. It took a moment before I realized that my father wasn't saying anything either amusing or reassuring."

She shuddered. "I saw him and panicked again. He was trapped. The chandelier was too big for our entrance hall, really, just a small cottage-style home. But Father loved that chandelier, said it reminded him of Mother.

"He was crushed," she whispered. "Beneath the middle of it, the branches splayed on top of him like a crown. I managed to push it to the side, I don't know how, I couldn't lift it afterward. But Father didn't move. No breath moved his chest, no beat pumped beneath his skin. And then the clock began to chime, the rhythm mocking the lack of any beat within his body, the chimes endless and unstoppable." She shivered, and he pulled her nearer.

"Is that what you are running from?"

She shook her head against his chest, relieved

to finally be speaking to someone. She couldn't stop herself from letting it all out, especially as a confession shared in the dark.

"My father left me a small dowry. Enough to be comfortable. My half-brother wants it, since the rest of my father's monies are legally tied at the moment, and he struck a deal with one of his cronies to take me off his hands and split it. I have one week before I am of age. I just need to stay out of his grasp for a week and then I'm free. My aunt wrote that she would take me in. She's a stickler for propriety, and I can stay with her for a little bit before deciding what to do. She would not turn me over to my brother if I have funds and a possibility for making a suitable match among her circle."

She touched the buttons on his shirt, hoping he didn't think her a snob for some nebulous reason. "Not a brilliant match, of course; we are only on the fringe of society. And I know that until my—"

She cleared her throat. It had gotten stuck at the point where she almost confessed about her ear.

"—until things are more settled I will be at a very major disadvantage. But I have to deal with things the best I can."

She couldn't help the wistful note that entered her voice. "I don't particularly care for high society and their airs. I just want a nice family in a small house, maybe by the sea."

Her father had always talked favorably of living at the shore. And in so doing there would be a connection to him. He had always fussed that she should be looking at potential mates, but she had been happy to stay in their little house outside the village year after year. She knew he had been secretly pleased, for all his talk about having grandchildren.

Christian's head bent down and rested against hers. "Maybe I can help."

She smiled. It felt nice. Sometimes things were so much easier in the dark. "Perhaps we can travel to London together. You are headed that way later, correct?"

"Yes, but I meant maybe I could help with your situation with your brother."

She jokingly tapped a finger on his chest. "You're going to make sure I get to the solicitor's without being abducted?"

"Well, you could always marry me instead of your brother's awful friend."

She laughed as she felt him jerk against her. She could only imagine the horrified look crossing his face as he suddenly realized what he'd said.

"A bachelor like you? I'm sure you *Runners* get

all the girls you can handle." She shook her head, her cheek brushing against the soft fabric of his jacket. "I know I am a diversion. I accept that." It was a painful admission.

He brushed his cheek against her hair. "A diversion?"

"Yes. I'm not bothered. Well, not too bothered. I want this." She chewed her lip and touched her ear. "Are you sure you want this?"

He lifted her chin and ran a finger down her cheek.

And with that he gently lifted her and placed her on the soft counterpane as he began to undo her shirt.

Chapter 15

❦

*. . . and if I'm not there to see you swept from your feet,
know that I trust your judgment in all things.*

George Simon
to Kate, age seventeen

Kate's breath caught as he slowly opened her
shirt as if he were unwrapping a package he
had been waiting to receive. Smooth fingers pulled
the shirt open and ghosted over the skin revealed.

"Modified stays. Ingenious, that," he said as he
lightly turned her over so that he could remove
her shirt and stays.

She had made the stays herself based on an old
Elizabethan design to completely flatten the front
of her figure.

"Well, I *am* posing as a tailor," she quipped, though her voice was husky as Christian's fingers worked.

Christian finished undoing the latches and pushed both edges to the side, where they flopped on the bed. He picked up the edge of the modified undershirt and pulled it slowly up her body. She rose a bit so that he could pull it off fully and the shirt got stuck under her freed breasts, pulling them upward, the cotton creating a friction on her nipples as he tugged.

He placed a kiss on the back of her neck and she arched up, the shirt finally coming free.

"Beautiful," he murmured, quickly discarding the shirt, and running fingers through her short, silky hair.

His fingers continued down her neck to her shoulder bones, pushing her down into the mattress, her bare breasts rubbing against the underside of the stays that still lay beneath.

"You have a long, strong neck. Silky-smooth skin covering inner strength." He placed a kiss at her nape. "A determination of character, perhaps?"

His fingers ghosted over her shoulders. "Strong yet delicate shoulders and arms. Far too delicate to belong to a boy. Far too strong to belong to a submissive lady."

He straddled her suddenly and pressed lightly against her lower body, where a good concentration of the heat in her body had pooled. He rocked into her as he continued massaging her back and arms, and she couldn't help but press further into the bed beneath, seeking something.

"Mmmm, we must do something about these trousers, Kate. They are all wrong on you."

She made to flip over but he held her in place. "No, no, that would be too easy, and not at all the real game we are playing."

She stiffened and he placed a gentle kiss at her nape once more. "A real game, Kate, not a diversion."

She relaxed as he bestowed light kisses and gentle touches. His finger strokes became stronger and bolder as he brushed them down the sides of her body, lightly brushing her breasts and pulling his fingers beneath her and down her stomach. His fingers made short work of her trouser catches, and she found the trousers slipping off her body quickly.

He nipped her hip, startling her. He laughed low in response. "I could feast on you all night, Kate."

The air hit her exposed flesh, and she didn't know what to do. She was suddenly self-conscious and buried her head in her pillow. He gave a low laugh and ran fingers up her calves, over the sensitive backs of her knees and to her thighs. He spent a few moments kneading the flesh of her thighs.

"I'll let you hide for the moment, Kate. But not for long."

His fingers moved up her thighs and touched her between them. She jumped and ended up half on her front, half on her side. He chuckled and took advantage of her new position, which was more open to him. Dragging both hands up so one was in the front of her body, one in the back, they converged on the spot where the heat collected.

Her eyes shot open as he began to massage her there, a different type of massage. Playful and demanding in turn. Her body began to move against him, responding to the tune his hands created.

He flipped her completely onto her back, and she arched upward as he captured a breast in his mouth, the fingers of one hand quickly rediscovering their warm target, his other hand holding her close. A stream of sounds continued issuing from her mouth as he pulled on her breast with his mouth, and his fingers and thumb found spots inside and outside her she never knew existed.

He released her breast. "You taste as delicious as I thought you would. Like raspberries." He licked her other breast playfully and then moved his body up so that he was nuzzling her neck, her chin, her good ear. He sucked on her earlobe, his fingers still working their magic, his body pressed against her providing breathtaking friction to the rest of her body as he rocked against her.

He shifted, and a small puff of warm air entered her scarred ear. Kate jerked upward as her body exploded. Christian captured her lips, swallowing the moan and panting cries she couldn't keep inside.

She couldn't stop shaking, and he pulled her against him and tried to tuck her under the covers at the same time. She didn't know how to tell him that she wasn't cold. She was far from it. The shivers that racked her body had nothing to do with the cold.

She looked up to find him watching her in the faint moonlight provided by the open drapes. A lazy fondness mixed with something else in his gaze. "You should see yourself in release, Kate. It's gorgeous. I won't let you leave the lights off next time. Perhaps I should fashion a looking glass to the ceiling so that you can see for yourself?"

Kate didn't know how to respond. So she threaded her hands through his hair, drew him toward her, and kissed him instead. His lips tasted as she imagined moonlight would taste. Smooth and mysterious, with a bit of the chilling shivers of a cloudless night.

He responded until they pressed against each other, trying to get closer and omit space that was already not present. Christian was the one to pull away, although he did it with reluctance.

"Let's let you recover. I'll be back in a second, sweet Kate."

She watched him dress, putting on just enough so that he was decent. He winked, and she knew she must look quite wanton, even in the mostly dark room. She was spread naked across the sheets, but she couldn't dredge up an urge to move.

"I'll only be a second. Don't move an inch."

It was a request she was happy to follow. Although that didn't stop her from arranging things so that he wouldn't be able to see her scars should he come back with a lit lamp.

Christian strode from the room, shutting the door softly behind him. Kate's darkened features in the throes of passion flashed through his brain, and he decided that he wasn't going to need to spend much time behind the common room screen relieving his own pressure.

He could have sated his lust back in the room

with Kate. He knew he could have. And with any other woman, he would have. What was different about this one?

With Kate he wanted to do things right. So, well, perhaps "right" in the strictest sense would mean marriage before consummation, but . . . wait a moment . . . had he just thought of marriage?

Yes, the thought certainly had appeal. And imagine the look on his father's face if he brought home a ragamuffin dressed in boy's clothes. Not that Kate was a ragamuffin out of those clothes; no, not in the least. In fact, just thinking about her smooth skin, her milky flesh . . . Christian picked up his pace as he entered the common room and headed for the privacy screen. He wanted to feel that silk again. He moved his hands to the buttons of his trousers. To slip into—

Christian tripped over something, and an ear-piercing wail shrieked through the room. He stumbled into the wall and caught himself at the last moment, jarring a piece of the wallboard with the side of his hand.

"What the devil?" He pushed himself back off the wall and turned to see Nickford rush in with his lamp, his nightcap askew, his feet bare. Mrs. Wicket, surprisingly enough, was right on his heels in full dress, followed by Olivia Trent in an entirely too revealing nightrail, and her companion, Francine, buttoned up to the neck.

"Where is it, Mr. Black?" Nickford was bouncing from foot to foot, whether from excitement or the cold floor, Christian couldn't tell.

"Where is what, Nickford?" he snapped, good mood gone but body still aching.

Christian bent down to examine the cord—*cord!*—that was tied from the screen to the door, waiting to viciously topple any guest who entered. There were strange little things hanging from the cord, and Christian had to bend farther to see them.

Most of the rest of the inn's occupants tumbled in, piling on top of the ones in the door.

"What is it?"

"Has there been another murder?"

"What was that racket?"

"Can't a person get a decent night's sleep around here?"

Nickford continued to bounce from foot to foot and look around excitedly. "I caught the ghost!"

Christian considered the multiple ways he could commit murder as he gazed evenly at Nickford's excited countenance. "Pardon me, Nickford, but I believe I heard you just say something about catching a ghost?"

"Oh, dear me, yes. I rigged everything up just so. Should have caught it this time."

Christian plucked the cord and it twanged violently as the attached bells hideously jangled. "You tied a cord with bells to a privacy screen. A privacy screen, may I add, that any guest in his or her right mind might want to use? And then you left it here in the dead of night for anyone to trip over?"

"Oh yes, the ghost makes the rounds this way. Couldn't tell anyone and tip the ghost off to what I was doing, now could I?"

Everyone was staring at Nickford with expressions ranging from curiosity (Olivia) to horror (Benji) to humor (Tiegs) to disapproval (Crescent). Christian saw Kate standing in the back, dressed again and fiddling with her head wrap.

He sighed. And he had had such pleasant intentions with an empty common room, privacy screen, and thoughts of Kate's delectable body. Now he had none of the above; well, thoughts of Kate's delectable body still loomed, but—he looked down at his trousers—the immediacy was gone.

Mrs. Wicket stamped her foot on the floorboards. "What have you done, Mr. Nickford? What is this about a ghost?"

"There's a ghost that haunts this inn, Mrs. Wicket," Nickford said in an earnest voice. "I've been taking samples and running tests. There's a ghost sure as I'm standing here."

"Of course there's a ghost, Nickford." Christian rubbed a weary hand across his face. No journal, no Kate, no peace. "Mrs. Wicket's the ghost. You said so yourself the other night."

Nickford rocked back on his heels. "Ah, but that has yet to be proved. I was attempting to do just that, only I caught you instead!"

Christian didn't deign to reply. It was useless to state the obvious and tell Nickford he was off his rocker. He did notice Olivia Trent giving Nickford a thorough once-over. Dear God. Could this week get any stranger?

"Good job, Mr. Nickford. Everyone can now go back to bed."

No one moved.

Christian gave Mrs. Wicket a deadpan glance.

"Everyone out! To bed, to bed." The innkeeper's wife started shooing everyone back into the hall.

Everyone shuffled out, people casting glances between Nickford, Christian, and Mrs. Wicket. There were also some leers given to Olivia Trent's scant outfit, which merited a second glance by any standard.

"Oh, Mrs. Wicket?" Christian asked.

"Yes?"

"Could you send Sally in?"

"Of course." He didn't look to her for the reply, still content to give Nickford the evil eye.

Sally appeared a moment later and Mrs. Wicket left to complete her rounds, or at least that was what Christian assumed she was doing. Mr. Wicket scurried off after her.

Kate remained, as did Nickford. Christian sent him a pointed glance.

"Ah! I need to get my experiment journal to make some notes." He skipped off.

Sally gave them a small smile.

"Sally, could we talk to you for a few minutes?"

"Of course, Mr. Black."

She seemed overly skittish around Christian, preferring to stick close to the open common room door. Christian gave Kate a pointed look, so she began the questioning.

"Did you clean Julius Janson's room and change his drapes?"

She nodded. "Yes, Mr. Kaden."

"Why?"

Sally shuffled her feet. "They were dirty and I was told to."

"Who told you to?"

"Mrs. Wicket."

"She told you to clean and change the drapes?"

"Yes, sir."

Christian looked thoughtful, so Kate plowed on. "What did you do with the old drapes, Sally?"

"I gave them to Tom, sir."

"Why?"

"Tom disposes of things we can't fix."

"You tried to clean the drapes?"

"Yes, sir."

"Why?"

"I was told to, sir." She started to look scared. "I didn't mean to do anything wrong, sir. I was just doing as I was told."

"I know, Sally," Kate tried to soothe. "We just have to ask you a few more questions since we noticed them missing."

Sally was the weak link in the servants' chain. Kate knew it, Christian most definitely knew it, and Sally seemed quite aware of it as well.

Christian leaned forward and Sally leaned back almost unnoticeably, looking ready to bolt. "When did Mrs. Wicket tell you to clean the room?"

"That morning," she whispered.

"And the drapes?"

"I couldn't get the stains out, so she sent Tom to pick them up."

Christian's eyes grew sharper. "Did Mrs. Wicket tell that to you, or did Tom?"

256

"Well, Tom did. But that's not unusual, sir."

"Hmmm . . ."

Sally started to look even more uncomfortable, and Kate sought to reassure her. "You aren't in trouble, Sally. Did you hear anything the night Julius Janson was murdered?"

"He was upset about something. Demanded an extra towel around two in the morning."

"You saw him at two in the morning?"

"Yes, sir. He was on the gallery smoking. I brought him the towel and he snarled at me. I went back inside."

"Did you see anything else?"

"No."

"Did you know Mr. Janson?"

"Yes. He stayed here a few times. He was always after Mary." She bowed her head. "He wasn't a very nice person, Mr. Kaden."

"Do you know anyone who'd want to kill him?"

Sally paused, but then shook her head, not looking up. "I hope it doesn't make me a bad person, sir, but I'm glad he won't get to Mary." The words were faint, but Kate heard them clearly. It seemed as if all the servants were in agreement on that point.

"Why did the Wickets like him so much?" Christian asked.

Sally looked at Kate when answering. "Mrs.

Wicket feels the same as everyone else, but pretends to go along with Mr. Wicket. She was trying to work him around without jeopardizing his cricket."

"Did you hear anything else that night?"

Sally paused and then shook her head.

"Thank you, Sally. You've been very helpful. I hope you have a pleasant evening."

"You too, Mr. Kaden, Mr. Black."

As soon as Sally had left, Christian turned lazily toward Kate.

"You scared her," she said accusingly.

"I don't see why. She didn't seem to have a problem with you."

"That's because you are scary."

He shrugged. "If you say so. She's protecting someone, hiding something."

"Yes, probably Mary."

"Or Mrs. Wicket."

"The mysterious Mrs. Wicket who chastises Lake for besmirching Janson, walks the halls at night in ghostly form, and faints when she finds out Janson is dead, only to immediately order the maid to clean his room. Something just doesn't figure."

"We should have asked her to stay."

Christian nodded. "Tomorrow." He shifted and dusted his hands off on his trousers. Kate lifted her lamp as Nickford skipped back into the room.

"Are you hurt?" she asked Christian.

He shook his head as he straightened. "No, just an unpleasant shock is all." He gave Nickford a pointed stare as the man continued humming to himself and looking around the room.

Christian gave the room a derisive, cursory glance, but his attention locked on to the wall where he noticed the wood boards skewed together.

"Ka— Mr. Kaden, will you hand me your lamp?"

She did so, and he held it up to the wall.

"Nickford, hand me that fire poker, so I can pry this free."

Nickford quickly obeyed. Christian inserted the poker and pried off the wall board. Instead of another layer of wall, the darkness stretched into a deep cubby. He held the lamp close and smiled as Janson's bloody bat was finally found.

Chapter 16

Comfort? There is nothing you can give me. There never has been.

The Marquess of Penderdale
to Christian, age nineteen,
upon the death of Christian's brothers

"**W**hat did you find?"

"Janson's bat." He knew his grin was smug.

Kate eagerly leaned forward. The color was still high in her face, and he felt himself growing hard again. One look at Nickford forestalled that. As much as Christian didn't care about exhibitionism, he didn't think Kate would much appreciate being taken over a common room chair.

"Oh, this is interesting—let me get my other journal. I'll need a fresh one for this new development, after all. I need to run some tests on that."

Before Christian could reply, the man had scrambled off, his cap bobbing, perilously close to falling off.

Kate put a hand on his arm, and warmth spread through him. "Are you sure it's Janson's bat?"

Christian held it up. The wood was scarred and darkened in places. A bat accustomed to being used hard and often. And there were some stains that looked new. There was no doubt in his mind that this was Janson's bat and that it had been used to murder him.

"I'm sure. Otherwise, why would someone stash it in a hidden compartment?"

He noticed something else. "Look here, at the base. It's crusted with blood."

Kate leaned in and he felt her breasts through her shirt. She obviously hadn't had the time to put her modified stays back on, and they bounced loosely on his arm. Perhaps they could compromise about the common room sofa?

"Christian?"

He shook himself to see Kate peering at him, a questioning look on her face. His face split into a wide grin. He really needed to watch himself. If he wasn't lucky she would break him completely.

"Yes, Kate?" he whispered and felt her shiver, her breasts moving ever so slightly. He pushed into her, putting the barest pressure against her nipple and watched as her eyes widened in awareness.

Nickford chose that moment to scramble back in.

"I have my new book! Let me see the bat."

"No."

Nickford blinked. "No?"

"We are investigating a murder, Mr. Nickford. A man is dead."

"Yes, I know. There's a ghost."

Christian stared at the other man. "Janson is your ghost?"

"Well, has to be now, doesn't he? Unless some-one else was murdered." He leaned forward, wetting his lips. "Have you heard reports of any others?"

"No."

"Pity." Nickford sighed and peered at the bat before picking up the journal on the top of his stack, leaving the second one uncovered.

Christian froze.

No. It couldn't be. They had checked Nickford's room thoroughly.

"Nickford." Christian swallowed, his throat

suddenly dry and scratchy. "Where did you get that journal?"

"Oh, this?" Nickford picked up the second journal, the gold embossment gleaming like a lighthouse in a storm. "Found it the morning Janson died when I was in the dining room. I needed a new journal to record my ghostly observations. The inn has probably been readying itself for a ghost for days, perhaps weeks. Buildings know these kinds of things, or so I've been told."

"You didn't think that the journal might belong to someone else?" Frankly Christian didn't care why Nickford had picked it up; he was just exultant that he had. The hard knot in his stomach turned into a river of fire.

"I needed it. Very important work to be done."

Christian nodded and reached for the journal. Nickford pulled it toward himself, a suspicious look in his eye.

"I know the owner of this journal, and he has been searching for it. Allow me to return it to the rightful owner and perhaps you will find yourself with a benefactor for your work."

Nickford perked up. Christian noted Kate's suspicion, but he ignored her for the moment. He needed Anthony's journal, with its lustrously embossed cover, safely in his possession, and then he could deal with soothing his partner's ruffled feathers.

"Really?" Nickford looked cautiously hopeful. Christian had no idea where the caution sprang from. Nickford hadn't seemed to possess an ounce of the quality previously.

"I have some high contacts. I think you will be pleased. But I need the journal."

It took Nickford only a moment to decide. "I suppose it is just as well. I only have some side notes in there, nothing too important. Most of the pages were used. You wouldn't happen to have a spare book, would you?" His gaze turned hopeful and Christian smiled widely.

"It just so happens that I do, Nickford. I just happen to have the perfect book for you."

Christian swept the lamp back into the opening of the wall hole and saw nothing else inside. He replaced the board and led the way to his room.

He gave Nickford a clean writing journal. Nickford nearly skipped to the door in his ecstasy.

"I will give you a full report on my progress, Mr. Black. Good night!"

As soon as the door shut, Kate turned to Christian. "What was that all about? Should we return Freewater's journal now or wait until morning?"

Christian unconsciously tightened his grip on

the journal. "We aren't giving the journal back to Freewater."

Her gaze sharpened. "Why not?"

"Because it isn't his."

"It most certainly is. I saw the gold embossment. The journal looks exactly as he described it."

"Yes, but it isn't Freewater's journal. He stole it."

Christian stroked a hand over the cover, his relief warring with triumph. He hadn't failed his friend after all. The niggling doubts about his worth quieted amid his exultation.

"How do you know?" Kate's voice had turned deadly. "What are you hiding? Why are you really at this inn, Christian Black?"

He looked up, surprised at the vehemence and the beginnings of betrayal shining in her eyes.

"I came for the journal, Kate. This book contains very sensitive information that can be very damaging to my friend if it falls into the wrong hands."

"Who are you? Are you a Runner after all? A spy?"

He shook his head. "No, just a man retrieving something for a friend. I wasn't lying the morning that we discovered Janson's body when I said I was on a personal retrieval mission for something sensitive. I just never said what the retrieval mission was."

She looked down. "I don't know why I'm angry. You never pretended otherwise."

A little of his excitement faded and he hugged the small book. "I know. I'm sorry, Kate."

She shook her head and then smiled. "I was worried for a second that you really were someone else in disguise."

Someone must be stoking a fire in the kitchens below because he could feel sweat beginning to break out on his brow. "Er, that would be something, wouldn't it?"

Tell her! Tell her!

She smiled broadly.

The voice withered and died. Would she still smile like that if she knew he was slightly higher on the social scale? Most women would be ecstatic. He should know. He had used his status in seductions before. But Kate didn't seem to hold much stock in titles.

And he wanted her to like him for himself. Not for some stupid title that neither he nor his father wanted him to claim.

"So what are you going to tell Freewater about the journal?"

He shrugged uncomfortably and willed his body to cool. It was best to leave such revelations till later. "Freewater stole this book; he doesn't deserve an explanation. His intent was to publish its contents in the press and embarrass people I care about. It will serve him right to forever mourn its loss not knowing what happened."

She raised a brow. "A bit bloodthirsty, aren't we?"

"He should never have taken it." Christian knew he sounded harsh, but he couldn't help it. Anthony was the closest thing he had to family. He would do anything for him. "Freewater was intent on ruining a good man."

"Mustn't there be something bad in there in order to be ruined? How do you ruin a good man?"

Christian turned away from Kate. How indeed. And how do you redeem a ruined man?

He could leave in the morning. Now that he had the journal, he was free. He didn't have to answer any uncomfortable questions. He didn't have to make the extra effort for Kate. There were plenty more women in the country. He could probably find ten willing, buxom maids in the next village over.

"Christian, you are still going to help find Janson's killer, aren't you?" The skeptical note in Kate's tone made him pause. He looked at the mussed bed and the bat they had recovered.

"Of course I am," he replied, unsure of his intent

until the words popped out of his mouth. He turned to face her, and something shifted inside. Yes, he had found Anthony's journal by a freakish piece of good luck, but he had also found Kate, who had broken through his constant state of ennui.

There weren't a hundred women in the next village that could compare to Kate.

He smiled. "I won't leave you, Kate."

And when she flashed him a grateful smile, he realized he meant it.

"Good." He could almost imagine her relief was due to wanting to keep him around rather than wanting him to help her solve the mystery. Just this once he was going to forgive himself for the thought.

"I can't believe you found the bat inside a cubby in the common room wall," Kate said.

"I know." He paused, considering the bat. "How many people would know about the spot? Not many, I'm sure."

"The servants probably."

They exchanged a look. Neither of them wanted it to be Mary.

"And anyone exceedingly lucky or clever. Although not so lucky because we discovered it," he said.

"No."

Christian paced back and forth in front of the bed, still clutching Anthony's journal and trying to think of other scenarios.

"Donald Desmond was jealous of Lake and Janson, although he hid his jealousy by flattering Janson and being his spineless second. What if Desmond got tired of always being second best, and knocked Janson off at a time when the blame could easily be placed on Lake? Desmond has verbally attacked nearly everyone in the inn, and has made it his duty to pin the blame on Lake. He would be killing two birds at once by getting rid of Janson and then having Lake tried for the murder."

Kate seemed to understand where his thinking was going because she sat down and pulled out their paper, nodded, dipped her quill, and jotted notes as he talked.

"Then there's Tiegs. And Tiegs's two underlings, either of whom would comply with Tiegs's orders. There was a connection between Tiegs and Janson. Perhaps he too planned to frame Lake after the fight in the taproom."

Christian tapped a foot and smiled blandly. "Olivia Trent and Francine seem innocent enough, but who knows, maybe one of them is a long-lost cousin or aunt who will profit from the death of the town squire's son. Or perhaps it is a two-part plot and at this instant the squire is lying dead somewhere, his carcass frozen and stiff, his—"

Kate stopped writing, a look of complete exasperation gracing her features. He grinned, and it felt good, as it always did with her. "No? Moving onward. Nickford. Just doesn't strike me as the violent type. Unless it would further his experiments. And in that case he would just leave the body where it dropped, or else drag it into his room, not to the stable. Unless he is a long-lost uncle looking to profit from the same—"

He smiled again at her expression. "No again? Does that mean I can't apply that theory to the Crescents either?"

"Christian."

"You are ruining my enjoyment."

She rolled her eyes.

"Moving forward. Freewater was in his room all night."

Kate raised a brow.

"Believe me. I listened and waited for the blasted man to leave all night. Why do you think I took the bed?"

"Because you aren't a gentleman. I clearly remember you telling me."

"Well, there is that." He gave her a slow once-over and proclaimed victory when color infused her cheeks. "But also because the bed is against that wall. I planned to retrieve the journal as soon as the blasted man left, but he never did. Quite annoying really."

Christian was in high spirits now that he had Anthony's journal in hand. He saw Kate frowning though and thought maybe he should avoid the topic of the journal until he could bring her around.

"Freewater was passing through, in any case. We have no evidence that he knew Janson prior to arriving here at the inn. I suppose he could be a spy for the French. He slipped from his room in the dead of the night, rifled through Janson's room, found his bat, crept up behind him, and . . . *wham*. What do you suppose?"

"Freewater is as dull as dull can be. I highly doubt his ability for any type of stealth."

"Wouldn't that be a perfect cover for a spy?"

"Christian, how many spies do you know?"

"Too true. So that leaves us with Lake, who we both thought was next door the entire time. You were closer, since I had my ear pressed to the other wall. I wasn't paying much attention to him. His door was oiled and he could have slipped out with ill intent. Other than Mary or one of the servants, the man had motive and opportunity. More than anyone else he may have wished Janson dead. He made little effort to hide the fact."

Kate scribbled furiously.

"And that brings us to the servants. Mary was as good as betrothed to the cur. According to you, the man spouted terrible things about Mary when he was out of range of the Wickets. Mary's face closed down whenever Janson was mentioned, and she has been canoodling with Lake since Janson's death. She had plenty of reason to dislike Janson."

Kate tapped the quill against her mouth. "And she could have hired anyone in this inn to murder him."

"Exactly. But it could have been Mary herself who did the dastardly deed. She could have immediately hidden the bat; this is her inn, after all, and she would know every nook and cranny. She could then have called in one of the other servants, or even Lake, to help toss the body over the railing and drag it into the stables."

Kate nodded. "But it snowed and they couldn't bear the body away with ease."

"As I said before, they should have just left the body on the ground, covered in snow. I think the guilty party or parties panicked."

"I think you make a valid point."

He had perfected the art of preening under false pretenses, but Kate's real praise made him want to sweep her into his arms.

"At least one person involved in Janson's death knew where the wall cubby was located. I don't think someone carried the bat around the screen to relieve themselves, thinking about where to hide the murder weapon, and just happened upon the hiding place. A little too convenient and unlikely."

"I agree, Inspector Black. I think you should hire on as a Runner after all."

He winked at her. There was no way he would ever be allowed to be a Runner. Although he would love to see his father's face contorted in horror, society wouldn't allow it. Bow Street wouldn't allow it. The unfairness of life, he thought. He was sure that someone like Kate would scoff at any self-pity on his part should she learn who he really was. But then she didn't strike him as being someone who appreciated self-pity in any case.

"Christian, we can't forget Mrs. Wicket. She may have even more motive and opportunity than Mary. Responsible for both the cover-up and the cleaning up. If Tom really did get the instructions from Mrs. Wicket to clean up the evidence, we may have a case of mother protecting daughter."

Christian had never experienced the protective

feelings that parents felt toward their offspring, but a few of his friends had good family relationships, and he had observed how oddly people acted when a family member was in danger.

Then again he was taking risks and doing strange things to save Anthony, so perhaps those feelings weren't just relegated to blood family.

Kate frowned. "But Mrs. Wicket had a choice to go to Mr. Wicket and stop the farce, cricket be damned."

He touched the rough wooden wall. "Mr. Wicket seemed ready to sacrifice his own daughter for the sake of the team."

She tapped the quill against the paper, and small flecks of ink landed in a haphazard pattern. "No, I don't think he would have. I think Mr. Wicket was willfully blind to Janson's faults, but I don't think he would have sacrificed his daughter to Janson. I think Mr. Wicket knew there was something wrong with the man. He tried too hard to make excuses for him, calling him passionate, headstrong, and competitive. I think he was just hoping and praying that 'his Julius' would lose his wild streak and become the perfect man to protect his daughter."

"If you say so."

She frowned more deeply. "You seem awfully

willing to believe that Mr. Wicket has or had ill intentions."

"I just think the man is plain daft."

"Daft doesn't equate to evil."

"No." He sighed heavily. "No, it doesn't." He would have taken daft any day of his childhood over the alternative.

"What do you say we talk about it in the morning? We can question both of the Wickets. We'll have to do it early. Mr. Wicket said the roads are likely to open up tomorrow, and we need to get this damn thing solved."

He looked at the clock. It was almost four in the morning. It had been quite an eventful night. And he still had half a mind to visit the screen to finish up what had been started earlier.

He looked to Kate, who had put down the quill and was chewing her lip in earnest.

"What's wrong?" he asked.

She shook her head. "Nothing. I agree. Let's turn in for the night."

He nodded and was surprised to find Kate a bit skittish. For some odd reason he found it endearing. He really was going soft.

She kicked off her shoes and climbed under the sheets. For whatever reason, she continued to wear her head wrap. He hesitated for a second. He had left earlier because he wanted to take things, well, not *slowly*, but at a pace that was comfortable to Kate. He perched on the edge of the bed and slowly removed his boots.

The hall clock started to chime the hour and he felt the stiffening of his bed partner. He turned toward her to offer comfort and was surprised when she toppled him forward and began kissing him in earnest.

Christian recovered quickly and took the lead. If she was going to up the pace, far be it from him to complain. He muttered soft words into her hair as she clutched his back. Settling light kisses in her hair and around her face and neck, he felt her begin to relax.

He ran soothing hands over her arms and back. She turned her head to look at him and he kissed her. A light kiss, just a taste really. She responded instantly, and the kiss progressed to a deeper passion and turned hungry and demanding.

Christian wasn't quite sure how her shirt came off, or his, and the removal of trousers was completely beyond his memory, but he did remember dipping his fingers into liquid fire and the taste of her mouth and skin, raspberries and desire, fire and song.

And he saw the determination in her eyes right

before the small, smooth fingers took him in hand. She had obviously never done this before. It was in her eyes and her, at first, tentative touches. He responded to her touches, letting her know what he liked, and moved into her hand to help her with others. The touches became bolder; the fire in her eyes smoldered as he continued to reciprocate.

He had never let his guard down during sex. Had never let his partner see any deeper than what he wanted. He didn't know if his inability to hold the mask was due to his desire to allow her to experience this first foray into her own sexuality without doubt or if it was just an extension of his increasingly hard grip on the mask while in her presence. Maybe it was just Kate herself.

He looked deep into her eyes and gave in to the feelings and emotions. Just as he reached release and knew that she had reached hers, he saw an emotion in her eyes, one he wasn't accustomed to seeing, and he could have sworn that just for a second her features turned golden.

Chapter 17

Did you think that showing off for the tutor was going to elevate you above your brother?

The Marquess of Penderdale
to Christian, age seven

Kate woke to the steady drip of snow melting from the roof and birds chirping noisily outside the window. She opened her eyes slowly, watching the jagged beams of light filtering around the edges of the drapery. She felt better than she had in weeks. Four weeks, to be exact.

She paused. It worried her a bit to feel such pleasure. The last time she had awakened this happy, her father had died.

An arm, warm and heavy, held her securely.

Closing her eyes, she nestled farther into the warmth, afraid to check if Christian was awake. She had confessed a number of things last night in the dark. In the dark she could believe that she was still attractive and desirable, the kind of woman Christian would want.

She bit her lip as she thought about the wonderful things Christian had done to her and they'd done with each other. Would he still have done them had he seen her ear? Had she just gotten herself further into trouble by not showing him the scars up front and dealing with the consequences then? Instead she had cast reason to the wind and involved herself emotionally and physically with a man who was already mercurial in his moods.

She gently slipped out from under Christian's arm without looking at his handsome face, walked to the window, and pulled back the drape. She briefly checked to make sure her head wrap was in place. It was. The steady drip was coming from the downspout, the ice melting from the warmth of the sun. The snow would soon be gone, leaving the countryside in wait for the next dumping.

It took a moment for her brain to catch up to her thoughts. Melting snow. She looked sharply across the horizon to the roads and could barely see the crews of men working to clear the lanes. They were almost through.

She let the drapes go.

The guests would be leaving today. And so would Christian.

She looked over to where he lay, tangled within the sheets. She half expected him to still be sleeping because he had that gentleman's way to sleep in late. But he was staring at her, his eyes watchful.

"You looked pensive, Kate. What were you thinking on so bright a morning? Are you sore?"

She blushed. "No. I was just thinking that the roads will be cleared in a few hours, and we still don't know who killed Janson."

"The locals will sort it out, if we don't." He swung his legs over the side of the bed and stretched, arching back like a cat.

She tried not to stare at the gorgeous man sitting before her in the altogether.

"But we should be able to solve the case," she persisted. Of course, he had volunteered to participate in order to get his friend's journal back. Now that he had the journal in hand, he could just leave. Leave the inn, the mystery. Leave her.

He gazed at her evenly, and she wondered from where this new calm exterior had emerged.

"If you wish to remain to solve it, I will stay as well, as I promised."

She studied him as a wave of relief coursed through her at his words. She hadn't realized that she had been holding her breath awaiting his response.

"I *have* to stay," she said tightly. The money that she would save on the room was enough to arrange a seat, albeit an uncomfortable one, to London, and she still needed to avoid her half-brother.

"No, you don't."

"I need to arrange fare to London, and my arrival needs to be well-timed."

He tilted his head. "I'll take you to London when you are ready."

She raised a brow. "And how is that?"

He smiled easily. "In my carriage. And I have a place we can stay just outside of London, only a few hours' ride from here."

She scrutinized him. "Your carriage? I thought you lost money at the races? And you want me to stay with you, unchaperoned in your house, wherever said house is?"

He raised a brow and waved off all but the last question. "And being unchaperoned is any different from what we have been doing the last few days? Where we are going you can even have your own room, if you like." He spread his arms in a magnanimous gesture, a smirk curling the corners of his mouth.

She wished she had a pillow handy, especially after a few gently sarcastic comments by Christian concerning her request to dress where he couldn't see her, after what they had done the night before. Christian tsked when she covered her breasts.

He surprised her by rising from the bed, lifting her and gently depositing her on the bed. "Let me be your maid," he whispered.

Although the water was cool, her body heated as he stroked a wet cloth across her body, cleansing her skin and reminding her of their activities the night before. She groaned with pleasure as he pulled the cloth over her breasts and covered her lips with his.

An hour later, sated, cleansed and garbed, they walked downstairs.

Tiegs and his thugs were already seated at a dining table. Tiegs lifted his cup in a mock salute as they entered.

Kate sank into a chair. Daisy smiled broadly and returned to the kitchen to bring tea and breakfast.

The guests trickled in until finally, with Mr. Freewater's arrival, they were all present. Freewater looked worse for wear—dark circles, pinched lips, and a haunted expression on his face. Kate had to assume the loss of the journal was the cause of his depression.

Desmond also wore a tight expression of distaste and condescension.

Mr. Wicket bustled in excitedly and clapped his hands together. "Good, good, everyone is assembled. I just received a report that the roads will be open soon, and the first carriage is due in town around noon."

A small cheer from Francine, a sigh from Nickford, and an even more haunted look from Freewater accompanied the announcement. Mrs. Crescent gave Francine a haughty glare, but even she had a relieved smile tugging her lips.

Christian leaned across the table. "We still have a few hours left. Let's talk to Mrs. Wicket."

Kate nodded and they stood. Tiegs walked a bit ahead of them as they exited the room, and turned to face them before they could enter the office.

"Solved it yet?"

"Hopefully by lunch," Christian said with ease.

"I do think you actually might. Where are you off to now?"

"To question Mrs. Wicket."

Kate looked sharply at Christian. What was he

doing sharing their strategy with him? Tiegs was still considered a suspect.

Tiegs nodded. "Very good choice. I believe she is upstairs on the second floor. Good place to be this morning."

Kate narrowed her eyes. "What game are you playing, Mr. Tiegs?"

He switched his gaze to her, looking vaguely amused. "Aren't we all playing a game, *Mr.* Kaden? You are looking quite bright-eyed this morning."

Kate felt her face redden. Tiegs's comment only confirmed what she had previously thought. He knew. Why he chose not to say anything publicly, however, was something she didn't understand. Tiegs seemed to find enjoyment in the dilemmas of others.

"Games are generally for the titled, but we poorer folks must do as needs dictate. Isn't that right, Mr. Black?"

Christian lifted his head in a strange sort of male acknowledgment. "Indeed. A good day to you, Mr. Tiegs."

"And to both of you."

As soon as he was gone, Kate turned to Christian. "What was that about? Shouldn't we question him? He obviously knows more than he is telling."

Christian shook his head. "Wouldn't do any good. Men like Tiegs know when to keep their mouths shut, unless you have excess money you'd like to spend to loosen his jaw and tongue?"

She stared pointedly.

"No? Well, let's see what we can do this morning and if nothing works out, we'll consider a little bribery."

A visit to the office confirmed what Tiegs had said. Mrs. Wicket was in the servants' quarters on the second floor. The innkeeper told them to go on up.

Kate had been on the second floor once before while assisting Mr. Wicket. The rooms were best termed "cozy." She hadn't been in the Wickets' chamber and was curious to see the innkeepers' private domain.

Two flights of stairs found them by the servants' quarters, which were nestled on the top floor. They passed the Crescents' maid, who looked harried and barely paid them any mind, and Benji, who issued a tentative smile.

Kate took the lead and knocked on the Wickets' door.

Mrs. Wicket opened the door and gestured for them to enter.

"I knew you'd be along sooner or later." She

gave them a long, piercing look. "Shall we have tea?"

"No, thank you," Kate demurred, and Christian declined with a charming smile.

The room was a decent size, as large as Freewater's room and complete with a fireplace and cozy furniture. A number of colored wall hangings were positioned near the window casings, adding a touch of color and warmth. Unlike the first floor, the heat of the kitchens didn't extend quite this far.

Mrs. Wicket motioned toward a beautiful oak table in one of the room's dormers, a good place to question servants privately or dine away from the bustle of the guests.

They seated themselves, and Mrs. Wicket leaned forward, resting her elbows on the tabletop and folding her arms, a bold move and one that Mrs. Crescent with her prim airs would surely have disapproved of. Kate leaned forward as well, trying to imitate a manly gesture with her right arm and hand while her left hand awkwardly remained in her lap.

"Now then, gentlemen. What can I help you with?"

"We were curious about your whereabouts on the night Julius Janson died. Can you tell us what you were doing that night?"

Mrs. Wicket didn't sigh or hesitate. "I made my rounds on the ground floor, as usual, going over meals with Bess and tasks with Elias and Benji, then returned here. I sent Sally with some towels and talked to Daisy briefly about personal conduct matters. Then Mr. Lake started yelling, and I walked downstairs to speak with him. I expected more from Mr. Lake. Quite a bit more than he was showing that night, as I informed him. We said good night and I returned here. I made my nightly rounds at three. No one was up and about and everything was in order, so I returned to bed within the quarter hour. I discovered Mr. Janson's fate along with everyone else in the dining room the next morning."

Christian frowned. "Why did you do your rounds so late? Nickford seems to be under the impression that your ghostly rounds are completed an hour earlier."

She raised a brow. "Ghostly indeed. But, in answer to your question, I was late that night."

"Why?"

"I was up late speaking with Mr. Wicket about Lake and Janson."

"What about them?"

Mrs. Wicket deflated, although it was barely noticeable, as if a breath of air left her shoulders just a tad slumped and her head the tiniest bit hung. "Mr. Wicket was a proponent of our daughter Mary marrying Mr. Janson."

"And you weren't?" Kate asked, three days' worth of curiosity contained in the question.

Mrs. Wicket shook her head. "I was not. My husband's head was turned by Mr. Janson's prestige and athletic prowess. Not only was he the squire's son, nearly the closest thing one gets to nobility around here, but he was *the* force behind the town's cricket team. We take these things seriously around here, Mr. Kaden."

As she said that, she suddenly squinted and leaned forward, looking more sharply at Kate. Kate held her breath for a second. The only way she had kept her secret from the hawk-eyed woman thus far was to stay out of her sight. As she had mostly dealt with Mr. Wicket, Sally, and Benji, it hadn't been difficult. One of Mrs. Wicket's fingers tapped rhythmically against the surface of the table as she continued to study Kate.

"Of course. We took these things seriously back in my village too. Never much of a cricket player myself," Kate said, more than a little nervous.

Christian seemed to take pity on her. "Your husband thought Janson would be a good provider and raise Mary's standing in the community."

Mrs. Wicket thankfully turned back to answer Christian. "Of course, Mr. Black. But Mr. Wicket doesn't always look beneath the outer trappings, doesn't always want to, the poor man. So I do it for him. Alas, he was quite adamant on Mr. Janson. Julius had been sweet-talking him for months, years even. He could be a charmer when he wanted something. But most of us knew he was rotten to the core. I just needed a little more time to convince my husband to deny Janson's request and look elsewhere."

"Lake."

Mrs. Wicket inclined her head. "Mr. Lake is being held to a higher standard, as he is well aware. It was the reason for his dressing-down that night. If I had so much as a whiff that he was like Mr. Janson, I would have pulled my support for him immediately. I'd like to think Mr. Lake is good for my Mary. I believe she enjoys his attentions as well. With Julius out of the way, the relationship between them has bloomed. I am hopeful for their future together."

"A compelling reason to murder Janson."

"Perhaps. However, I did not murder Julius Janson."

She said it so calmly, so directly, that Kate was inclined to believe her. There were so many things working against her, however. She had the motivation to murder the man and the opportunity with her wanderings. She knew the inn, probably better than even her husband. She would surely know of the hiding space in the wall.

"We found Mr. Janson's bat, the one that killed him, in a hollow space in the common room."

Mrs. Wicket didn't even blink.

"Do you know how it could have come to be there?"

She gave an elegant shrug, in contrast to her roughened hands and slightly bowed shoulders. "All of us know of the crooks and nooks in the inn. Many a guest has accidentally stumbled across them as well. I assume that is how you discovered it?"

"Literally," Christian said smoothly. "But if you knew about these spaces, why didn't you tell us about them when we started our investigation?"

She gave another elegant shrug. "It never crossed my mind. A man we all knew had just been murdered in my inn. Mr. Wicket was strongly concerned with what the squire would do and how it would affect our business. Under the circumstances why would I even think about a tool used to murder Mr. Janson or suggest possible hiding places for it?"

Kate really couldn't think of a good reason, but Christian's charming smile grew lazier, a sure sign that he held an ace.

"You heard us talking about not finding a weapon. Benji even mentioned that he had talked to both of you in his report that first day about how we were searching for a weapon around the inn. You *knew*, Mrs. Wicket."

Kate smacked the heel of her hand to her forehead. Mrs. Wicket, to Kate's astonishment, smiled. A small smile.

"You caught me, Mr. Black. Well done. I did know, yes. And I chose not to tell you about the cubbyholes, that is true as well."

"But you didn't murder Mr. Janson."

Christian's voice was sure, almost resigned.

"No, Mr. Black. I didn't murder Julius Janson. Unfortunately, I have a feeling that you have an idea who did."

Christian tilted his head in acknowledgment. "You will not interfere?"

"Oh, I will most definitely interfere, Mr. Black. What I choose to do depends on your intentions."

Christian looked toward Kate, and must have recognized that she had started to piece the puzzle together as well. The time of the murder. Of course. And she had a bad feeling that the motivation for the crime was well within the bounds of self-defense. She was sickened by the thought of what might have occurred to motivate it.

Christian nodded at her, seeming to take her silence as agreement. "Thank you for answering our questions, Mrs. Wicket. I believe that we will be talking with you later?"

At the woman's nod, Christian pushed back in his chair and led the way to the door. He had a hand on the knob when a soft but firm voice stopped them.

"Please. Please be kind, Mr. Black, Mr. Kaden."

Christian nodded curtly, and Kate gave the woman a sympathetic look.

Benji was sitting in one of the armchairs in the small common area near the stairs. Christian paused and cast a speculative glance in his direction.

"Benji, would you like to accompany us? We are about to solve the mystery of Julius Janson's death. You deserve to take a part in the proceedings for your help."

Benji's eyes widened, but he quietly rose as

Christian knocked on the door Kate indicated. Footsteps echoed inside and then the door was pulled open, a friendly, pretty face staring at them in question.

"Good morning, Mary."

Chapter 18

There's nary an intelligent bone in your body, boy.

The Marquess of Penderdale
to Christian, age nine

"**G**ood morning, Mr. Black. Can I get you something?" She peered around Christian's shoulder to where Kate and Benji hovered behind him. "Is something amiss?"

Kate felt a heavy weight settle in her chest as she gazed past Mary to the slight figure who had stepped up behind her. "Hello, Sally."

Christian's gaze focused on her as well, and Kate watched as the lines on his face grew resolute. "Mary, would you mind if we talked to Sally alone? Benji will be with us."

Mary's eyes held innocent confusion, but Kate caught the darting look she threw Benji. They all knew. She'd bet every last farthing that the entire staff of the inn, possibly barring Mr. Wicket, knew what had happened to Janson.

"Sally?" Mary turned to her, an obvious question both in her voice and on her face.

"It's all right, Mary. Please."

Mary studied her for a long moment and finally nodded. She gave Christian a cool glance and cast an imploring one on Kate. Kate understood. She was supposed to understand and as an employee of the inn, if only temporarily, help them. Mary's gaze held a hint of betrayal as well, which confirmed that Mary had been aware of her gender all along.

Kate nodded to her. "I will do all I can."

Mary's eyes lost the chill, and she nodded sadly before filing past them.

Christian walked into the room and Kate watched Benji close the door. He looked devastated and close to tears. She looked between Sally and Benji. Of course. More than two people were involved. Had she and Christian been so caught up in each other that they had missed the obvious? On the other hand, if one were to look at the possible suspects from the outset of their investigation,

Sally would be at the bottom of their list, with Benji not far behind.

"You know, don't you, Mr. Black?" Sally's soft voice asked.

"What happened that night, Sally?"

The maid's eyes grew filmy, but she lifted her chin, showing more spirit in that moment than she had in all their previous encounters combined. "Mr. Janson was not a nice man, Mr. Black. I learned that from his previous stay at the inn." She rubbed her arm, and Kate could see a wicked bruise peeking from under her cuff.

"He threatened you?"

Sally's expression turned bitter, a look not suited to her usually kind demeanor. "Mr. Janson didn't threaten. No, he always made a point that he promised. And that his promises were always kept."

Kate moved forward. "He hurt you."

Sally tried to maintain a stiff upper lip, but the look was compromised as a tear slipped down her cheek. Kate felt another burst of outrage on Sally's behalf. Janson had been a monster.

"Mr. Janson was very spoiled. His parents gave him everything he wanted and he took whatever else he desired. He was the chief cock of the walk, to borrow Tom's phrase. The community loved him for his status and prowess on the field, and those who did not learned quickly to either move on or remain silent."

"What happened that night, Sally?" Christian's voice was low and soothing.

"He tried—he had done—he already—" She broke off on a sob, and Benji rushed around them to hug her tightly. She latched on to him.

Christian allowed her a few minutes to compose herself. Kate's heart was heavy. It was obvious what had happened to Sally. Christian had warned her days ago that she probably wasn't going to like what they uncovered. But why had Janson done such things in an inn whose owners he was trying to woo?

"He did it because he could." Benji answered her unspoken question grimly. "He did nearly everything because he could. You don't understand how things worked around here. It happened before—he caught her behind the stables. After he was done he threatened, no, promised, that no one would believe her innocent, even if she were to yell down the inn. Said he would say she had approached him and had taken advantage of him. I told Sally to tell Mrs. Wicket or Mary all of it, but she wouldn't. Only reason I know is because we found her afterward, me and Tom."

He looked devastated at the memory. "Mrs.

Wicket and Mary rightly guessed, though I could see it in their eyes. There wasn't much we could do about it. The Jansons rule this district. Even if Mrs. Wicket and Mary had protested against him, it would have done little good. Nothing ever stuck to Janson," he said bitterly. "It took a long time for Sally to walk around the inn without a fireplace poker in hand, even when Janson was out of town."

Kate's mouth fell open, stricken. "Oh God, oh no. I took the poker from you, Sally. I can't—I don't—"

Sally raised her head and stayed further comments. "It's not your fault, Ka— Mr. Kaden. Mr. Janson attacked me long before you took the poker. I could have retrieved it. I was trying to believe it couldn't happen again, especially with so many folks staying here at the inn."

Kate saw Benji flinch. He had probably been trying to boost her confidence.

"I took some towels down, and he grabbed me outside his door. He was drunk." Her chin rose again, and Kate had the feeling that she wanted everything finally out in the open. "He dragged me inside and threw me on the bed. I was dazed at first, but when he began to undo his trousers, I just grabbed the first thing at hand. He slept with his cricket bat," she said darkly. "I hit him once, just grazed him across the shoulder and ran toward the gallery door. He lunged at me. I just . . . I just brought the bat down again. He fell into the drapes and they dislodged. He never got up."

She shuddered. "There was so much blood. I had Mr. Crescent's trousers that I was taking to press. I tied them around Mr. Janson's head to stop the flow, but there was so *much*. I ran from the room."

"Were you by chance wearing a green calico dress?"

"Yes." She seemed surprised. "How did you know? Oh." She seemed to realize something. "There was a tear in it, a piece missing. I assume you found it?"

Christian nodded. "What happened after you ran from the room?"

Sally looked Christian straight in the eye. "I dragged Janson out to the gallery, tossed him over the railing, and pulled him into the stables."

Christian sighed, clearly not believing her obvious lie. Benji forestalled him. "I did it, Mr. Black. Sally ran from the room and into me."

"No, Benji, no!"

Benji touched her cheek. "It's all right, Sally." He turned back to Christian. "I tossed him over the rail and dragged him into the stable."

"You tossed him over, then you and Tom dragged him into the stable," Christian clarified.

Benji looked as mutinous as Sally had. "I did it alone."

Christian shook his head, in obvious denial. "You may have started dragging the body by yourself in your panic. I can't see Tom succumbing to panic. But you couldn't have dragged Janson all the way on your own. Tom was in the stable, on the night shift, and probably more than willing to help after he heard what happened. You moved Janson's belongings at that point, because it was too late to act as if his death were an accident. If the weather had been more cooperative, you might have been able to get rid of the body. Alas, it was not. So you moved Janson's things to make it look as if he had left. Then someone had to hide the murder weapon, his bat."

They stood tight-lipped.

"Mary hid the bat," Christian said.

"No!"

At that moment Kate knew it was the truth.

Christian cocked his head. "Benji hid it, then.

It was really just the two of you acting in self-defense."

Both of them were so visibly relieved as to wilt where they stood, still clutching each other.

"Thank you, Mr. Black. What will happen to us now?" Benji asked, head high.

"I'll talk to the Wickets and take you with me. I don't think it would be a good idea to leave you here with the likes of Donald Desmond ready to whip up a mob against you."

"Where will you take us?"

Christian cocked his head. "I have a house near London and connections. We will see what we can work out. Do all the servants know what happened?"

Benji cocked his head in return and seemed to come to a decision. "More or less. Since the guests' servants are bunking with us, conversation has been limited. We all knew what a rotten bastard Julius Janson was. Only Mr. Wicket was blind in that regard, and even he could only hold on to the blindness for so long. He was getting desperate, if you hadn't noticed. Desperate to keep intact his ideals about the town's number one cricket player and handsome man-about-town."

Christian nodded and turned to Kate. "Anything more you wanted to ask?"

She shook her head, still in shock.

"Both of you stay up here while we sort things out with the Wickets. As soon as the roads clear we will be leaving. The less you see of Desmond or any of the other guests, the better. In fact, can you both stay here until we call for you?"

"Yes. It won't take me long to pack. And Mr. Crescent's valet has left our room, so all is clear for that."

"And Mrs. Crescent's maid?"

"Staying with Daisy and Bess."

"Good, good. We'll see you in a bit. Stay strong, Sally." Christian gave her an encouraging smile, but stepped no closer to her. It was obvious why Sally was skittish around men she didn't know well. Kate could have hugged him. Sally's answering smile was still a bit timid, but no less sincere.

They exited the room and Christian closed the door behind them. Kate leaned against the wall, shock and anger still brimming. He took hold of her and nudged her down the stairs and into their room.

As soon as they were inside, he pulled her into his arms. She trembled and hugged him back tightly.

"What will happen to them? Oh God, I knew

Janson was bad. I *heard* his threats. And I did nothing."

He pulled back and lightly shook her. "No, Kate. It's not your fault either. It's Janson's fault. Let it go."

"But—"

"No."

Although the high-handedness of the statement might have caused her outrage at another time, she felt the tension ease from her body.

"Janson got away with so much because he was the son of a squire," Kate said. "Like the nobility, just what Mrs. Wicket said. And Sally is a by-blow, did you know? I found that out accidentally the first day I was here. Sometimes even servants can be careless when they think they are alone. The daughter of a baronet and an upstairs maid. Of course, her father never acknowledged her. Kicked them right out."

Christian wasn't sure he liked where this conversation was headed.

"Just like the titled, powerful aristocrats to care about their own pleasures and use those in lower classes before throwing them away like so much waste."

"Yes, well—"

"Happens all the time, Christian. Surely it sickens you?"

"Yes, well—"

"You are a gentleman at heart, no matter what you claim, and you must have seen this type of thing before." He saw her shudder. Funny, his collar felt tighter than when he had fastened it earlier.

"The upper classes just take and take. And they get away with anything. Worse, they *know* they can."

Yup, definitely tighter.

"My brother's friend is a minor baronet. He's the one my brother, half-brother actually, wants to sell me off to. Says I should be happy with what I can get. The man is repulsive, though. Not much better than Janson, really." She shuddered again, and Christian couldn't even appreciate her sudden chattiness as he felt a familiar curl of rage building inside.

"What?"

"I'm running, of course."

"You aren't marrying him."

She patted his arm. "Of course I'm not. And it's kind of you to offer to help."

"You will tell me their names."

"Oh, I doubt we will run into them."

"You will tell me their names."

She seemed to finally catch on to the fact that his words were clipped and his face a thundercloud.

"Christian?"

"You won't be marrying this baronet. I don't care what your brother threatens you with."

She ran a hand down his arm in a soothing manner. It worked. A bit.

"That's sweet of you. If it came to it, he could force me, and there is nothing you could do. He is a baronet. My brother will gain custody of me if I can't outsmart him for a few more days."

He touched her cheek. "I'm not worried. And if they are stupid enough to come near you before you are ready to claim your inheritance, they will be very sorry."

"It's not much of an inheritance. Probably a pittance to you—unless you really have gambled it all away. But money is money, as my half-brother has always said. And I could live off of it. Maybe get a little place of my own with a garden and no clocks," she said wistfully.

"I'll get you a little place with a garden *and* clocks. You won't be afraid of them anymore."

She gave him a strange look. "Christian, you can't just say you'll buy me a house."

"You're right. I *will* buy it instead."

"But—"

A knock on the door interrupted her. Christian grabbed the knob, happy for the excuse.

Elias stood there with his hand ready to knock again.

"The carriages will arrive in half an hour, sir. Will you be needing one?"

"Yes. Wait. On second thought, would you be willing to run to the Green Toad?"

Elias looked at him strangely, but agreed to visit the other inn. Christian gave him the description and name of his driver and pressed a coin into his hand. Kate gave him an odd look as well, but he just shook his head.

"I need to talk to the Wickets and make arrangements. Will you be all right here, Kate, or do you want to go downstairs?"

She looked outraged, and he almost smiled.

"I can handle myself quite well, thank you."

He gave her a small salute. "As you wish, my lady. I'll track you down in the dining room or here in fifteen minutes or so."

He had an innkeeper to appraise, a deal to work out, and a problem to solve. He had tangled his own web and deceived Kate, and now he was going to have to work out how to get rid of the snarls. The snarls had never been a problem in the past; he had simply left and started over. But he didn't want to start over. He wanted Kate. He wanted honesty. Honesty from her and for her. And he hadn't the first clue how to be in an honest relationship with someone else.

He had less than one hour to tell her he was really an earl in disguise before the evidence beat him to it.

Chapter 19

*Just when you think things are at an end, watch for a
new beginning.*

George Simon
to Kate, age thirteen

Kate watched as Christian closeted himself
in the office with the Wickets. Benji and
Sally were fetched a few minutes later, and Tom
followed a few minutes after that.

Christian had said something about buying her
a house. He couldn't have been serious. But what if
he was? Was he proposing something more concrete between them?

Everyone was milling about the dining and tap
areas, even the servants, because it was obvious

that something important was going on. Donald Desmond's eyes were narrowed as he surveyed the closed door and everyone in the room. His eyes narrowed further when they landed on Kate.

Kate looked away. She had already gained more attention from trailing Christian than was wise. Honestly, if she had been using her head, she would have stayed as far from him as possible. But something told her that she would have regretted that more. Regretted it more than—

"So did you and the idiot discover who did it? I hope it put a little more hair on your chest. People mistake you for a girl often, I bet."

—her identity being discovered.

Kate gripped the bench with her left hand and tried to look unruffled as she traced the carved patterns in the table with her right forefinger. "I'm sure the Wickets will inform everyone of the proceedings soon enough, Mr. Desmond."

"They'd better." There was a dark, feral look in his eye. "And I want the murderer strung up by tonight. Too many servants in there to be anyone else. Which one of them did it? That bloody creep from the stables?"

"Mr. Desmond, you will find out when everyone does. You just need to wait a few minutes more."

"No." He stalked toward her. "I want to know now."

He grabbed her chin and forced it up. She tried to pull away, but his grip was too strong.

"Now see here, Mr. Desmond—" Elias started toward them.

Desmond pointed a finger, shaking with rage and a bit of madness. "Stay right there. I will deal with this."

"Let the lad go, Desmond," Tiegs said in a lazy voice.

Desmond gripped her chin for another second before roughly releasing her. "Tell me, boy."

She started to say something scathing, but noticed the change in his eyes. He gripped her chin again and started laughing demonically.

"Oh, ho, ho. Mistaken for a girl, I had that reversed. Black isn't a complete idiot, I see. Do this often, do you? Black like his women only when they look like men? What does that cost a gent?"

He released her chin and leaned into her space, his hands planted forward on the table, directly in front of her. A malicious smile curved his thin lips.

"Pardon me?" she asked, completely unnerved.

"Answer my question, whore."

Kate blinked. "What?"

"I said, how much does he pay you to dress as a man?"

Kate looked around the room. Most of the people were staring in fascination at the two of them. Really, these people had had more than their fair share of entertainment these last few days. Mr. Wicket should have been charging stage fees.

A few people looked confused, while Daisy shot her a look of sympathy.

It didn't take long for the confused, few though they were at this point, to catch on, especially after Desmond ripped her cap and head wrap from her head. Her short curls spilled free.

She heard Mrs. Crescent gasp and fought to regain her composure. Hadn't she just admitted to herself that the adventure had been worth her discovery? Well, here it was put to the test.

Desmond grabbed her shirt and pulled her forward. "What's your name, whore?"

She grabbed his wrist and twisted just as she'd seen Christian do. He hissed and raised his other hand. Her vision slowed. Tiegs gestured to his thugs. Elias, eyes wide and mouth open, started to lunge forward. Olivia put one slender hand to her mouth. Mrs. Crescent looked outraged, her eyes trained on Kate. And then there was nothing but a blur of flesh as Desmond's fist descended.

Kate's eyes closed waiting for the blow. There was a shout, and a whiff of air brushed her cheek.

"What is going on here?" Christian's tone was low, the words perfectly enunciated, ice in every syllable.

Kate opened her eyes to see Christian's hand closed around Desmond's fist, mere inches from her face. Christian's knuckles whitened, and Desmond's mad expression turned pained as his face whitened as well.

Christian pushed him backward. Desmond clutched his fist and turned hateful eyes on him. "Your whore here was about to tell us what you pay her."

"Kate is not my whore," he said calmly, as if talking about the weather. "You have obviously been stuck inside too long, Desmond. Perhaps a brisk walk outside and away from this inn would do you good. Perhaps you would care to make it a permanent trip."

"Not until I find out who murdered Julius."

"Ah, yes. Julius's death, an unfortunate accident. I'll be taking it up with the constable when he returns. Mr. Wicket has promised to take care of the body so that it will be ready for burial when his parents return."

"What about them?" He pointed at Benji, Tom, and Sally, who was partially hidden by the men.

"Ah, yes. They have key information about Mr. Janson's accident. They will be coming with me until events are sorted out with the constable."

"Which one of them did it?"

Christian raised a brow somehow appearing bored. "What makes you think one of them did it, Desmond?"

"It's bloody obvious."

"Tut, tut, swearing in front of the ladies."

"There are no ladies here," he sneered.

Kate took a quick peek at Mrs. Crescent and saw her ire finally switch from Kate to another target.

"Now, wait just a moment—" Mr. Crescent started to say, obviously angered.

Christian tapped a well-manicured nail on the tabletop. "I think that does it for this discussion."

He started to turn when Desmond grabbed his coat. Christian immediately twisted his wrist, much as Kate had done, but with enviously more force.

"Under Section Five Hundred Forty-two of the Runner's Code I could have you thrown into Newgate. Ever been to City College, Desmond? It could teach you a whole new meaning of the word 'bloody.' "

Despite Desmond's twisted body position and the obvious pain, he still forged on. "Julius deserves justice. I want them strung up. One, all, I don't care."

Christian leaned in to whisper in Desmond's ear, which was close enough for Kate to hear. "Listen here, you ignorant maggot, unlike you and that misbegotten bastard Julius, the rest of us don't attack innocent women. If I see you again, I will make you very, very sorry."

He pushed Desmond away and brushed off his sleeve. "Under Section Seven Hundred Eighty-nine of the Runner's Code I am not allowed to reveal the details of what occurred until the full investigation has been reported to my superiors."

He turned to address the other guests. "Be at peace, patrons, that justice has and will continue to be done. Thank you all for your cooperation in this matter. I hope everyone has a pleasant trip."

Nickford started to clap, ignoring the way the others turned to stare at him.

The patrons and servants began to murmur to each other, and Kate saw Christian give Tom, Benji, and Sally a signal. They disappeared, probably to retrieve their belongings.

The Crescents made a beeline for Christian and Kate. Unfortunately, there was no way to escape without pushing them over.

Just as Mrs. Crescent started to open her mouth, Christian leaned in. "May I introduce my betrothed, Kate Caps."

Kate wasn't sure who blinked harder, the Crescents or herself.

"A veritable tizzy it was when we discovered this was the only place left to board with the weather closing in as it was, and no way to get through the storm. Kate is helping me with cases. Arrived a few days early. Somewhat of my secretary on the road, if you will."

Kate was too shocked to react. He had just announced her as his betrothed, albeit with the wrong last name. And had he just used the word "tizzy"?

Mrs. Crescent frowned, looking somewhat irritated for being outmaneuvered. "You should have arranged for something else, Mr. Black. It isn't done."

And Kate knew in that instant that the door to her aunt's home was now closed. Mrs. Crescent was just the type to socialize in the same circles as her aunt. They would assuredly meet at a function were she to actually make it to London, obtain her inheritance, and be taken in by her aunt. Kate bowed her head.

"Be that as it may, the next time we see you, we will be a happily married pair. Good day, Mrs. Crescent. Mr. Crescent."

Mr. Crescent stepped in Christian's path. "Forgive my wife, Mr. Black. Perhaps we should sit down and discuss what happened?"

Ah, yes. The information gathering. Both of the Crescents planned to be first to Town to share the news.

"I'm very sorry, Mr. Crescent." Christian looked contrite. How he managed it, Kate didn't know. He didn't have a contrite bone in his body. "What I told Mr. Desmond stands. I am not allowed to discuss this case until I get the say-so from my superiors. Good day to you both."

Kate saw Desmond conversing with Freewater. Desmond directed an evil stare their way as Christian herded her from the room.

"Let's pack. I want to get you out of here as soon as possible."

Surprised, Kate let him lead the way back to the room.

Christian convinced her to dress in women's clothes again, stating that her disguise didn't matter anymore, and it would be better for where they were going for her to be dressed as a female.

She put on a real bonnet, one that covered her ears. Somehow when he had pulled her hat loose, her curls had managed to keep her bad ear undetected.

Packing took little time and soon they were back in the dining area. Bess had put together food for their trip. Kate was surprised to see how much. Bess squeezed her hand. "We are thankful, miss, for what you two are doing for three of ours. Blessings to you and your betrothed."

Olivia gave Christian and Kate a sly smile, taking in Kate's lovely white morning dress trimmed with a cherry ribbon, and scarlet merino cloth pelisse and fur muff. "I see now why you didn't take me up on my offer, Christian. It was very interesting meeting you both."

Tiegs just gave an enigmatic smile, and she saw Christian put a card in his pocket after shaking Tiegs's hand. "His Lord and Ladyship depart. Whatever shall I do for amusement now?"

Kate shook her head, partially confused, and found herself vigorously shaking hands with Nickford.

"Anytime you want to experiment again, you just let me know."

Christian smiled. "We'll be in touch, Nickford. I keep my promises."

"Oh, very good, very good," Nickford crowed.

Mr. Wicket came scrambling in, panting. "My lor—, er, Mr. Black, your carriage is outside. Everything is set."

"Excellent. Thank you, Mr. Wicket, for your excellent hospitality. Please let me know if I can be of further assistance."

"Oh, very good, my l—, sir. Yes, very good."

Mr. Wicket scraped and bowed some more, leaving Kate confused and uneasy. Mrs. Wicket gushed a bit too, furthering her unease. What tales had Christian spun while talking to them?

She turned to see Freewater slumped in the corner near Desmond, two empty mugs in front of him.

After a few more well-wishings they were standing outside in front of a well-appointed carriage. Kate turned a suspicious eye to Christian.

"Come, Kate, we must be off. Very nice of Lord Canley to give the Runners the use of his carriage. In you go."

She stared at the carriage as the last piece slid into place.

Did he think her stupid? She might have been willing to believe he had lied to the Wickets, but when added together with all the hints he had unconsciously dropped and the concrete evidence in front of her, a new alternative seemed quite apparent. She looked him in the eye and saw an expression that was both pleading and promising. She grudgingly stepped into the expensive conveyance, Christian entering immediately after.

Neither of them saw the angry, dark eyes watching from the window.

Chapter 20

Always remember that your dear old father will always support you no matter what.

George Simon
to Kate, age sixteen

"Who are you?"
The question was clipped.

He responded with his most charming smile, hiding a sigh of relief as the carriage picked up speed. She wouldn't try to jump from a moving carriage. "I'm Christian, pleasure to meet you."

"Christian *who*? Who are you?"

"I'm the same person you met that first night at the inn."

Her face was tense. "Don't play games with me. What is your real name?"

"Christian Black."

"*Please.*" Something moved across her face, anguish or despair, and he lost all amusement.

He leaned toward her. "My name really is Christian Black. Black is our family name." He hesitated. "My father is the Marquess of Penderdale."

"And you?"

He sighed, leaning back into the plush pads. "I am the only surviving son, which makes me the Earl of Canley."

"You are a peer," she whispered.

"No, I am the heir. Unfortunately for all of us." He grimaced.

Her eyes were intensely focused on her clutched hands. "How you must have laughed."

"No, Kate." He tried to take her hand, not liking the direction the conversation was taking, but she shied away.

"Did you find the situation amusing? No, don't answer that, I know you did. Even without knowing you were an earl, I saw the arrogance. Has this all been a joke?"

"No, Kate—"

She laughed somewhat hysterically. "You called

me your betrothed. When really you should have stuck with Desmond's claim of whore. Really, there is no need for you to escort me anywhere, Your Lordship."

"Stop."

To his amazement she did, though her shoulders began to shake, whether from hysteria or grief, he wasn't sure.

"Oh, Christian. I knew there was something off about you from the beginning. But I just thought you were only the careless blood who had the world at his feet."

Her words hurt, but he wasn't going to let it show. "Well, there's that too."

She met his eyes, her gaze more piercing than usual. "Why is it unfortunate that you are the heir?"

Damn. He wasn't sure which was worse, her upset or her ability to rally and attack his weakest points.

"Well, that is the way things work, you see."

"No, I don't."

"You have two older brothers who can do no wrong, and somehow you are always the one breaking the family heirlooms and putting others in danger and getting them killed." Damn, he hadn't meant to say that.

"What do you mean? Are you referring to your mother?"

"Mother for one. Father seems to think that the deaths of my two older brothers were also my fault, as they were returning from a party that I had chosen not to attend. If I had, perhaps the accident would never have occurred or perhaps it would have been me in the ravine."

Her mouth opened, but no sound emerged.

"It's not important. Just the curse of being the youngest," he said flippantly and tried to adopt his most vacant expression. It always seemed to work on his father.

Kate's eyes narrowed and she turned to the window. He had succeeded in putting her off the conversation, but the victory was hollow. Suddenly his persona chafed more than he cared to admit.

He wanted back the Kate who made him forget to use the mask. Had he lost her by not speaking to her earlier? He *knew* he should have admitted the truth to her last night. Caring what someone thought was just as frustrating as it had been before he had attended Eton and adopted his devil-may-care attitude. He couldn't get hurt if he didn't care.

Blast. Those walls had been bloody hard to erect in the first place. Now as he stared broodingly out the window, he began the laborious process of reconstructing them.

Kate tried not to look at her companion. She wanted to strangle him *and* soothe his hurts. He was so capable at times; his behavior in the inn and how he had handled the people proved that. But at other times he seemed little more than a recalcitrant child. She supposed it had to do with the lousy upbringing he hinted at, but never fully divulged.

The gap between them had widened with his revelation of being an earl, and she was left standing across the chasm, waiting for the edge to crumble as she slipped inside.

When she fell had yet to be determined. "Christian, it is important. *You* are important. Do not dare think otherwise."

He gazed at her steadily and his lips quirked. "And here I thought you were exasperated by my arrogance, Kate."

She frowned. "You know to what I refer. And if I ever meet your father, I think I may well do him harm."

"I hope you never have the displeasure."

After a moment he smiled faintly. "But I do know what you mean. Or I wish to believe I do."

He held her eyes. "My sweet Kate," he whispered.

They lapsed into silence for a few moments, a slightly charged, but comfortable one.

She inspected the carriage while Christian frowned thoughtfully in the corner. The workmanship was beautiful. Gold filigree and gleaming squabs. Plush cushions and luxurious curtains. Just like him. Beautiful and posh.

Nothing like her. Plain and damaged.

She touched the bonnet covering her damaged ear and felt tears prick her eyes.

The journey took a little under three hours on the newly cleaned roads and they mostly discussed what it would be like to open an investigations firm. Christian's eyes lit as he talked about what they could do with one.

The carriage slowed and swung to the right. Kate drew the curtain aside to look out the window. A magnificent drive stretched before them. Christian grew silent.

Statues and stately, mature trees lined the drive, which was covered in snow, haunting but beautiful. The structure loomed ahead, majestic yet lacking. The lines were too straight, the symmetry too perfect. No ivy curled lovingly through the stones, no snow clung where it shouldn't. The manor said, *Look and marvel, but touch me not.* Apart from the beauty, she couldn't picture Christian growing up here.

The carriage stopped beneath the front portico and Kate let the curtain slip from her fingers, the cloth a shroud encasing them in shadows with only a sliver of light showing through a crack. Christian continued his silent vigil. She didn't know how to respond to the austere grandeur of the manor or what to say to him.

A servant opened the carriage door. "My lord, good to see you." The man turned to her and held out his hand. "Miss."

Kate smiled awkwardly and stepped from the carriage, Christian exiting behind her. A stern elderly man, presumably the butler, engaged Christian in conversation. The man spared Kate a glance, then surreptitiously dismissed her.

The gulf between Christian and her widened. She wondered if it had been that wide all along and she had just been unwilling to see it.

House servants gathered their luggage, Christian's surprisingly small amount of baggage and Kate's unsurprisingly pitiful few cases. Another carriage pulled up and Kate observed Benji and Sally gaping in wonder and some apprehension. Tom merely stood with his arms crossed, as unapproachable as ever.

Christian gave instructions to the butler for Benji, Sally, and Tom to be taken around back. He held out his arm to Kate, and she reluctantly put her hand on top. He didn't smile as they walked inside. He didn't so much as crack an expression.

"Are you well?" she whispered as they entered a large hall dominated by a portrait of a ruthless-looking man.

"This is the house of my birth. I'd much prefer to be at my home in the north, but given our present circumstances, this will have to do," he muttered, his tone holding a distinct chill.

She pulled to a stop. "Why are we stopping here then? Chri— I mean, Lord Canley."

His eyes turned wintry. "Don't refer to me as that, Kate."

She fidgeted. "Well, I certainly can't refer to you as Christian inside the house of your birth."

He turned so that he was fully facing her. "I don't care one whit what anyone else in this house thinks, Kate. You will refer to me as Christian, as you have been doing."

She searched his face. "I don't think that is true, Christian," she said slowly. "I think you do care."

His face closed and he led her forward. "I prefer not to discuss this or anything else of importance here in the hall. Too many enemy ears. And I need to send a note to Anthony."

"If you find it so unsettling, why are we stopping here?"

"Its close proximity to London for you, and to Anthony for me. I only plan to spend one night, maybe two at the most. You can meet with your solicitor in two days, correct?"

"Yes."

"Excellent. That gives us plenty of time."

"Are you going to take the journal to Anthony?"

Christian sent a surreptitious glance around the hall as they continued. "Yes."

"You never explained why it was so important."

"Because Anthony is more family than the ones I have by blood." His muscles were bunched beneath her fingers. "I'd do anything for him."

There was a lot of emotion packed into that sentence.

"But why would anyone want the journal?"

"Blackmail. Circulation for the papers. The opportunities are endless."

"The journal is damaging enough to be used as blackmail?"

"Oh yes. But it doesn't matter. I won't let anyone touch it now that I have it."

"You would do anything for your friend?"

Christian stopped at a door and turned to her. "Yes, Kate, I would."

He opened the door and led her inside. It was a spacious room with tasteful furniture and accessories; however, there was little personality to be found. Then by chance she spotted a small chest in the corner as Christian spun her around. The chest was oddly misshapen and there were a number of strange things on top. The chest was hidden where it normally wouldn't be seen or noticed. She would bet they were Christian's things. Hidden beneath a carefully cultivated image, just begging to be explored. Like their owner.

The misshapen chest gave her some hope.

Christian drew her forward, lowering his lips to her neck. "Now that we are here, I suggest we don't leave this room until we are ready to travel to Anthony's or London."

She tilted her head; a wave of heat and longing surged through her body. She was so confused about most everything in her life, but oddly enough not about this. She just knew that she felt safe in his arms. And that she wanted more. "What about dinner?"

"I'll have trays sent up."

He stopped to take off his jacket. Anthony's

journal poked from the pocket, and he draped the jacket over top of a chair. He loosened his cravat and dropped it to the floor.

"I think I will burn these clothes." He gestured to the clothes that had been part of the wardrobe that had never quite fit him. And as nicely tailored as they were, they were undoubtedly much less fine than what he was used to.

"And perhaps I'll have you for dinner instead." He touched her cheek. "And this time, Kate, I won't let you hide in the dark."

Kate swallowed nervously as he untied her dress. He left it hanging loose and threaded his finger through the ties of her bonnet. She pulled away as he withdrew the cap and she heard it plop on the Aubusson rug, her eyes tightly closed.

Silence.

She held in a sob, unwilling to open her eyes to see the disgust on his face.

"Kate?" His voice was low and flat.

She opened her eyes and started fumbling with the ties of her dress.

"What is this?" His voice was harsh, and she thought she detected an underlying hint of betrayal beneath.

"I'm sorry. I—I couldn't tell you. I'll go."

He grabbed her wrist. "Why?"

"Because I couldn't bear it."

"I don't understand." He looked pained.

"The chandelier hit me. It caused this."

She reached down for her bonnet, but he pulled her up and lifted her chin. There was question in his eyes and a hint of relief.

"What are you talking about?"

She stared at him. Why was he making her spell it out? "My ear."

"So you aren't rejecting me because of something else? This house? The situation? Or just . . . me?"

Kate could do nothing but blink. He thought she had rejected him when she had frozen up. That *she* was rejecting *him*.

She couldn't reassure him; her thoughts were in too much disarray. "Aren't you horrified?"

Christian looked at her ear and lifted a tentative finger to touch it. The light stroke sent a not unpleasant shiver through her. "It's not your best feature Kate; I think that distinction belongs to your bright eyes or luscious lips. But horrified? No."

She licked her lips and stared at him. Willing herself to believe him, to believe the look of need in his eyes, that he still wanted her.

Christian could be brash and careless and

sometimes insincere, but he was also warm and funny, smart, caring, and genuine.

And she was falling in love with him.

She closed her eyes.

"Kate?"

She pushed the thoughts aside and opened her eyes. "Yes?"

"Did you think that I would think the less of you because of a scar? That it would make you any less beautiful?"

Kate couldn't answer as tears welled in her eyes. Of course she had. Her brother and Connor had claimed that she was disgusting and no one would ever want her. And Kate had been all too willing to believe it.

Now here was a man, himself a catch by any woman's standards, who claimed she was beautiful, scars and all.

"Yes," she whispered.

He touched her forehead and brushed a curl away. "Ah, Kate. So little faith. Have I impressed you so little?"

"No, I mean, yes, you have impressed me. I—I value your good opinion." And that had been the trouble really. She hadn't wanted to lose him, even though she barely had him.

He rubbed a finger along her cheek. "How could

you think that one minor flaw would make you any less desirable? It only makes you, you. And I find you irresistible."

It wasn't a minor flaw. She could hide it with the judicious use of hats and hairstyles, but it was far from being unnoticeable otherwise.

"I'm going to show you exactly how much that scar doesn't bother me," he whispered as he tilted her chin and brought his lips to hers.

The kiss was sweet. So sweet that Kate could have cried. To have this man . . . to stay with him instead of going to London . . . even to stay with him as his paramour . . .

"Kate?"

"Yes."

She answered the unspoken question and he lifted her under the knees and walked into the bedroom. He laid her gently on the soft, velvety counterpane. His hands shook slightly as he undid her dress, and as she touched his shirt, hers did as well.

Soft hands brushed over clothes, then skin, and soon there was nothing to separate them.

He pulled back the covers enough for her to slip inside and followed her beneath. The room had contained a distinct chill before they had started moving. Now there was a peaceful, languid warmth that infused the air around them.

"Beautiful, lovely Kate."

Christian dragged a finger down her throat and chest, and circled her belly button.

"No one around to hear you scream and moan tonight. These walls are much thicker than those at the inn."

His finger continued downward, circling the curls below and then skirting back up to catch a breast.

"I'm going to make sure we use the soundproofing to our advantage."

He kissed, no *claimed*, her lips, and she arched into him, unable to help herself. Not *wanting* to help herself. She pressed against him, arching off the bed, and she heard his harsh intake of air. He pushed back into her and her lower body pressed against his, a desperate searching of his body for hers as they rocked against each other. He slipped inside her folds, rubbing gently against the spot that he had teased so much the night before.

She kissed him more hungrily, her body demanding more as they clasped together and his body rubbed against, and nearly inside, hers.

He broke the kiss and dipped his head to pull her right breast into his mouth. She arched again, and the thought briefly flickered past that her body liked the position.

"Raspberries."

Her fingers reached up and curled into the soft dark strands at his nape. His deep blue eyes searched hers, and he held the contact as his hand played with her nipple and his body continued to move against hers. There was something building in her body, just as there had been both times before. Christian smiled, a real smile that lit up his eyes and spread happiness across his face. A mischievous glance replaced the smile a moment later as he slid down her body and disappeared from view.

"Christian, wha—"

Kate gasped as his tongue swirled around her, doing things that his fingers had done before, but more *maddeningly*. He swept and licked and even nipped, as if he were truly enjoying a dessert laden with luscious fruit. Her fingers found their way into his hair and she could only hold on as he made her buck and moan and thrash. And then there was that beautiful light, made of gold—sweeping from the tips of her toes to the top of her head, making its way up and down, penetrating her very being, and converging where Christian was.

She heard a sound caught somewhere between

a scream and a moan and vaguely wondered if it had been her making the sound as she went boneless on the bed.

Christian appeared from under the covers a few moments later, a rather smug grin on his face. "I love the sounds you make. And that they are just for me."

Kate felt too lazy to respond. Her entire body hummed pleasantly, and it felt as if she had just run to London and back. But she didn't think that running would make her feel *quite* so wonderful.

Christian pulled a cord. Kate gave him a questioning glance, but he just smiled.

Minutes later there was a knock at the door. Christian threw on a robe and padded into the sitting room. Kate couldn't see the door from her vantage point, so when he returned with two trays of food, she just stared at him.

"Thought you might be hungry. And it's only gentlemanly of me to allow you to rest a bit your first few times." He said it with a leer. Her insides warmed as he verbally extended their relationship beyond today.

"I thought you said you weren't a gentleman?" she quipped and forked a piece of pheasant.

"I'm not. I have completely dark, ulterior motives for you, my dear."

"Thank goodness."

Christian twirled his forked meat. "What do you plan to do after you receive your inheritance?"

She shrugged, but her mouth was suddenly dry. "I had planned to stay on with my aunt in Town. With the extra money she would forgive a few of my less than stellar qualities."

His eyes tightened, but he remained quiet as he continued to eat and listen.

"However, that forgiveness doesn't encompass dressing like a boy and sharing a room with a man for several days, so I think that plan is definitely out." She tried to keep her voice light.

"You don't want to be with your aunt anyway. Stuffy existence, even worse on the edges of the ton. You'd suffocate. And I'd be most put out." He reached over and tucked a strand of hair behind her ear, her damaged one. His fingers lightly traced the outside, not hurting, but making her shiver.

He pulled his hand back and resumed eating. "They don't deserve you."

"My brother said I would be lucky to marry his friend. That I would have no other options." Kate abruptly shut her mouth, not sure what devil had made her admit that.

Christian looked up. His eyes were serious. He set his tray on the floor and removed hers as well.

"Your fool of a brother is an ass and knows nothing." He touched her cheek. "You are beautiful, inside and out. And any man would be lucky to have you." His fingers trailed down and traced her shoulder bones. "Beautiful, beautiful, beautiful."

She took a deep, shuddering breath. "You are beautiful as well, you know. I can see you, Christian Black, and I like it when the real you comes out to play."

He tightened and she saw him swallow. And then he was kissing her with an intensity that took her breath away.

As opposed to the last few times they had engaged in such activities, this time his hands stayed near her head, wrapped around her chin, then the back of her head, slowly pulling through the strands and then returning to frame her face. Almost reverently. He kissed her as if he were branding her, but also with an underlying gentleness that brought tears to her eyes.

His lips touched her eyes, her nose, her cheeks, chin, and ears.

"Christian," she breathed, trying to grab onto a single thought as he continued his investigation.

"Don't worry, Kate. Now that I have you, I won't ever let you go."

His kisses proceeded to caress her shoulders

and chest, down to her stomach and thighs, and lower to her knees, calves, and toes. Warmth spread everywhere he touched, and there was a heightened edge, as if something very important was taking place.

Something more than mutual pleasure between friends for Christian. Something more than discovery for Kate.

She ran her hands down his sides, touching him as she had the previous night, and his eyes smoldered. "Playing with fire, Kate?"

She smiled back.

Touches continued to be soft and reverent, strong and needy. Lips to her breast, fingers in her short curls. Hands stroking velvet and steel.

Christian rose over Kate and took in her flushed face, her parted, pink lips, eyelids at half mast. He kissed her softly and then met her eyes.

"Kate?"

She nodded, her short curls bouncing on the pillow, and reached for him. He gladly complied, nudging her body and finding her slick and ready.

He pushed forward, then withdrew. Push, withdraw, push, withdraw, until her face looked as glossy as his felt, until her breath echoed his own.

He leaned down and whispered in her ear. "I think I've fallen in love with you, Kate."

Her hands tightened around his back and her body arched upward. He thrust forward and entered her completely, deeply, a shiver racking his body. It was like coming home. A feeling he had never before known.

Moving in earnest, whispering all the things to her that he had been thinking these last few days, he expressed how he loved her smile and cherished her opinion. How just being in her company made the day that much brighter.

Her breathing increased with each word and her body moved in tune beneath his. It was a perfect harmony.

Barriers he had worked to recreate in the carriage crumbled completely. He didn't *want* to have them with Kate.

And as they both peaked and echoed the other's name, Christian knew it was he who had been branded.

He was deadly serious with what he had said. He was never going to let her go. Walking into this house today, he had shed the last of the blinders. Making love to her had sealed his destiny.

Kate was his.

His dreams were warm and welcome. His arms wrapped around Kate, hugging her tightly.

But just as he was sleepily trying to decide whether to keep bundled in the covers with Kate all day or to fix all their loose ends so they could stay under the covers for a few weeks, something woke him fully from his sated slumber.

"Well, well, well, isn't this a cozy little scene," a vitriolic voice announced from the doorway.

Chapter 21

You will never be rid of me. I will always be here.

The Marquess of Penderdale
to Christian, age twenty-one

Christian whipped around to see his father standing in the doorway, back ramrod straight and nose firmly in the air as if he had just smelled something unpleasant.

"I know you are hopeless, Christian, but you really should be more careful with what you are saying, especially when in a house with, how did the servant say you phrased it? Ah, yes, with enemy ears. Careless as always, especially letting things out of your possession just so that you can get a tumble with any villager ready to spread her legs."

"Don't call—"

Christian's breath died as his father said two words. "Interesting journal."

He froze. No, he couldn't have. He looked toward the sitting room and realized he had left it on the chair when he had carried Kate into the bedroom, too far gone in lust and love to care about anything else. *Careless. Careless, useless, wasteful.* All the words he had grown up with swirled in his head.

His father had Anthony's journal. Oh, not on his person, assuredly, but in his possession. He wouldn't allow his son to try and physically remove it from him, no matter how crass an action that might be. His father thought much worse of him than just being crass, Christian knew.

His father had Anthony's journal. His father, who had more power in one finger than Freewater with his small paper could ever dream. His father, the bane of his existence, the one whom he had tried and tried to please before nearly going mad. If it hadn't been for meeting Anthony at Eton, he didn't know what he would have done. Not even when his two elder brothers had died had his father given him a thought beyond criticism. So Christian had lived up to every thought his father had had of him. It had been a damn sight better to live that way than to live under an ever heavier boot.

Christian looked at Kate. He had worried about her having that power over him, but the more he knew of her character, the more at ease he felt. He trusted her. Twenty-five years' worth of damaged trust with his father, and Kate had managed to slip past his defenses in under a week. And after last night . . .

But Anthony's journal . . . He looked at his father, who was too noble to smirk, instead wearing a chilly, distant look, disappointment permanently creased in the lines on his face.

"You will follow me downstairs. Now. And I want your strumpet out of this house."

Christian saw Kate shrink into the bedding.

"No," he said calmly, tugging his trousers on.

"What did you say?" his father asked in his usual low and deadly tones.

"I said no. Kate is not a strumpet, and she's not going anywhere."

"You dare say no to me, in my own house?"

"It is my house too, unfortunately for you. And Kate is staying. You were not to return for another week. I do not know why you came back earlier, nor do I care. We would have assuredly bypassed the property if I had known, but as we are here

344

now, we will be staying for two days and then will be gone."

"Would that you could have died instead of your mother, instead of your brothers," he said harshly.

Christian let the words wash off him. "I know, Father. I am well aware of your preferences, and have been most of my life. Unfortunately for you, I'm still here, and none of them are."

He watched his father turn red, trying to control his rage. The marquess shot a poisonous glance toward the bed. "You will follow me to the study, Christian. I will not have this conversation in front of the hired help."

"Kate is not the hired help, but do lead the way. I'm sure I've forgotten where your study is by now. It has been far too long since I've been disciplined."

The marquess turned sharply on his heel and stalked from the room. Christian apologetically turned to Kate, whose mouth was hanging open. He concentrated on the anger in her eyes rather than the pity. "Stay here, and don't let anyone tell you otherwise. If Sally comes by, have her stay with you too. I should have thought of that last night."

She began to speak, but he forestalled her with a sharp hand motion. "No, Kate, please. I can't let

345

down my defenses to explain right now. I need them to speak with the marquess. Say you understand."

She swallowed and nodded.

He allowed a small bit of relief to overtake him, and he briefly closed his eyes as he kissed her. "Thank you. I'll be back soon."

His father deliberately took his time. It had proven an effective maneuver in putting Christian at a distinct disadvantage in the past. He poured a glass of port, swished it around, sniffed its aroma, then sipped. Christian held himself perfectly still throughout the ritual. It had long ago been beaten out of him not to fidget or interrupt, and even though he had occasionally used the tactic to stir his father to anger during the past few years since he had come of age, he didn't want anything to distract him from what his father might say.

This was it. His father thought he finally had something concrete that he could use to bend Christian to his will. The swished port and calculating air always boded ill. His father was nothing if not predictable.

"I have been talking to Lord Palmer. His daughter is on the market this year. Diamond of the first water, most assuredly. You will wed her by the end of the season."

Christian had met Palmer's daughter. Nice enough girl, but not the one for him. That designation belonged to Kate.

"No."

The marquess stroked his glass. "Oh, you will, and furthermore, you will do so with a smile on your face."

"Why the sudden interest in my wedded state?"

"Because even if you are a worthless son, there is still a possibility for the future generations. They will still be of my seed." The marquess's face twisted.

"Most regrettably, of course, as they will carry Uncle Charlie's legacy as well," Christian said smoothly, trying to stay calm.

Christian closely resembled his uncle on his mother's side. While his father had blamed Christian for the death of his mother, his uncle had blamed his father. Very vocally.

Somehow it seemed fitting that he looked like his uncle. The marquess had always hated his brother-in-law. Still did, in fact, even with him four years in the ground. Christian could only thank the fact that his uncle had hated his father with equal vigor and had left all his assets to Christian, as a final twist of the knife. The largesse had emancipated Christian from his father in a way that he never would have been able to achieve otherwise.

"Always one to state the obvious, Christian. It is one of your many failings."

"Being born to this family has to be by far my worst." He had long since mastered the bored tones that drove his father to drink.

The marquess's hands gripped the glass tighter. "You will marry Palmer's daughter. The betrothal contract will be here in the week. You will sign it, and only then will I return your friend's journal."

Christian unclenched his muscles. He had known something like this was coming, but it still burned.

Bargaining for time and trying to sound as unconcerned as he could, Christian said, "I need to speak with Anthony, of course."

"Of course, go speak with your friend. I expect you back here by three. Then we will discuss how things will be from now on."

Christian made his feet take him toward the door and back to his room.

Kate looked up as he entered and moved toward him. "What is going on?"

Christian looked at her, and she placed a hand on his sleeve as if to comfort him. He pulled her close and hugged her to him, her arms automatically circling behind.

He had a lot of maneuvering to accomplish in a very short amount of time. He pulled back and lifted her chin. "Kate, I need you to stay here. I'm going to talk to Anthony, who lives a short distance from here. I'll be gone for an hour or two."

"May I come with you?"

He wanted her to, damn but he did. But this was something he needed to do himself. "No, but promise me that you will not leave this room. Promise me."

She bit her lip and nodded. He gently touched her cheeks and kissed her. "I love you, Kate. Everything will be fine. I'll explain later."

She nodded again, and he hoped that the love he saw reflected there was enough. That she would continue to look at him that way in one year, in ten years. That he wasn't doomed to be a disappointment to all those he loved.

Chapter 22

> *If you find love, grab on to it with both hands and never let go.*
>
> George Simon
> to Kate, age seventeen

"The marquess said you were to come with us."

Kate looked warily at the two brawny men. They were wearing the livery of the house, but they looked like hired muscle. "Why?"

"Don't ask questions, just come with us."

She shook her head. She had no idea what was going on, but she was damned if she was leaving, especially after Christian had looked at her so seriously and told her to stay in the room. "No. I'll just wait for the earl to return. But thank you for the offer."

"It wasn't an offer, bitch. Now come with us."

"Well, I'm definitely not going with you now."

"You are, and you will."

The man doing the talking stepped forward. Kate took an immediate step back and looked for a weapon. The man was across the room and had grabbed both her arms before she had a chance to fully lift the table lamp. It shattered across the wooden floor as he wrenched one of her arms behind her back.

"You are coming with us, and then we are going to contact your brother in London and let him take care of you, just like family should."

Kate wondered if this was a personal servant to the marquess, or if all the servants were infected with this odd, hostile madness. And how did they know about her brother?

The man had her out the door in a matter of seconds. As he half pushed, half carried her down the hall—she was kicking and hissing for all she was worth—the marquess emerged from a room with Donald Desmond in tow. Desmond looked the worse for wear.

"What are you doing here?" she hissed. His presence explained how the marquess knew about her brother. Freewater could have heard one of their more lively conversations if he'd been intent on listening, and she had little doubt that Desmond had plied him for all the information he could after they had left. Freewater had been well on his way to drunk. Damn it!

Desmond shot her the usual look of hatred, but it was tempered with fear. It looked as if he too had been treated to the marquess's impeccable hospitality.

"Mr. Desmond here was found lurking around the grounds. We don't like spies or poachers in these parts, but Mr. Desmond assures me that he was just trying to follow my son, the Earl of Canley."

Desmond nodded fiercely.

"I assured Mr. Desmond that though it was my right to punish my son, if he tried to do the same, I would take action. We can't have the house shamed any more than already threatened, now can we? And Mr. Desmond, though kind to share his knowledge of the past week's events, including yours, is now going to forget ever having witnessed any of it. Aren't you, Mr. Desmond?"

Desmond nodded even more vigorously.

"Wouldn't want that barrister's post in London

jeopardized in any way, or to have charges filed against you, would we?"

Desmond shook his head, and a bit of spittle flew from his mouth. She couldn't work up much sympathy for him.

"Stewart, please see Mr. Desmond out."

The other servant grabbed Desmond's shirt-sleeve and pushed him down the hall.

The marquess looked at her as if she were some odd thing stuck to his boot. This man was all that was wrong with the nobility. The corruption of power. That he would help Christian surprised her, although on second thought she supposed it was about self-pride.

"Dressing as a boy, behaving like a common strumpet. I'm sure my son finds you fascinating. He has always enjoyed dirtying himself with his friends. But now that will all change. He is to marry someone of my choosing, and I need you to, how should I put this . . . disappear. Mr. Desmond, such a *nice* young man, told me about your brother's search for you in London. I doubt it will be hard for us to locate him, even without your help. A young woman on the run with your"—he looked at her ear—"deformity will be easily identified. I'm a generous man, though. I'll make you a deal. Give me your name and the name of your brother, and I will give you a thousand pounds. A heavy fortune for a girl like you. So speak up, what's your name?"

Kate made sure to enunciate properly. She was in the presence of nobility, after all. "Go. To. The. Devil."

Her arm was twisted back farther and she couldn't help the cry of pain that escaped.

"Now that wasn't very nice. I will, however, give instructions for the offer to remain open until you reach London. I'm sure that you will see the wisdom of taking the money once you reach Town. Off with you now."

Kate's last glimpse of the man was a cold smile and the back of his expensively tailored coat as he strode into a room. What was worse was that she could see the outline of a book in his pocket. Most assuredly Anthony's journal.

The servant began pushing her down the hall again. Kate continued to resist, although some of her verve had given way. What was she doing? Surely she had reconciled by now that there was no way for them to be together. Wouldn't it be better to just let Christian go? Let him marry a girl of his station? Take the marquess's thousand pieces of silver and escape before they located her brother?

She saw the image of Christian as he had leaned over her last night and whispered that he would never let her go, and recalled the feelings those words had produced inside. If she loved him, really loved him, she would fight for him. She would at least fight until Christian himself retracted those words. She would not allow some callous, unconscionable man make those decisions instead.

Kate renewed her struggles with vigor. The servant swore vociferously and tried to get a better grasp on her arms. She splayed her legs in front of her, planting them on the doorway leading down the servants' stairs. Lucky for her, it was a narrow entrance, and she could effectively stop them from moving forward.

Unlucky for her, the servant was smarter than he looked. He released her. Without the force of him pushing her forward, she dropped to the ground like a stone. Pain radiated from her wrist up her right arm, and her rear didn't feel much better. The servant bodily dragged her down the stairs.

In pain and more than a little fatigued, Kate continued kicking out. If he got her in a carriage, her fate was sealed. If she could just wiggle from his grasp, she might be able to outrun him. Where she was going to run was a different matter.

She was definitely in deep trouble.

"Where are you taking Miss Kate?"

The servant stopped abruptly, and Kate stopped struggling when she saw Tom standing in their path, arms crossed and looking incredibly intimidating. The sunlight formed a mock halo around his head. She swore she heard the angels start playing, so overwhelming was her relief.

"Out of the way. Direct order from His Lordship."

"From the earl?"

The servant sneered. "No, dimwit, from the marquess. Now get out of the way."

"'Fraid not. I only take orders from the earl. Seeing as you ain't him, you'll be letting Miss Kate go."

"Get out of the way, I say."

Kate winced as the servant grabbed her injured wrist.

Tom went still. "You will let go of Miss Kate right this moment."

"No, now get out of the way!"

Tom took two steps forward and his fist flew past her head. And just like that, she was released. She hugged Tom, who went rigid under the embrace. "Uh, Miss Kate?"

"Thank you, thank you, thank you."

"Miss Kate, we need to leave. The earl will find us."

She nodded. "No, wait. Anthony's journal. It's inside."

"We can't go back inside."

"Livery. Do you know where they keep the wash?"

"Yes, it's in the front room in the servants' wing. Why would—oh no. Miss Kate, we don't have time. We can't fight all the servants. There are hundreds of them. The marquess will arrest all of us."

She nodded and pushed him toward the stables. "You're right. You stay here. But I need you to undo the back of my dress."

"What?"

"Please."

Tom studied her for a second, stone-faced, and then did as she asked.

"Just ten minutes, Tom. If I'm not back in ten minutes, leave without me."

Kate tore back into the servants' entrance and repeated every thanksgiving she had ever learned when she found the wash. Grabbing a few less than pristine items that she had seen the upstairs maids wear, she ran behind the privacy screen. She nudged the chamber pot aside and peeled off her dress, swapping it for the ill-fitting maid's dress. She snatched a bonnet from the top of the pile and tied it as best she could. She just had to hope that no one chose to look any closer.

Kate walked as slowly as she could manage through the halls so as not to draw attention. She retraced her steps back to the hall where she had seen the marquess. This was where luck would be needed. If luck was smiling on her, she would enter the room, retrieve the journal, and be out again before the marquess was any the wiser. If luck was not with her, well . . . perhaps she was courting stupidity.

She spied a tea tray and lifted it. She had to rely solely on improvisation. She had no time to devise a plan.

Her father had always said that those in love sometimes act a little stupidly. He had seemed quite amused when he had said it too. He had followed up by saying that if she ever had cause to act stupid in the name of love, she should count her blessings, for it was better to have been stupid than to not have been stupid at all. Wait. That wasn't the saying.

She reached the marquess's study door before she could reorganize her thoughts. Ah, well. Time to be stupid.

The knob was cold in her grip. She knocked softly.

"Enter."

"Your tea, Your Lordship," she said softly.

"Put it on the desk and leave."

The marquess stood facing the window, arms crossed behind his back as he surveyed his domain, most likely secure in his knowledge that everything was going his way.

Kate spied Anthony's journal on the desk. Suddenly she felt light-headed and scared. Her breath came out in short, soundless gasps. Her stomach tied in so many knots that she didn't know if she would ever get them undone.

As she looked about nervously, she spotted another journal on a side table. It wasn't identical, but it was dark, rich, and similar in size. If the marquess didn't look carefully, he'd never notice the difference until it was too late. Kate walked forward and swept it up in her free hand.

She set the tray on the desk and did a mental cheer as she quickly swapped the books and turned to leave. Luck was finally with her.

"Wait."

Kate froze with her back to him. Every part of her body ready for flight.

"Tell Stewart to report to me immediately after he returns."

"Yes, my lord," she breathed.

"Now get out."

"Yes, my lord." She didn't think she had ever been so happy to follow an order.

She picked up her step as she hurried back downstairs and grabbed her clothing from the dirty clothes basket where she had hidden it. Not bothering to change, she raced to the stables to meet Tom, Benji, and Sally. She only hoped they hadn't taken her advice to leave without her.

Christian breathed deeply as he walked back into his room at Rosewood. His meeting with Anthony had been fraught with tension, and all he wished to do was crawl into bed with Kate and never leave.

But that wasn't going to happen. Not here. Especially not after the revelations of the past few hours, the past few days.

How was he going to tell her? His hands shook a bit as he gripped the handle to the bedroom.

Pushing it open, he was surprised to find the room empty.

"Kate?"

No answer.

A wave of unease passed through him. He shouldn't have left her here. No matter the outcome of the day's events, leaving her here had been a bad decision.

His eyes focused on the shattered table lamp near the bed, the pieces of glass strewn about the hardwood floor and nestled into the rich Oriental rug.

He turned abruptly and strode back into the sitting room, forcing himself not to panic and run. Kate's bag was on the floor behind a chair, her pelisse lying on top. He stared at them for a moment, then swiftly picked them up and marched toward his father's study.

His father's back was turned, his arms clasped behind him as he gazed out the window. His father was so sure of his success. Bitterness washed through Christian, but he swallowed it. He had to think about Kate.

"What have you done with Kate?"

"Back again and still without manners. What makes you think I touched a hair on the strumpet's head?" his father said, turning.

"I'm warning you."

"With what? You have nothing with which to warn me. You never learn, Christian. I hold all the cards. I always will. You haven't the talent to best me."

"What did you do with Kate?" he asked as calmly as he could manage.

The marquess waved a hand. "Not that it matters now, but I've sent her to her brother in London. Family needs to tend its own. Something you never learned."

"No, I believe that was something *you* never learned, Father."

The marquess's lips tightened. "You continue to disappoint me, Christian. Nevertheless, the girl is gone. Long gone by now. Took the money I gave her and ran like the trollop she is."

Christian took a deep breath. "No she didn't. I know Kate."

"You've known the girl for what, a few days? A silly infatuation, a dalliance. I could expect no more from you. Nevertheless, you will marry the Palmer chit and forget the damaged one chasing you like a lost dog. Unless you want your friend to suffer."

A strange calm settled over Christian.

He and Anthony had talked for a long time. Although the conversation had been tense at first, so many of the things they should have said long ago had finally been spoken. How Christian had hidden his painful childhood behind a careless façade and how Anthony had encouraged it.

They had both done their fair share of stupid things. Yet they were both finally growing up and taking the responsibility.

Their friendship was stronger than ever. It was *real*, not the illusion he had always feared. There was nothing his father could do about it. And Kate. His feelings for her were definitely genuine. And he might have been unable to trust in someone's feelings for him a week ago, but so much had changed in the last few days. He was willing to believe Kate's feelings for him were true as well.

He just needed to find the words to tell her what was truly in his heart.

"I'm going to marry Kate, Lord Penderdale. And there is nothing you can do to stop me. This is one ace you no longer hold."

The marquess's eyes narrowed dangerously. "Don't try me, Christian. There are worse fates I can bestow on you."

Christian cocked his head. "No, I don't think there are."

"I'll cut you off without a farthing. You'll get nothing that is not entailed, and I'll make sure those properties are so in debt that you'll never have a moment's peace."

Christian gripped Kate's pelisse. He gazed at his father, the man who had been the bane of his existence for far too long. His father had regained his usual look of calm superiority, but there was a tightening around his eyes. Kate did that too when she was trying to act composed. Surprise rushed through him and sudden understanding.

His hands relaxed their grip. "No you won't."

His father raised a brow, but something in his posture stiffened. Christian fought the shock. After all these years. The signs had probably been there all along, but he had been too young, impatient, or angry to read them.

"I will, boy, don't think I won't."

Christian slowly shook his head and straightened to his full height, two inches above his father's. "No you won't. You are too proud. You wouldn't be able to stand the scorn."

"You don't know what I can stand."

But he wouldn't, and they both knew it. Christian saw the dawning horror in his father's eyes, horror that he tried to conceal.

"You are worthless."

Christian smiled. "And you repeat yourself far too often. I'm going to marry Kate, and there is nothing you can do to prevent it, Lord Penderdale. You can ruin us socially, you can ruin the estates financially, and you can withhold anything unentailed. I don't care. I never have cared about any of those things. I had only thought them the ways to the family heart. But I have long since given up on receiving any good word from you. I will make my own family and never look back."

"You can't do this, Christian." There was a slight hint of desperation in his father's voice. There had been a time when Christian would have given almost anything to hear it. Now he just wanted to leave and find Kate.

"I can, and moreover I will. That's the thing about making someone into a person who doesn't care. It comes back to bite you in the end."

"I'll ruin your friend."

Christian nodded. "Yes, and Anthony is prepared for that. I spoke to him about it."

"Your friends will abandon you."

Christian smiled a real smile in his father's presence for the first time in years, decades even. "But they won't, Lord Penderdale. So I'm afraid you'll have to take these matters up with Anthony, pardon me, that's Lord Darton to you."

"How I hatched such a good-for-nothing spawn, I'll never know."

"I suppose it was the usual way. I'm sure Mother was bored the entire time."

"How dare you mention your mother. I will make you *pay*."

Christian cocked his head. He felt the first flare of true freedom. "I find I don't much care, Lord Penderdale. Now, if you'll excuse me, I have a lady to find. Good day."

He walked from the room at a leisurely pace, a last flip of the finger to his father, and one that belied his anxiety to find Kate.

He was halfway to his room to gather his overnight pack when he saw Sally. Her eyes widened and she waved him over. "Your Lordship. Oh, goodness, thank the Maker. Come quickly. We were just on our way out."

"Where are you going, Sally? And do you know where Kate is?" There was a desperate edge to his voice. He decided that he didn't much care if Sally heard it as long as she answered in the positive.

"She's with us. She got into a spot of trouble with the marquess's men, but Tom found them in time, thank goodness."

Relief rushed through him, so potent it made him stagger. "Kate is still here?"

"In the stables, Your Lordship."

He closed his eyes, then pushed forward, bags forgotten, and strode to the stables, Sally in tow.

Kate, beautiful, slightly bedraggled Kate, stood

arguing with Tom. She was wearing a godawful servant's dress that didn't fit, but that fact was completely unimportant next to the fact that she was *here*.

"Christian!"

She ran to him and buried her head in his neck. He clutched her the same way and inhaled the raspberry scent that seemed to surround her.

"I was worried you were halfway to London and I'd never find you," he murmured into her hair.

She raised a trembling hand to his cheek. "You'd have found me, I'm sure of it."

He smiled, feeling a little trembling in his joints as well. "Hopefully I will always find you, Kate."

She smiled back, love shining from her eyes. He shut his eyes and inhaled deeply, raspberries filtering through his soul. He hadn't been wrong. She really did love him.

"Marry me, Kate?" he blurted, passionate declarations momentarily forgotten.

She blinked. "What?"

"Marry me. It doesn't have to be today, or tomorrow or even in six months. Whenever we're ready. Just say you'll marry me."

She searched his eyes. "Christian?"

"You'll have to live with me for as long as it takes, of course."

She tentatively nodded, and then a smile of pure joy lit her face. "Of course. Of course I will."

"Good." He hugged her to him. "Now let's get out of here. Anthony said we were more than welcome to stay with him until we can get you to your solicitor. Your brother doesn't stand a chance. Even if he did, I have plenty of money. And while we are at Anthony's we can figure out what to do about his journal too."

She smoothed a hand down his back. "Oh, about the journal—"

He smiled into her hair. "Don't worry. We'll work it all out."

A muffled roar of fury resounded across the yard.

They drew apart to look toward the house. "I wonder what's wrong with the old goat now? What's he trying to do? Shake the foundations?"

Kate smiled, a slow, mischievous smile that could have come right from his face. "Sounds like he misplaced something. Shall we be off?"

Christian's heart quickened. Whether from the smile on Kate's face and the way she pressed against him or from her words, he wasn't sure. "What do you mean, misplaced something? What did you do?"

She leaned up and nibbled his ear. "Oh,

nothing. But I'll let you investigate and question me later. Maybe even search me if you're good."

She kissed the side of his neck. "But let's be gone from this place first."

"I couldn't agree more." He helped her into his carriage, which was hooked to the horses and ready to go—since Tom had already thoughtfully decided to steal it.

As they proceeded down the drive, the golden rays of the setting winter sun highlighted Kate's features, and he felt a fierce rush of freedom and love.

He thought he might just start that search now. He *had* been a good boy, after all.

Epilogue

*But most of all . . . just be happy. That is what I want
for you above all else.*

George Simon
to Kate, age eighteen

Kate leaned back against Christian as they
watched Tom hoist the sign for Canley Investigations. Christian's dream was soon to be a
reality. Inside, Sally and Benji were straightening
the storefront for tomorrow's grand opening.

Shortly after they were married, Christian had
announced to the ton that he was opening a personal investigations service. Tongues wagged for a
few weeks, but society decided to embrace the idea
in their own way, tutting about the eccentricity of

the handsome earl, his lovely wife, and their "club."

Kate hadn't thought she would like the higher ton circles at all, but was pleasantly surprised to find aspects she actually enjoyed. Watching her brother Teddy scurry out of their path whenever they met at a function also proved amusing. Christian had dealt quite effectively with the rat. Christian and Anthony held enough influence to pave a smooth path for her, and while things continued to be rocky in regard to her father-in-law, ever since Christian's proclamation, they had discovered a way to at least be civil.

And Kate had observed more than a few measured looks of respect on the marquess's face when Christian wasn't looking. She figured that as long as the man never hurt her husband again, she would let him live.

Christian stroked her round stomach and she leaned farther into him. The marquess was hoping to have some influence over their children. She and Christian privately joked about their cold dead bodies rotting in the ground before allowing anything of the sort.

Lucky for them their marriage was about as far from cold as it was possible to get. Christian was a passionate and attentive friend and lover, and she liked to think that she gave as good as she got.

They had their fair share of disagreements; with two such strong-willed people, that was bound to happen. But none of the arguments lasted long, and Kate cherished every one of them (after the fact, of course). Each day, each moment, uncovered new layers for both of them, and made their bond stronger.

The past year had been full of warmth, love, and laughter. Kate couldn't be happier.

She looked up at her husband, and he smiled down.

"Did you know that you are every woman's dream earl?"

He gave her a light squeeze and brushed his lips against the fading scars on her ear.

"As long as I'm the earl of *your* dreams."

Next month, don't miss these exciting new love stories only from Avon Books

Autumn in Scotland by Karen Ranney

An Avon Romantic Treasure

Charlotte MacKinnon will never get over being abandoned by her husband after just a week of marriage. Now he has returned, five years later, and he's far more handsome and charming than he ever was before. In fact, it's almost as if he's an entirely different person . . .

Passions of the Ghost by Sara Mackenzie

An Avon Contemporary Romance

In this conclusion to Sara Mackenzie's sexy Immortal Warriors trilogy, Reynald de Mortimer awakens from a centuries-long sleep to discover his castle has become a high society hotel. He finds himself strangely drawn to one of the hotel's guests—but will their love survive the demons that haunt them both?

For the Love of a Pirate by Edith Layton

An Avon Romance

The always-proper Lord Wylde is stunned to discover that he was betrothed at birth to the granddaughter of a pirate! True, Lisabeth is beautiful and intriguing, but she's the opposite of what he's always wanted . . . which may just make her the one thing he truly needs.

Confessions of a Viscount by Shirley Karr

An Avon Romance

Charlotte Parnell needs to prove her worth as a spy. When she meets Lord Moncreiffe, a man looking for a little excitement in his proper life, it's clear they make the perfect team. But will these spies-in-the-making really throw caution to the wind and unlock the secrets in their own hearts?

Avon Romantic Treasures

Unforgettable, enthralling love stories, sparkling with passion and adventure from Romance's bestselling authors